Paper

By

Emma Pullar

Also By Emma Pullar

Skeletal
Avian

'When searching for somewhere to escape the terrible realities of the world, I find the best place to hide is in stories.' – Beatrice Summers

I dedicate this book to those who are battling, or have ever battled, with mental illness. I've suffered with mental illness throughout my life; from depression and anxiety to obsessive compulsive personality disorder, premenstrual dysphoric disorder (PMDD) and post-traumatic stress disorder (PTSD). These days I'm feeling well, but I still struggle from time to time. I'm pretty sure the reason I'm functioning better than I ever have done previously is because I'm able to write every day. Writing is my medicine; without it my mind doesn't cope. If you're suffering mentally, tap into your creativity. It helps.

Killer

On your back, legs spread, his hand inside your knickers. You don't squirm. You take what he does to you.

'You like that, don't you?'

You nod and pretend you like it. You don't like it. You never have. The doorbell rings. You lock eyes. His worried, yours relieved. He wipes his fingers on his coffee-stained joggers. The doorbell goes again. There're shouts. The words aren't clear. With much trouble he gets to his feet.

'Stay quiet. I'll get rid of them.' His wicked mouth stretches into a smile, revealing crowded yellow teeth. He points to the coffee table. 'I got you a new book. Go on, have a look.'

You smile and nod as he lumbers out of the living-room. Once he's gone, you slide off the couch, summer dress riding up. You crawl over to the low, round table and reach under the glass. The new book is beside the stack, and on the other side is a clear plastic box with all your dolls and cut out paper clothes in it, scissors resting on the lid.

The new book is a princess one. You open it and flick through, marvelling at all the pretty gowns, dresses you will never wear. Princesses don't have to do what you do. You bring the pages to your nose and inhale the print. You wish you could take your books home, but he won't let you. You cross your legs and your knee accidently nudges the stack. The thin books slide sideways and fan out under the table. One shoots out further than the others and catches your eye.

The rag dolls on the front of the book grin at you, happy; they talk to you. *He treats you like a rag doll. Pulls you around, takes off your clothes, plays with you.* You close your eyes, but cruel memories press on your mind. Think of something else. You flick back through your new book and find Cinderella in vest and knickers. The clothes around her are a beautiful gown, her rag dress, glass slippers, a handbag, a tiara, a broom – and a vacuum cleaner? A memory you were trying to repress stabs you in the brain. His words were loud: *The vacuum cleaner would do a better job!* Then he rolled up the rag doll book and hit you with it until you started doing it the way he wanted you to. The smell was nauseating. You hated putting it in your mouth. Your bottom lip quivers. You take the scissors from the top of the plastic box, pull the rag doll book towards you, and stab the closed blades into the face of one of the rag dolls on the front cover. You stab and stab and stab, making several holes in its rosy-cheeked face.

The living-room door opens and makes you jump. The scissors drop from your hand and clack on the blond laminate floor. His melon head appears between the door and the frame.

'Vera from next door.' He smiles. 'Wanted a cup of milk. I gave her some. I'll pick up a pint for her later.' He talks to you like you're his wife. Like you're not here against your will. Like he isn't blackmailing you. How can he be so kind to that old lady next door yet do unspeakable things to you? 'Tidy your things away, Princess, I'm going to get the box.'

You cringe inside. His head disappears behind the door. He's going to get the 'toys'. The ones he will hurt you with again. You glance down at the red marks on your palm where you gripped the scissors tightly. Your eyes travel to Cinderella. She was a slave; not a sex slave but she was made to scrub the house and was treated badly by those meant to be her family. She became a princess with the help of her fairy godmother, but you don't have that luxury. You will have to rescue yourself. He always calls you 'Princess'; perhaps you should take the power back, own that name, as your friend Jess would say when people called her a bitch. Your gaze moves to the vacuum cleaner beside Cinders and then to the one on the floor beside you.

You nervously twiddle with your hair before reaching down and grasping the metal pole. It's hot in the tiny room, but despite the heat you're shaking like the temperature has dropped below freezing. You drag the round vac over to the door. Its wheels roll clumsily across the uneven floor. You raise the vacuum cleaner pipe and grip it tightly in both hands. You wait. Heart drumming in your chest, face throbbing like it's on fire. His heavy footsteps thud against the floorboards. They thunder louder and louder down the hallway. The door trembles in its frame as he comes closer. Your quick breaths are loud in your ears.

The door creaks open. He steps over the threshold. You hesitate. Tears threaten. You close your eyes and swing the metal pipe. Crack! It's a blow to the back of his bald head. The fucker goes down. He drops the box and his nasty toys spill across the scuffed laminate flooring. He hollers on his knees, hands over the back of his head. Crack! You hit him again. A little scream escapes you. The fucker falls sideways and goes limp.

Using his ropes, you tie his hands behind him tight – triple knot. He's heavy, and you struggle to move the unconscious lump. Summoning all your strength, you prop him against the peeling leather couch. Hands shaking, body trembling all over, you can't believe what you've done. You stare down at your abuser, a big lump of blubber. A switch flips inside you, the trembling turns off. You smile. Your eyelids feel heavy, a calmness wraps around you like a warm blanket. It's his turn to take it.

You crouch down and pat his exposed belly. If he were a woman, you'd swear there was a baby in there. To rouse him, you take up the scissors, open them wide and use the sharp edge against his hairy stomach. You carefully grip one side of the handle and blade, fingers either side of the sharp bit, and press down hard into his flesh. Blood gushes. He screams himself awake.

'Stop! Stop!'

The sight of his blood relaxes you. It's washing away the pain. It's like popping bubble wrap, so satisfying. You hum to yourself while he cries. Sing while he begs.

'*Take the knife, cut the skin, take the salt, rub it in.*'

He screams in pain when you take the table salt left on the coffee table from his fish and chip dinner last night and pour the grains into the gaping wound in his stomach. Then rub them in.

'Stop! Don't! Why are you doing this?'

'You always choose what we play. Now it's my turn to pick the game.' You use your baby voice. You've been told you look younger than twelve; 'babyface' is what your foster parents say. He says you mustn't tell. That no one will believe you. He calls you a dirty little whore and says your foster parents will send you away if they find out what you've done. But you're not a whore. He's the whore, and he'll pay for what he's done.

'Please; I'll bring you more books. Better ones!'

You want the books, but not as payment for the things he does to you. You push fingers into the gash; he thrashes about like a whale out of water and whimpers while you finger-paint a red flower on his hairy belly.

'When you were inside me, it was fun for you, but now I'm inside you…' You push in again, deeper, and he hollers in pain. 'You don't wanna play?' You'll have to stop him screaming. You take a silk scarf from the overturned box and tilt your head, ear almost touching your shoulder. 'You have to take turns. It's now my turn.'

You pinch his big nose which is covered in little black dots. His ruddy face is like a bright red balloon about to pop. He opens his lopsided lips and you shove in the balled-up silk scarf, push it up hard to the back of his throat. You smile sweetly. He tries to speak with his mouth full, like you had when you tried to tell him you didn't want him to do that. He didn't listen then and you won't listen now. The noise your 'foster uncle' manages to make with the cloth stuffed in his mouth sounds like a hippo's yawn. You close the scissors and plunge them into the cut. More blood oozes out; he thrashes about. You place the blood-covered scissors on the floor and push your salty fingers into the gash again, deeper still. It's warm and wet.

The cloth does its job, muffling the big man's cries. Tears stream from the corners of his fearful hooded eyes. You pull out, gently press your fingers to your lips and kiss the tips. The taste of salt and blood sends a shockwave down your spine. The big bastard loses consciousness again. You place your bloody hand on the collection of paper doll books he used to groom you with before you knew what grooming was. You pick up the rag doll book with the holes stabbed into it and the princess book, and compare the two. You are a princess. He's nothing but a dirty old rag and he'll never touch you again. He'll never touch anyone again – you'll make sure of that. Men should never touch little girls, but they do because there's no one around to stop them.

You'll stop them.

Chapter One

The Mime of Trafalgar

In the dark early hours of the morning, London had a dream-like feel to it. Victorian buildings bathed in a ghostly glow stood silent. Black cabs were parked up in a row, their orange TAXI signs on, and in the driver's seat the faceless silhouettes gave the impression dark spirits ran the nightshift. The roads were at their emptiest in the small hours, rumbling vehicle engines few and far between, only a handful of red double-decker night buses in service. The sole constants were Trafalgar Square's gushing fountains. Beside them several ornate iron lampposts shone soft light onto the shimmering fountain pools. Although the Square felt almost deserted, rather than the baleful creepiness felt in a cemetery full of ancient tombstones, the dark streets and old buildings of central London held a unique peacefulness.

Sun up and the quiet greyness of Trafalgar Square transformed into a place of honking horns and quick footsteps. Commuters erupted from the train station like ants spewing from an anthill. Mike glanced skyward as he shouldered his way through the bustle, with the wooden crate containing his props held close to his chest. The puffy charcoal clouds above and chilly breeze made the October morning feel more like midwinter. Despite the threat of rain, he hoped there'd be a big crowd today. He needed the money. Last month, he'd been short on the rent, and although his flatmates were always understanding he didn't want to risk losing his crazily cheap digs – a rarity in the inner city. He was terrified of running out of money and being forced to live out of his prop crate.

The suits weaved around him in haste, rushing to their boring office jobs. Some appeared in doorways, takeaway coffee in hand, newspaper under the arm. They'd probably spent the night in their office and who could blame them? The rental market in London was out of control. Cockneys would be extinct in a few decades. Someone should put them on the endangered list.

Gazing at the cold, grey buildings, Mike pictured what might be going on inside. In his mind, city offices were like hornets' nests. Workers buzzing around their desks, ready to sting someone. Did the suits ever worry about being made homeless? Nah. Too busy stealing. Bankers were the worst: bunch of pirates looting and plundering. Mike never trusted banks; he refused to use them. The only thing that had changed about pirates over the years was their uniform. Instead of big gold earrings, a hook for a hand and a peg-leg, they wore ties, suits and carried large umbrellas. Back in the days of sailing the seven seas, the parrot was the pet of choice – *pieces of eight, Polly wants a cracker*. These days the pet was a government official – *print more money, Polly wants a bailout*.

Apart from the workers, the other creatures who roamed the streets of London were tourists and beggars. Yesterday, some stuck-up prick had said that what Mike did for a living was begging. It wasn't. Sitting on the dirty ground with a sign that reads: *Homeless and Hungry* is not the same as performing for money. Mike wore his black-and-white Pierrot-inspired costume with pride. For now, the Square was his stage, but one day he would be in a West End show in front of a captive audience – the lead, no doubt. His name up in bright lights. Mike was as important as anyone else in the theatre biz. *Another day, another grand performance for my adoring fans.*

His position in front of the towering stone pillars of the National Gallery had the perfect amount of light and shade; he'd claimed the spot years ago. He was the most adored of all the cast of characters, the most original and the most talented. Everyone knew where the great Pierrot performed. But today there was a box in his way. Mike glared at the fuzzy butt crack of the fat oaf in Lycra who'd stolen his spot. The Lycra-legged buffoon turned round and, seeing the pale-faced mime's angry stare, placed one meaty hand over the bat logo stretched across his moobs while holding his other hand up in apology.

'Excuse me, your highness…' Fat-Bat's voice was gravelly, what you'd expect of a fifty-a-day smoker. Today he sounded worse than usual. Face full of head cold, his tone was gruff and gurgling, as if a family of snot gremlins lived in his throat. The fake superhero had arrived earlier than usual. The bakery must have been closed. Any more pasties and doughnuts for brekkie and Bat-Tit's tatty costume would split.

Mike glared. 'Glad you know your place, peasant.'

Mike's rudeness never bothered Bat; he often ignored the mime's quips and today was no exception.

'When you left yesterday…' He moved the plastic box stuffed with his rain jacket, bat gloves and mask out of Mike's way. '…A beautiful lady set up in your spot. I thought since you didn't mind her doing it, maybe you'd found a better place to perform … the West End, perhaps?'

He chuckled and began to cough, which turned into a face-bruising choke. *Serves him right for taking the piss.* A snide smile spread across Mike's thin lips, but faded when the middle-aged Bat recovered from his coughing fit. Mike waved his hand dismissively, the ruffled material at his wrist flapped.

'I don't know what you're talking about.'

Losing his one-armed grip, he quickly grabbed the side and hugged his box of props tight. He hated small talk and boring topics of conversation almost as much as he hated being mocked. He preferred silence to small talk. It was why he'd chosen to be a mime.

Batty shrugged his huge hunched shoulders. 'I guess, you won't share with me 'coz I ain't a beautiful lady.'

'I have no interest in women.' Mike rolled his eyes. The idiot really couldn't tell his sexual orientation?

'Beautiful golden hair. I tell ya, if I weren't married…' Bat-Stink's piggy eyes glazed over. Mike flung his prop box to the ground. The thud snapped him out of his daydream. 'I filmed her. Want to see?'

Mike had a tug-of-war with his inner narcissist. He wanted to see her, but he didn't want Fat-Tits to be the one to show him.

'I probably know her already.' Mike crossed his arms, slender nose in the air.

'Suit yourself.'

The big man twisted his body and went to tuck his mobile phone into the leather bum bag he wore backwards around his waist. Bum bags were a hideous accessory in the 80s and 90s. Mike's older cousin had one; he lived in America and called it a 'fanny pack'. Mike remembered being horrified by this name; later he found out that Americans don't call female genitalia a fanny. He could hardly believe the hideous waist bags were still for sale and that people still bought them. Why had they not all been burned along with shell suits and Hypercolour T-shirts?

Mike took a step closer until there was only about a foot between them. This was as close as he was prepared to get to the forty-something loser, who had not only let himself go but had shut the door and locked it so there was no coming back. A Jabba the Hutt costume would have been a better choice for him. He could stand next to the ropy-looking floating Yoda.

Mike tapped Jabba the Bat's beefy shoulder. 'Perhaps you should show me, in case it's one of my friends from Bliss.'

He knew this would sound impressive to Bat-Breath. 'Bliss' was a local nightclub in Soho. An exclusive place for VIPs. He'd never told anyone how he became a member, and he never intended to ever tell anyone how he'd sweet-talked the security guard, and then, when the guard's shift was over, he'd met the muscular but brainless bonbon in the back alley and given him a blowjob in return for a spot on the guest list. Just as he'd not known the name of the security guard before or after he'd sucked him off, Mike didn't know the real name of the chunky superhero he'd been working beside for the last two years, and even though he didn't care to be in the cockney Batman's company, he wanted to impress him. What Mike enjoyed most was impressing people. It didn't matter who. He had impressed the doorman at Bliss with his fellatio skills and now he would impress Bat-Bloke with his connections to beautiful creatures.

'It's here somewhere.' Bat swiped his finger across the screen quicker than Mike swiped left on Tinder. 'Sorry, the eldest is at college and she likes me to send her photos of the dog, I need to delete some of 'em … ah, here's the blonde beauty.'

He turned the screen around to face Mike. Mike leaned a little closer. He studied the video footage of a leggy blonde strutting through the crowded Square. Hair worn in Shirley Temple ringlets, tied with a crimson bow, her shiny locks bounced with every stride she took. The woman who looked to be in her late twenties was slender and wearing a glittery, powder-blue, babydoll dress, white tights and little red shoes. Mike's next thought was a glam Dorothy Gale. The young woman's delicate face was painted white like his, but instead of a teardrop she had pink blush circles on her cheeks. Her long false eyelashes were almost drag queen status and her ruby-red lips were in a permanent pout. She was stunning and she knew it. A work of art. Heads turned as she approached Mike's performance spot. The video stopped and the triangular play symbol appeared in the middle of the screen over a static image of the princess.

'Go on then.' Bat jabbed Mike in the ribs with his pork-sausage finger. 'Who is she?'

Mike flinched away from the intrusive digit. He knelt down and pulled a black cloth and a gold bowl out of his wooden crate, carefully placing the bowl front and centre for his fans to drop money into. Then he closed the wooden lid and turned the crate upside down.

'A dear friend, actually.' he lied.

'Is that right?' Bat's brow furrowed with suspicion.

Mike draped the black cloth over his makeshift podium and stepped gracefully up onto the overturned crate like a queen stepping up to her throne.

'Oh yes, I'd quite forgotten. A few weeks ago I offered my spot to a select few … to use when I'm not performing. Glad to see she's accepted my offer.'

He hoped his weak smile would cover the envy bubbling up inside him. He hoped this Dorothy Gale lookalike, who'd taken his place once he'd finished work for the day, wasn't stealing his crowd, his limelight. Mike noticed the lack of tourists mixed in with the office workers. It could be the weather, or train delays – or maybe it was her. Perhaps people were going to wait until later – to come and see her.

'What's her name, then?' Bat raised a wispy greying eyebrow.

'Never you mind what her name is.' Mike narrowed his eyes. 'She won't want to talk to a loser like you, especially not when she finds out you've been filming her … perv.'

Bat scowled, tucked his phone away in the pack at his back, pulled on his faded plastic Batman headgear and struck a superhero pose. Mike took a deep breath and puffed it out. He dropped his chin to his chest and the neck ruffles tickled his nose.

He whispered into the ruched material, 'Show time.'

Chapter Two

The Epileptic Journalist

Kerri slipped through the door and into the main office of *Trafalgar Times* headquarters, hoping that the editor-in-chief wasn't out on the floor. The boss rarely ventured out of her office, but it would just be Kerri's luck if she had done so today. The young journalist's nose wrinkled. The stuffy oblong room held a lingering smell of Caesar salad dressing and egg mayo sandwiches, which someone had tried to mask by spraying vanilla body mist. Kerri scanned cluttered desks. The coast was clear. She made her way past the rows of monitors, giant handbag slung over her shoulder, knocking into photo frames and other desk junk.

Kerri kept her eyes on the back door – the boss's office. Her heart pounded with the thought of it opening and that booming voice calling her name. Trying to be stealthy, Kerri caused more of a ruckus than if she'd walked to her desk normally. Moving like a slow-motion tornado, her oversized handbag knocked down things on one desk, and when she whirled around to put them back in their place, it knocked stuff over on the desk behind her. Most work stations were unoccupied, but those who had no time for lunch were sitting hunched over their keyboards, tapping away at lightning speed. Deadlines looming, not one of her colleagues gave her so much as an upward glance as she passed by.

'You're late again, girl.'

Kerri froze. Her heart bounced against her ribcage. She clutched the ruffles on the front of her blouse and exhaled.

'Jeez, Donna!'

Donna, a bubbly American who'd lived in London for most of her life but had nevertheless managed to retain her chirpy Californian accent, shot Kerri a disappointed 'headmistress' stare. With it came an unwelcome rush of nostalgia, reminding Kerri of the time she'd been caught sneaking back into class after bunking off first period. Donna was the same age as her old headmistress would have been, but radically different from the pearl-wearing, Hyacinth Bucket type. Backside resting against Kerri's desk, Donna was dressed in a designer, rose-gold satin plunge-neck jumpsuit with a matching sash around her head. Her shoulder-length black hair was perfectly straight and smooth, silky too, like she'd stepped out of a shampoo advert. Kerri always wondered how she got it so straight; no one had hair that perfect. Americans love their beauty-enhancing products, which also showed in Donna's blindingly white and perfectly straight teeth.

Right micro-blade eyebrow raised, the managing editor held a takeaway coffee cup in one hand, the other rested on her curvy hip. Her plum-painted full lips were pursed in preparation to dish Kerri a lecture. Kerri dropped her gaze like a naughty child and let it linger on the half-moon lipstick imprint on the white coffee cup lid.

Donna tutted. 'I can't keep doing this.'

Kerri heaved her giant handbag off of her shoulder and dumped it down on the desk. 'I know, I'm sorry…'

'Sorry? I've been covering for your ass for four hours! Told her grandness you had an emergency. Why didn't you call?'

'I had a seizure.'

'Another one! That's not normal, sweetie.'

'I don't think my medication is working.'

Donna took a sip of coffee and pointed to Kerri's forehead.

'That looks painful; maybe you should start wearing a helmet.'

Kerri leaned sideways and glanced past Donna at her dishevelled reflection in the wall mirror. Before she left the flat, she'd dragged her short hair into a messy topknot and rushed when applying her make-up. Her delicate pale face was blotchy orange, resembling an Essex girl who'd been heavy-handed with the tanning lotion and drunk when applying her lipstick. Kerri wiped her mouth, transferring the glittery red gloss to the back of her hand, but instead of making things better her smudged and faded lippy meant she now looked like a drunk Essex girl who'd snogged half the pub.

'I'm such a state!'

She fussed with her bird's nest hair while Donna gawped at her.

'Never mind your make-up fail; how did you get that massive bruise?'

Kerri's gaze lifted to check her forehead in the mirror and, sure enough, on the right side near her hairline was a large purple splodge.

'Shit!' She touched it and winced. 'I came to in the shower. Must have hit my head.'

As soon as she'd seen the bruise it started to throb.

'You shouldn't be alone; have you considered moving in with Mark?'

Donna placed her takeaway coffee-warmed hand on Kerri's shoulder, gold-painted nails resting on the journalist's red blouse. The colours made Kerri think of Christmas and how fast it sneaks up at this time of year. October. Blink. Christmas Day. She patted Donna's hand.

'I'm not alone. Bea and Mike are busy people, but I can call on them if I need to.'

'Bea and Mike?' Donna scoffed. 'Mike is a weirdo who can hardly look after himself and Beatrice is a hermit. You said she never comes out of her room.'

'She's an author, not a hermit.' Donna rolled her eyes as if to say 'same thing'. 'Anyway, I'm not ready to move in with Mark.'

Kerri glanced at the framed photograph of Mark propped up on her desk beside the computer monitor. Slumped on Mark's shoulder was Mash, his Persian cat, named so because as a kitten he used to mash his face into Mark's affectionately. He was also white and fluffy, and when curled up he looked like a dollop of mashed potato. Mark wasn't traditionally handsome, but that wasn't important to Kerri; she'd dated hot guys and it had always ended badly. Kind eyes and a warm smile was all she needed. He was funny and loved animals as much as she did; he had a job and owned a flat in a nice area. What more did a girl need? She cared for him a great deal, but wasn't ready to take such a big step; they had only been seeing each other for six months and he already had one divorce under his belt.

Donna drained the last dregs of the takeaway coffee and threw the paper cup into the small round bin under Kerri's desk. 'Don't wait too long; you don't wanna end up alone like me. Dinner parties, spa days and exciting sexual encounters with gorgeous strangers…' She winked. '…You'd hate it.'

Kerri smiled. Donna led an exciting life, but Kerri would rather stay home, snuggled up under her duvet with a good book and a mug of hot chocolate. Her homebody lifestyle was partly because of her struggles with epilepsy and her anxiety about having a fit somewhere potentially unsafe. Although Donna would never show it, Kerri sensed the highflyer felt lonely from time to time.

Kerri's phone screen lit up with a message. She glanced down at the light coming from her open handbag. The screen clock caught her eye: it was almost half one.

'I'd better get on before I fall too far behind.' She plucked out the phone and considered the message: social media notification, not important. She shoved the mobile in her pocket and rummaged in her handbag. 'Can I borrow some foundation?'

'Girl, you must have hit your head hard.' Donna placed her hands over Kerri's ears and gently turned her head back to face the mirror. 'You wanna be a shade of orange? That's all good, but you can't be black.'

Kerri smiled weakly. 'Sorry, I'm not thinking straight.'

'White Brits be constantly burning their pasty skin to try and get close to this beautiful shade. It's tragic.'

Kerri's smile strengthened with the memory of her late teenage years and her friends spending their days in tanning salons or home spraying their legs like streaky bacon. Donna grinned and batted her long eyelashes like the most innocent of models. Kerri had expected Donna to be straight-laced and stuffy given that she was in her mid-fifties, but in fact she acted more like she was in her thirties, while Kerri acted in a way society deemed a middle-aged woman should behave.

Donna would often crack jokes about Kerri being an old lady in her head, but as clumsy and ditsy as a school girl. She was also fierce where it came to politics and would front anyone on race-related issues, especially when she had to stand her ground in a predominantly white middle-class company, where the privilege goggles were firmly strapped over most people's eyes. Their articles always had to be double checked for casual racism, and Kerri did her best not to add to that. Still, Donna refused to let prejudice turn her heart to stone. The things she'd gone through (and Kerri only knew the half of it) would crush even the strongest soul, and the managing editor had smashed her way through life's barriers with sunbeams shining out of her face and a smile forever on her lips. Kerri looked up to her in a big way. She sighed at her reflection in the mirror.

'I look like a half-peeled orange.'

'It's not that bad, darling.' Donna stepped into the aisle. 'Her majesty wants to see you, though.' The managing editor sashayed away, talking over her shoulder. 'Be careful, she's in a bad mood. She marched past the fruit bowl in the canteen this morning and I swear the apples and oranges started to rot.'

'Great.' Kerri rubbed her fingertips in a frantic circular motion, struggling to blend in the orange foundation streaks.

'Hi, Kerri.'

She stopped rubbing her cheeks. Five foot nothing, weasel-faced Spencer had appeared over her shoulder in the mirror. He'd stood behind her in that exact spot to make it look as if he was giving her one from behind. Not too close though; he didn't want to be accused of harassment, but even so the insecure maggot would push the boundaries wherever possible. Kerri turned around and gagged on the strong scent coming from Spencer's cheap suit. She coughed into her fist. What did he do? Take a bath in Pound Shop aftershave while fully clothed?

'What is it, Spencer?'

He grinned, and his enormous over-bite peeked out from under his over-stretched cracked lips that struggled to cover his goofy teeth.

'The boss lady told Sean to give your workload to me; it's already done.'

He dusted imaginary lint from his shoulder like he was some kind of superhero for doing Kerri's work as well as his own.

Kerri frowned. 'You'd better not have messed with…'

Spencer lifted his hands in a 'don't shoot me' fashion. 'Calm down, love. I was given new leads, meant for you, your existing…' Having the attention span of a gnat, the little man was easily distracted. '…That is one huge bag, what've you got in there?'

Spencer peered nosily into Kerri's open handbag. She snatched it away from his prying eyes, slung it over her shoulder, and glared.

'Never you mind.'

'Oh, I get it.' Spencer's eyes lit up. 'You keep all your one-night-stand stuff in there: spare knickers and make-up, just in case you get lucky.'

He raised his monobrow several times. Kerri scowled. *What. A. Penis.* That thought gave her an idea.

'That's right. I also carry around a double-ended dildo and lube, in case I pick up a chick.'

'Well, well. Dark horse.' Spencer stepped into Kerri's personal space and licked his lips. *Oh crap. He's taken that comment seriously.*

'Just a joke, Spence.' Kerri clapped him on the back. 'I carry lots of notebooks, like we all do.'

If this weasel had done her work, she wouldn't be needing notebooks today. A skin-prickling dread ran over her body like a thousand scratchy little rat's feet. That's why the chief wanted to see her. This little shit is after her job!

'I know it's a joke; only a virgin would say something like that, to throw me off the scent.' He raised his eyebrows several times. Kerri smirked. A virgin? She laughed, snorted, then covered her mouth, embarrassed at the loudness of the piggy noise she'd made. 'I'm going places in the world, kiddo.' Spencer was younger than Kerri; was calling her kiddo meant to belittle her? He swept his tiny hand through his gel-spiked hair and his fingers caught in a knot. He awkwardly forced them through, weaselly face twisting into a look of constipation as he tried to stop the pain of accidently ripping his hair out from showing. 'You could learn a lot from me. Maybe I'll teach you a trick or two.'

He attempted a suggestive wink, but couldn't quite manage it, his other eye partially closing. Kerri cringed. Spencer had one of those smarmy faces and dipshit personalities that could push a nun to murder. Kerri wouldn't hurt a fly, but right now she had an overwhelming urge to put her hands around Spencer's scrawny little neck and squeeze until there was no more hot air left in the little beast. Donna said he was a parasite, the office flea, feeding off everyone. Then Kerri remembered her mindfulness lessons. Last thing she wanted was another stress-induced fit. She concentrated on her breathing while Spencer jabbered on about himself. Serenity washed over her. She smiled at the general reporter. 'Thanks for the offer, but I prefer to learn from those higher up the ladder. No offence. See ya, Spence.'

Spencer made a meow sound and did a claw action with his hand. 'Watch this space, kiddo. Soon enough you'll be begging me for help in more ways than one.'

Kerri huffed to herself. *He's such an idiot.* She marched off towards the door at the back of the office. It was a door no one wanted to go through because the only time any of the lower ranks in the office ever did, when they came back out, they cleared out their desk. Kerri wasn't the lowest rank, but she was job-sharing with another journalist who was on holiday, and if he ever complained about having to pick up the ball every time she dropped it, Kerri could kiss her job goodbye.

Chapter Three
The Failed Author

Beatrice waited patiently by the entrance to St Pancras station where her agent had agreed to meet her. Sunlight forced its way through the clouds in irritating intervals. Bright. Sunglasses on. Dark. Sunglass off. In the end she decided glasses on; in darkness every few minutes when the sun disappeared back behind the clouds was better than being blinded by sunstrike.

St Pancras was a masterpiece of Victorian gothic architecture and was always chock-a-block with tourists and commuters. Having never met her agent, Bea was anxious that she might look as nervous as the desperate-faced forty-something clutching a designer handbag opposite her. Both she and the woman were dressed in expensive suits. Neither had a coat, but Bea had an umbrella in her bag. Autumn was a fickle season. Right now, it was warm and breezy but later it could turn bitter and start raining. Bea straightened her jacket and picked lint off the sleeve. Her outfit was a designer hand-me-down from the granddaughter of the old lady who owned the building she lived in, but who cared where the suit came from? Bea was wearing it and that made her important. Or at least she pretended it did.

Bea had picked a white blouse to wear underneath her navy jacket while the other woman attempted to rock a black bodice. The woman's confidence in her body wasn't there. Bea found this odd. The chick had a banging rack, and if she'd had big melon breasts like that, she'd have had them on display; she definitely wouldn't be half covering them under a jacket. Bea fell into a daydream. The mysterious woman was probably waiting for her

Internet lover. A muscular Greek god with dark, wavy hair. Maybe they were soul mates about to meet in the flesh for the first time – or maybe not, and instead of a whirlwind romance the saga would end in an awkward quickie in a seedy hotel.

Bea berated herself for zoning out. This was why her career had gone tits up in the first place. The writing side of things was easy; she dreamed up stories with no trouble. Writer's block, pfft, what's that? The problem was she was rubbish at the business side of things. Hence the new agent. She should concentrate on looking professional and in control rather than what she really was: a flighty writer addicted to people-watching who liked to dream up scenarios about passers-by.

Bea combed her fingers through her dead-straight bob. A nervous tic. Playing with her hair when anxious was soothing as a child, but it didn't have the same effect as an adult. Bea did it out of habit. She reached into her jacket pocket and lifted her phone to check the time. Her agent was late. *Great start to a new relationship.* Bea craned her neck to search the crowds.

A short woman in a chic floral dress and knee-high boots was striding towards her. Blonde pixie cut. Smiling. It had to be her agent, but having only seen an online photo of her Bea wasn't one hundred per cent sure. With a name like Jackie Highfield she'd expected her agent to be tall; somewhere along the line Bea's subconscious had decided Jackie was of super model height. That wasn't the only thing that seemed odd. She knew her agent was in her sixties, but the photo online had given Bea the impression Jackie had had plastic surgery or Botox. Nope. As she neared it was clear her face was as old as she was. Phone filters had to be the answer. Everyone used them. Some use stronger filters than others. It seemed Jackie was a fan of the extreme filter.

'Sorry, Beatrice darling.' She marched right up and planted an air kiss beside each of Bea's cheeks. Bea mimicked her and got a whiff of expensive perfume. 'The Bakerloo line was jam-packed. Had to wait for the next tube. Then I lost my ticket and found it on the floor behind me. Anyway, you look lovely; shall we go?'

Beatrice mumbled a thank you and a so do you, although lovely wasn't the word she would have used to describe Jackie's appearance. That awful saying 'mutton dressed as lamb' blinked inside her head. She clenched her jaw, angry at herself for thinking such a thing. The programming was hard to break. *Older women can wear what they want, and Jackie is rocking what she's wearing, super confident, unlike the younger woman in pastel blue with her bra showing.* Bea trotted along, wanting to keep up with the pocket rocket beside her who took long strides and strolled at a steady pace, but also wanting to stick around and see who the mystery woman was waiting for.

Over her shoulder Bea spied the forty-something getting into a black cab with a hot young woman in a tight-fitting red dress. She wasn't meeting a man at all. Daughter? The young woman's hand slipped to the backside of the woman in blue. Not her daughter. Ugh! Stupid brain. How could she call herself a writer when her mind couldn't even think outside the box society had created for her? Her heart sank. Her new novel was probably shit. This meeting was going to be a disaster. Fuck. Shit. Bollocks. Arse.

'Beatrice.' Jackie looped her arm under Bea's. 'The restaurant's this way.'

They crossed the road arm in arm. Bea felt slightly uncomfortable with the intrusiveness; she hated being touched, especially by strangers. She assured herself that Jackie wasn't really a stranger: they'd been emailing back and forth for a few months. Still, it was too touchy-feely for her. Bea gently unlinked her arm, pretending to reposition her handbag over her shoulder. Jackie strutted across the road, a black cab honking at Bea and almost hitting her when she hurried after her agent.

Jackie talked fast, and Bea felt under attack from the verbal machine gun fire. Her agent spat out words so quickly she struggled to keep up with what she was saying. It wasn't long before they were outside Punk Station: a quirky, upmarket place that looked like the inside of a Steampunk blimp. Jackie held open the glass restaurant door. Bea whispered thank you and gingerly stepped inside. It was like walking into another dimension. London had been left behind and it seemed she'd walked into a world of wizards and witches. Golden exposed pipes, cogs and clocks, bleak paintings and eclectic junk covered the walls. Eccentric well-to-do folks, sitting with straight backs, were making intelligent conversation. An aura of importance surrounded them like an invisible shield; nothing could touch them, they were above it all. Jackie collared the maître d' and shortly after a waiter directed them to their reserved table.

Jackie slid behind the table and settled herself on the leather booth type seating which ran along the back wall. She shrugged off her jacket, pulled a case from her handbag, and perched a pair of trendy black-framed glasses on her slender nose. Bea lowered herself onto the seat opposite.

Jackie picked up the menu. 'Sharing okay with you, Babes?'

Babes? Bea's chest tightened. Too casual. Can't cope. This is why I don't go out. She glanced down at the tapas menu. Asparagus Eggs Benedict, a fish dish, chicken.

Jackie ran her painted nail down the front of the menu card. 'I'll pick three and you pick three.'

Heat rose up Bea's face. She took her sunglasses off and tucked them into her handbag, then wriggled her arms out of her jacket and draped it over the back of her chair. Bea didn't know what to pick. The food was super expensive and she was super broke. Jackie offered to pick for her. Bea agreed. Her agent clicked her fingers in the air for the waiter, which Bea found a bit cringy. Then, even more cringingly, Jackie ordered a bottle of wine in an inappropriately flirtatious manor. The young man – obviously sick of older women coming on to him – smiled weakly and backed away.

Bea uncrossed her legs and casually hooked her foot under the strap of her handbag, dragging it along until it was safely under her chair and there was no risk of the Italian waiter tripping over it while trying to get away from Jackie's innuendos and double entendres. The waiter popped back with some olives. He stood next to Bea and lowered them in front of her. Jackie leaned across the table and took one before he had a chance to set the ramekin down. She pushed it between her glittery pink lips and winked at the young guy. He hurried away.

'Isn't he just yummy?'

Bea followed Jackie's gaze, which was on the waiter's firm arse in tight trousers. She cleared her throat. 'Um… I was thinking, for the new book…'

'Fuck the new book.' Jackie popped another olive in her mouth, as if what she'd said was no less polite than 'Would you like a drink?' Bea struggled not to let her mouth hang open.

'Excuse me?'

Jackie held a green olive between her pink-painted nails and studied it.

'I don't wanna read it.'

She popped the olive into her mouth and bit down. Bea frowned. *How bloody rude.* Her anxiety shifted to annoyance. Not rage; Bea could never muster enough stamina for that emotion, but she was definitely irritated.

'You haven't read it?'

'Nope.'

Bea frowned. 'Then what are we doing here?'

'You need to write something new, a different genre. Something fresh.'

Here we go. Agents are all the same.

'I thought you signed me because you liked my new novel.'

'I signed you because you can write. Now, *what* you write, that's the problem.'

Bea crossed her arms in a huff. The waiter was back with their first little plate of food: the asparagus and eggs. Jackie took a fork and dug it in to the long green stem nearest to her. Bea didn't feel much like eating any more.

'What would you have me write?'

Jackie sucked the tip of the asparagus, her eyes on the waiter. He bowed to excuse himself. She bit off the tip. Her gaze shifted from the waiter to the other patrons. She grabbed Bea's forearm.

'Don't look round too quickly, but is that Tom Hardy?'

Bea remained perfectly still like a mannequin. She moved her eyes to the left.

'I think it is.'

That was not unusual for London restaurants. Bea had seen many celebrities and actors over the years eating in one restaurant or another. Jackie took another bite of the asparagus.

'I just adore him. It's taking all my strength not to go over there and lick his face.'

Bea's eyes widened. 'Lick his face?'

What was wrong with this woman? Was she on some female equivalent of Viagra?

Jackie smirked. 'A little taste, that's all I need.'

Bea sighed inside. This woman didn't have books on her mind; her head was clearly filled with thoughts of bonking younger men. Bea picked up her knife and fork and cut though the egg. Hot golden yolk ran over the greens.

'So … if you don't want my supernatural novels, what do you want from me?'

She delicately pushed a forkful of food into her mouth. The egg dripped and she caught it with the tip of her finger. Jackie gave her attention back to her client.

'Crime. It's a sure thing.'

Bea's inner critic spouted words inside her head: *Ha! You can't write crime. You're a crappy writer and your concepts are rubbish. X-files for youngsters. Yeah, right. That hooked the little fish and then they realised it was garbage. They wriggled off the hook and swam away as fast as they could.* Her paranoia piped up: *Maybe you should go back to teaching.* The timid inner child came next: *Your ideas aren't rubbish … are they?* Back to the critic: *They are, they're bullshit!*

The morsel of Eggs Benedict she had eaten was laced with a little too much pepper. Bea coughed and spluttered, tickle at the back of her throat. She poured herself a glass of water; a couple of ice cubes and a slice of lemon slipped over the spout of the jug and sloshed into the tumbler. She sat quietly and sipped. The coolness shocked her teeth and doused the fire burning in the back of her throat. Jackie had stopped stuffing her face and was lavishly applying burgundy lipstick, with an old fashioned, round compact mirror perched on her palm. Bea hoped to God she was not going to approach the actor and try to flirt with him.

Bea gripped the tumbler and moved it in a circular motion until the lemon was swirling around the melted ice. Her eyes unfocused and refocused as she thought about her past. When Bea had quit her teaching job to write novels, she'd been confident she would be earning within a year. She knew it would happen for her. That magical six-figure deal. Living the dream. That was in her future … but how wrong she was. Not about the deal. She got that. Won the literary lottery, or so she thought. The fame was fleeting. The fortune wasn't much of a fortune once her agent, publisher and the taxman had taken their cut. Marketing had been left to her – more of her advance spent. Soon there was nothing left and everyone had forgotten about Beatrice Summers. In a matter of months, they'd moved on to the next bestseller.

Her old agent was like a broken record: *It's not what they're looking for. Try writing romance, that's always popular.* Bea wrote it. No dice. *How about something for children?* Bea did that. More rejection! This new agent says she should write crime. *It's a sure thing.* For fuck's sake! Bea swore she wouldn't do this. Writing for the market never works because the market changes so quickly.

She put down the glass and locked eyes with her agent. 'I don't have an idea for a crime novel.'

Jackie snapped the decorative silver compact shut. 'Think of one.'

Jackie's gaze travelled back to Mr Hardy, who wore a Bond-esque suit and was thanking staff at the bar. Bea pressed on despite her agent being distracted.

'It's not as easy as that.'

'Why not?'

The actor laughed heartily, patted a waiter on the back and moved towards the door. Jackie's hungry eyes followed him. Their waiter was back with two more tiny plates of mini dinners. Jackie didn't acknowledge him. He was nothing compared to the hunky actor. Not wanting to snap her fingers in her agent's face, Bea slid the fish dish towards Jackie.

'Have you ever written a book?'

Jackie glanced down at the plate Bea had pushed in front of her. She stabbed the tiny fillet with her fork and placed her hand like a safety net under it as she lifted the morsel of fish to her mouth.

'Several.' She chewed and swallowed. 'They were shit. That's why I'm an agent.'

Bea allowed herself a chuckle. With the attractive actor out of the door and the waiter gone back to the safety of the kitchen, she had Jackie's full attention.

'But if I write to trends, by the time it's published the trend will be over.'

Jackie poured Bea a glass of red. Bea shook her head, but Jackie pressed the glass into her hand. Bea dutifully took a sip. Jackie picked up her wine glass and pointed it at Bea.

'Listen, Doll.' She swigged. 'You're not writing to trends. Supernatural has trends, dystopia has trends, genres like romance and crime are staples: they're always popular. What's important is how you write and what you write within these genres. Don't do what everyone else is doing. Write something fresh. I'm not asking you to be a hack. I'm telling you to write what people want to read, but in your style.'

Bea sighed. She liked writing stories about aliens for the young adult market, but the fact was, apart from a few loyal fans, her books weren't selling in any great volume. The inspiration for writing crime was not there; she couldn't write all that complex police stuff. She didn't like to read it, so how could she write it with any passion? Readers can see right through writers with no passion for the genre. But she'd have to try. Otherwise it would be back to teaching, and somehow, with all the cuts being made to school budgets, it felt better to earn very little as a somewhat failed author than go back and earn very little as an overworked, under-appreciated servant of small children.

'Okay, Jackie. I'll write a crime novel.'

'That's my girl.'

Jackie patted Bea's hand who quickly withdrew it to the safety of her lap. She cleared her throat.

'But…'

Jackie drained her glass.

'But?'

Bea took a deep breath. She wasn't good at confrontation, but she needed Jackie to know she wasn't going to be pushed around, not this time.

'I want more control. I did everything asked of me last time and it turned out badly.'

'So, there *is* some fire inside you, Beatrice Summers.' Jackie clapped her hands together. 'Good. Writing for adults can be harder than writing for children. Not because the work is trickier – writing for kids is tough – but because people will try to tear you down at every opportunity. That cow of an agent you had before was an amateur; she fucked you over royally. Not me, Babes. I got ya back.' She topped up Bea's glass, which didn't need topping up, then filled her own almost to the brim. Bottle empty. She slammed it down on the table. 'Let's make some money!'

Jackie clashed her wine glass against Bea's just as the waiter appeared with more food. Bea pushed her lips into a weak smile, a little unsure of what she'd got herself into, but happy that Jackie was at least honest and enthusiastic.

With any luck, this would be the start of something big.

Killer

You read the text again.

Bring the girl in a sundress. No knickers. School shoes and white ankle socks with a frill. I have the keys to the warehouse. Use the backdoor in the alleyway. You may wait in the alley or watch. Your call. Cash on delivery.

You stride confidently down the deserted alley. The sky is clear, but you sense a storm is brewing. The air is thick with that familiar smell of rain before it arrives. Blonde wig in perfect ringlets, flawless make-up, glitter on your cheeks. You look adorable. Will he recognise you? What a stroke of luck to find him on the dark web. It's fate. Meant to be. Your heart races with anticipation, but your head throbs with anxiety. He should have been your first. A stab of disappointment turns your lips down. What if he dodges death again? You take a deep breath and chew your bottom lip. Taste the ruby-red colour like that childhood memory of tasting a red crayon. You can do this. You want to do this. You smile and skip along, song in your head: *Dolly, dolly, number three, he shall die and bleed on me. It might be slow, it might be quick, I might even cut off his dick.*

You take Uncle Dolly out of your jacket pocket and study him. You're happy with the paper doll and clothes. Not so much with the stuck-on photo. You wanted one of him smiling, but couldn't find a single one where he wasn't grimacing. This one taken from a newspaper article you found online isn't the best quality, and looks even worse when compared to the paper clothes; you flicked through the book for a long time before settling on this particular patchwork dress. You're wearing something much cuter. A 1950s fire-engine-red poodle skirt, black glitzy top, fitted jacket and a red scarf tied at the neck. It makes you feel pretty and powerful.

No idea what he wears these days, but you guess his slobby style hasn't changed much. You also have no idea what he looks like now, but you know it's him you're meeting. He let slip that he doesn't use paper doll books to groom children any more; they're out of fashion and kids these days like different things. Sweets and puppies work best according to his handle: HardforUnders69.

How many has he abused since you? One is too many. Being on a list of sex offenders doesn't stop them. If only you'd killed him back then… No matter. He goes today. By your hand.

Creating wounds in evil men alleviates your pain. It's your medication. It's the only thing that works. Pills do nothing. Talking therapy…? Ha! They'd lock you up. Patient/doctor confidentiality? It's all good until somebody dies. You're addicted to death – to causing it. It's a rush like nothing else. You tried to stop after the last two, but the urge was too strong. You can never stop, and you don't have to. There are plenty of rats in this world for you to exterminate and there always will be. Plenty of paedo bastards, easily lured. They never see it coming. They're big, strong men; what could a little woman like you possibly do to them?

The thrill of the kill never lasts. The thirst is quenched once they're dead, but it isn't long before you're thirsty again and the hunt is on for a new toy. The dark web is seething with filth. Your advertisements are popular. A few fake five-star reviews and the rats come scurrying. Taking photos of the children you entertain at parties is the down side. Doctoring them to look like they're being abused churns the stomach, especially the sweet little five-year-old boy who you made open his mouth to show you his blue tongue after you'd given all the kids sweets at his birthday party. As soon as he turned to show his mother, mouth wide, you snapped the photo and asked his parents for permission to use it on your website. Permission granted, you did use it, but not on the site the parents thought. You photoshopped a naked man standing next to the child, positioned it so his erection was in the boy's mouth and then turned it into a cinemagraph, the man's hips moving back and forth. The punters loved it. "Oh God, that makes me so horny." "Can I get this exact boy please?" Sick fuckers!

These men delude themselves into thinking kids want them. Many believe children can give consent. They can't. Your uncle deluded himself into thinking you enjoyed what he inflicted on you, but you knew he wouldn't enjoy what you inflicted on him. That day, all those years ago, is as clear in your mind as the smell of freshly cut grass. After they found him, they came for you. A soft-spoken doctor asked all sorts of questions to find out why you did what you did, but you never told. You said he attacked you and you were defending yourself. He did and you were, but you didn't talk about the years of abuse and the paper doll bribery. You pocket the doll as you pass by what looks like the backdoor of a restaurant. He worked in a restaurant once, as a wash-up, he said.

He said lots of things, but the words he used most often were 'don't tell'. Your silence in exchange for the books and to keep the roof over your head. You couldn't face going back to that depressing orphanage. Things would be worse there. You'd heard whispers about the staff abusing children. Better the devil you know. One abuser who gives you presents versus many with no presents, and judging by the bruises you saw on the kids when they got dressed in the morning the staff were violent too. You made the deal with the devil uncle and you kept your promise. Unfortunately, he lived to tell of your torturing him and you were sent to a centre for disturbed kids. Unfortunately for him they worked out he had been molesting you. Don't have to be a genius to work that out. The sex toys scattered around him were a dead giveaway.

Your footsteps echo inside the empty warehouse. The dilapidated building smells of old boxes and mould. Machinery that was once there is gone, shapes on the floor lighter in shade where they once stood. Dwindling daylight stripes across the dirty concrete. A figure stands in the darkness next to a rickety wooden bench; particles dance in a shaft of light which exposes a thick layer of dust on the worktop. A bark echoes upwards and wind whistles through, rattling the high single-paned windows. A small sausage dog darts out from the shadows; held back by his lead, he struggles to get to you. A deep voice commands the dog to sit. It obeys and lowers its snout to the ground. Button-brown, sorrowful eyes dart around, eyebrows lifting one after the other as he waits patiently for you to get close enough so that he can jump up. The dog's thoughts play out on his innocent face; as soon as you're a foot away he's going to get his jump on. The scolding will be worth it.

'Where's the girl?' His croaky tone is followed by a phlegmy smoker's cough that echoes loud against the emptiness.

You slink towards the decrepit voice of your abuser. No longer scared, anxiety gone. He can't hurt you any more, but you can hurt him, again. This time, to death. 'My business partner is bringing her.' You hold out your gloved hand. 'Pay.'

'Payment after.' He steps into the light. Still an overweight slob, but with more wrinkles and white hair sprouting from everywhere except his bald head. He looks like he's made of rice pudding with dog hair clippings thrown over it, then poured into the baggy tracksuit he's wearing. Skin and body, all lumps and bumps, drawstring pulled tight under his beachball stomach. You know why he wears the tracksuit bottoms. Easy access. You glare at the nasty piece of shit and your fist tightens around the handle of the dagger concealed up your sleeve.

You lock eyes with him. 'Payment first.'

His hooded eyelids droop. He looks straight through you. Doesn't recognise you.

'You never said anything about a business partner.' He's twitchy. Knows something's up, and it's not gonna be his cock. A smug smile creeps across your lips. His dull eyes spark. 'You're one of those damned hunters, aren't you! Get out your phone and film me, why don't ya? I don't give a shit.'

He spits at your feet, white foam centimetres from the tip of your ruby-red high-heel. His little dog raises his head but doesn't dare bark. Animals can sense danger.

'I'm not here to film you, old man.' You lick your lips in anticipation, suspense tingling over your skin. 'I'm here to kill you.'

'What?' You push the blonde curls off your face so he can get a good look at you. He narrows his eyes.

'Don't you recognise me?' You pout. 'I'm hurt.'

His eyes widen. He stumbles backwards. 'Princess?'

The dog leaps up and starts barking. His yaps bounce off the walls and echo upwards as he runs frantically around his owner. The dog's lead wraps around your uncle's legs. The fat man falls. Déjà vu. He hits the dusty ground with a thud and a groan. The dog continues to yap at his owner's feet. You crouch down and put your free hand on the dog's head. The small animal is soothed. You unclip his lead from his collar and the little brown sausage dog scampers away and out of the door. So much for man's best friend.

You step over your abuser, legs wide apart. You clip the side of his head with your heel and he turns his head away from the blow, face now in line with your crotch. He opens his eyes to a view of what he asked for: no knickers. He grabs your legs. You laugh as he tries to pull you off balance. You kick out of his weak grip. Wrinkled hands are no match for your strong calf. You take the paper doll out of your jacket pocket, dagger handle resting in your other hand.

You hold the doll up. 'This is you.'

He doesn't speak. Doesn't beg. He knows he's fucked. He tries to lift his head and winces in pain. The hard floor has jarred his back. You place the doll on the dusty table, unfolding the little cardboard stand you made for the back so it stays upright.

'This…' You slip the blade from your sleeve and turn it on him. '… is *for* you.'

He points his shaky index finger at you. 'Those murders, the man and his wife … that was you?'

In one swift movement, you drop to one knee and plunge the knife down into his eye socket. He hollers and thrashes. Blood spurts. A rush of excitement zaps through you like an electric shock. Jelly oozes as you thrust the blade further. He falls silent and still. The light has left his other eye. You pant with the euphoria.

Hands tight around the handle, you feel the pattern imprinting on your palm through the leather. You pull the blade and it makes a slurping sound, his eyeball coming away from the socket. 'Yes…' Blood drips down the handle, down your black glove. '… that was me.'

The wind rattles the windows above. The dog is nowhere to be seen. You wipe both sides of the knife clean across the right leg of his tracksuit bottoms then use the tip of the blade to lift the dead uncle's T-shirt. Between tangles of black hair is the scar you gave him all those years ago. It gives you a thrill to see it. You lower his shirt and stare at the bloody knife handle, pondering whether to pleasure yourself with it. The urge is strong, but you don't want to risk an infection or worse. You lower your other knee, sit back next to the lifeless body and tilt your head. You'll have to clean his face before you paint it.

Chapter Four

Mike's Audition

Mike fidgeted on the hard wooden chair, hands resting on his knees, partly because he was wearing tight ripped jeans and the exposed skin was cold, and partly to keep the nerves from knocking his knees together. The hallway was cold and dank. The wood panelling behind them smelled of musty costumes and decades of cigarette smoke. Mike glanced skyward and sure enough, the ceiling was that unmistakable dirty yellow.

To his right was a beefy-bottomed girl, arse spilling over the sides of the wooden chair, with an expression on her face that implied her brain wouldn't be fully charged before midday. She was probably a student, and judging by her stripy rainbow top (two sizes too small) and charity shop orange trousers, she was probably studying something useless like classics or ceramics. She yawned without covering her hippo-wide mouth. Mike leaned away from her. Disgusting, lazy cow. He was up at the crack of dawn most days, and she couldn't even handle a 9am start.

To his left was a tall guy with a long neck that could rival a giraffe. His dowdy appearance made Mike think of Lurch from the Addams Family. The lofty fellow had come lumbering in a few minutes after Mike and had asked if the chair next to him was taken. Lurch had a curious accent, Eastern European with British undertones. The chair next to Mike was empty and he had to stop himself being a smartarse by positioning his hand on the chair and proclaiming the seat was taken: *You know Thing, right? Doesn't he live with you, Lurch?*

While they waited to be called, Lurch cleared his throat several times, which made Mike irritated enough to point out the water cooler. Before long more rag-tag hopefuls joined the queue, and Mike wondered what on earth had made him think he was anything like these sorry creatures. They were all beneath him and most certainly talentless.

He reminded himself of why he was there. Why he wanted off the streets of London. He stayed in the Square for the fans. The public adored him. At least, that's what Mike told himself and everyone else. If you lie to yourself and others enough, eventually everyone will start believing, until one day the lie becomes the truth – or something like that. Mike constantly told himself he was worthy of the West End. Worthy of being paid big money. Possibly, deep down, he didn't really believe it; maybe that's why his dreams had not come true and he was still broke and struggling to get by.

He loathed those who came to the Square for a free show. Those who stared, hands firmly in their pockets. The type who buy an outfit, wear it to a party once and then send it back for a full refund. Take, take, take. He'd often had the urge to yell DROP SOME CHANGE OR FUCK OFF! He never did, but if Mike could have gouged out their eyes, he would have done so. They can look all they want at dreary grey buildings and statues covered in bird shit, but they shouldn't watch him without paying. He'd be rolling in it if everyone that watched him dropped a pound or even fifty pence. Mime was artistry. Pierrot was a master performer and he admired and embodied the sad clown. He was going to show the world just how talented he really was.

A young woman caked in heavy make-up took a seat next to Lurch and the princess who had used Mike's spot while he was off flashed up inside his mind. Jealousy bubbled. She wasn't like the rest. She could easily take his crown and become the new favourite. That's why he had to get a new job. He needed today to go well. He'd bombed out of every audition he'd ever gone for, but today it was his time to shine. He could be as glam as the mysterious princess.

After seeing Bat's recording of her, Mike couldn't get the gorgeous creature out of his mind. Although it pained him to admit it, even if it was only to himself, she was everything he wanted to be, everything he should be. His 'friends' at Bliss took great delight in mocking him. The queens tell him he's either one of them (ugh, drag, ghastly!), or he's lying to himself about who he truly is, or else he's trans-confused. What even is that? A slur, that much was obvious. Why couldn't he be a man by day and a woman by night? Why is it always one or the other with these people? Mike wasn't overly camp, but he was more feminine than masculine. Who cares? He didn't need a label to tell him who he was. Let them stick labels all over each other and leave him out of it.

He had to admit he was desperate to know more about the new fairy princess. The living statue girl said the princess was handing out flyers. A children's entertainer drumming up business. Mike didn't buy it. She was there to steal his place, he was sure of it, and if he aced this audition she could have it.

After failing so many auditions for parts in top London shows, Mike begrudgingly decided to go down a gear and try out for a part with a travelling theatre company that visited community centres and retirement homes. The money was crap, worse than what he earned in the Square, but it would mean he'd have a proper credit and be a step closer to his dream of performing in shows like *Wicked* and *Cats*.

He puffed out the nervous tension when the memory of his most humiliating audition touched his mind. He'd tried out for the role of Scorpius Malfoy in the Harry Potter play. The actual name of the play escaped him. The panel had expected him to be a fan. Apparently, everyone else had read all the bloody books and watched the movies. Ugh! Too much prep. Who has the time? Mike wished he'd found the time, done his homework and pretended he was a Potterhead. Regret is the keeper of future fears.

Now he was prone to over-preparing and panicking about what he might be asked and whether he would have to lie through his teeth. His cheeks flushed with the thought of that face-burning moment when he announced he was not a Potter fan and thought the books were overrated. Stupid. Stupid. Stupid!

'Michael Gloss.'

Mike glanced up. A young woman dressed in a pinstripe suit, holding a clipboard loaded with headshots, had appeared in the doorway.

'Yes.' Mike held his head high and slowly stood up like a king rising from a throne.

'Come with me.'

He followed the suited lady up a narrow winding staircase into a large space on the first floor. At the back of the room was a long table. Two seats were occupied and one was empty. Sunlight streamed in from large sash windows, casting golden oblongs across the worn floorboards. Mike's heels clopped in time with the women leading him towards the trestle table.

'Good morning, Mr Gloss. May I call you Michael?' A confident male voice boomed before he was close enough to get a proper look at the figures sitting behind the table, notepads in front of them.

'Good morning. Just Mike is fine.' Mike stopped striding and stood in the centre of the room, hands clasped behind his back. The woman took her place at the table and sat down in the empty third seat.

The exuberant man in the centre, wearing a dickie bow tie, rubbed the back of his bald head then shuffled papers in front of him. 'You're auditioning for the part of Belle?'

'Yes.' Mike nodded.

The two men, clearly a couple and slightly reminiscent of Laurel and Hardy in stature, exchanged cocked eyebrows. The woman placed Mike's headshot in front of the plump one who began perusing it, while his boyfriend sat back, cross-legged, straw-thin arms folded. Mike took an instant dislike to him. The thin man reached forwards and picked up a biro, holding it between his skinny fingers like a cigarette; he probably wouldn't feel out of place wearing a ball gown and sipping a Martini. He stared Mike down, dark eyes drilling into his soul. It was going to be tough to convince this diva he was right for the job.

'You're currently working as a mime in Trafalgar Square?'

'Pierrot. The sad clown.' Mike shrugged off his cardigan and tied it around his waist. It had been chilly this morning but the tiny hall was a hotbox.

'Surely, you'd make more money doing that?' Baldy shot Mike a smarmy smile, thick lips sealed. 'Why do you want to work for us?'

Mike fluttered his false eyelashes.

'I've wanted to play Belle since I was a little…'

'Boy?' The skinny guy smirked.

Mike wrung his hands. That spiteful, biro-chewing bitch was eagerly awaiting an opportunity to pounce. He wasn't going to let it rattle him.

'Although my fans will miss me, it's time to move on and be part of something that will advance my acting career.'

Mr Spiteful leaned close to his partner to read the information on Mike's resume. 'You're a little old for that, aren't you?'

Mike kept his face plain despite the anger bubbling up inside him. Late thirties isn't old! In the gay world men over thirty-five were treated as past it, sure, but that didn't make it true, and anyway Mike didn't look his age. He knew he should have lied and put down twenty-eight.

'Talent is what's important.'

The skinny guy stopped chewing the end of his pen to retort, but the bald man cut him off.

'I agree.' Baldy had put an end to his razer-tongued lover's jabs. 'Let's hear your ballad first.'

Mike took a deep breath as the intro played. He sang the first verse and then the music cut out. He glanced over at the woman in the suit. Why had the music stopped? Was the equipment playing up?

'Mike…' The bald man took the stack of headshots from in front of his assistant and flicked through. 'I'd like you to sing one of Gaston's numbers.'

Gaston? That part wasn't right for Mike. He was not at all muscular.

'I haven't prepared for that.'

Sweat was beading on Mike's forehead. He didn't want to play Gaston. He was Belle. Beautiful Belle.

'Shame.' The smirking snake raised his hand. 'Show in the next one please, Emily.'

'No, wait!' Mike cleared his throat. 'I'll give it a go. I've watched the movie so many times. I know all the lyrics to every song.'

Mike kicked off his heels, took a deep breath and squared his shoulders. Legs locked apart, he was going to be as manly as possible. *You're an actor,* he told himself, *fucking act! You need this.*

'Off you go.' Mr Bald rested his elbows on the table and perched his chin on his linked fingers.

Emily started the music. Mike sang in his gruffest voice and moved around the small hall as if he was the most muscular and manly man who ever lived. The small casting team smiled, the skinny one swaying along to the music. They liked him. They really did! When the number was finished, Mike stood breathless. He'd done it.

'That was great!' The bald man clapped with enthusiasm and his skinny wife tapped his palm delicately to simulate clapping. 'Can you bring in one of the girls waiting outside, Emily. I want her to do a reading with Mike.'

Mike beamed. They wouldn't be bothering if they didn't think he had what it took. This audition was going great. Skinny passed Mike a crinkled script and he cast his eyes over his lines. When Emily opened the door, the big-bottomed student slouched in. Mike's smile fell from his face. Surely this girl was here to play the beast?

'Welcome, Lindy.' The bald one grinned. 'We'd like you to read a few lines with Mike and then we'll hear you sing, okay?'

'Sure thing.'

She tugged at the bottom of her two-sizes-too-small top in a futile bid to cover her bulging stomach. Mike seethed with anger. Belle means beautiful. This girl was no Belle. How could they choose her over him?

'Mike, I want you to gaze into Belle's eyes like she's the most beautiful creature you've ever seen.'

Mike stared at his competition. No make-up and a lazy eye behind rectangular glasses. The girl smiled back and her piggy nose twitched, it looked like a pimple in the middle of her moon face. Reflected in the beast's glasses was Mike's beautifully made-up face. His sorrowful eyes, framed with black liner and false lashes, welled with tears.

'FUCK THIS!' The words shot from his mouth before he could stop them.

He threw the script in the girl's face. She gasped.

'You'd pick her as Belle over me?' He pointed straight at her, but remained facing the panel. 'She should be the beast!'

They all gasped, except for skinny. He clapped his hands with glee like he was watching his favourite soap opera.

'How rude!' The bald guy stood up in mock-outrage. 'I'm so sorry, my dear.' He cooed to the Belle auditionee. Mike knew none of them really cared about the woman's feelings; Mike's reaction was what they were hoping for. Men like them consume a steady diet of drama. They must have been hungry this morning. Bastards.

Mike scooped up his heels and stormed out of the door, middle finger up as he left. He hurried down the stairs, sheer pop socks snagging on the wooden steps, tears threatening. He pushed past the others waiting in the hallway, knocking into Lurch's knees. Out of the entrance door, the cold air hit his flushed face and cooled it, tears stinging like frostbite. He bent down and slipped his heels on, one after the other.

Why couldn't people accept him for who he was? He'd have made a great Belle. He wiped away the tears, trying not to smudge his eyeliner. He took his cardigan from around his waist, slipped it on and hugged it tight around him, sheltering his body against the chilly wind. Head down, he moved into the flow of tourists. Pedestrians barged past him, battling against the gale. A newspaper page blew towards Mike's legs and got stuck. He reached down and grabbed it. Who reads newspapers any more? About to screw it up, he stopped when he saw a black and white picture of the princess who'd stolen his spot.

He moved close to the wall of a building, turned his back to the wind, and held the page up. In a square box was a photo of the princess Bat-Tits had caught on film. She was wearing a Cinderella-inspired dress and tiara. Next to her smiling face was a list of quotes from happy customers and a phone number to book a party. It was true, she was a children's entertainer. The sounds of London's busy streets – horns honking, hurried footsteps and cabbies craning their necks out of their car window to yell at people – were drowned out by Mike's inner voice: *You could do that. Join forces with the princess. You could be Belle. It might be fun.*

He hated kids, but that was a minor detail. He had to get in contact with this woman. Her company was called Pretty Princesses. The tagline read: 'A magical experience for those who wish their favourite princess would come to life.' He scanned the number and reached into his trouser pocket for his phone. He hesitated; he couldn't phone her up having never met her. What was he going to say? *Hey, want a new partner?* That would never work. He had to meet her in person first. Show her how perfect he would be as one of her princesses. She'll probably come back to the Square. A rush of excitement tingled over Mike's skin. A wonderful new opportunity awaited; he could feel it!

Chapter Five

Kerri and Sausage

K erri walked the streets in a daze, kicking fallen autumn leaves across the ground and pondering the very real idea that she might lose her job. The angry-faced, pointy-finger telling off she'd received earlier from the editor-in-chief was playing in her head on a loop like a demented GIF. The woman hated her. Said as much. Well, she didn't say those exact words, but that's what Kerri had gathered from the meeting. If the boss could have breathed fire, Kerri was sure she would have done so.

Management, not counting Donna and Sean, were totally intolerant of Kerri's condition. The boss spoke as though it was all in Kerri's head and she could somehow control her fits. Sadly, her boss also thought the same about depression, anxiety, and other mental illness. According to her, these 'illnesses' were controllable; it was only the weak who lost control of their minds. The editor-in-chief's words rang in Kerri's ears: "You're allowing your mind to shut down your body. Control your thoughts and you won't have fits. Find a way to stop this happening or find another job. Are we clear?" No amount of education on epilepsy was likely to change her mind.

Sean had orders to punish Kerri. He'd been giving her the most tedious non-stories to rehash or follow up. He kept adding the word 'sorry' at the end of every email. So far this past month Kerri had covered the local desperate housewives' book club, affairs and scandals of some boring accountant, and the last one involved a ghastly common-as-muck cow fighting with a gormless and toothless git about him shagging her aunt/sister/cousin, probably all them and all at once. Kerri had at least had fun with the headline: 'Toothless Terry Pulls More Women Than His Dentist Pulls Teeth.'

It was hard to decipher Terry and his wife's emails. Slang, textspeak, spelling and grammar mistakes galore. In the end, Kerri had to use video chat to get the story, but that was even worse. Both spoke the way they typed. She did what she could with the information, but probably got it wrong. Who cares? Given the opportunity, these people would sell out their own mother for a quick quid.

That piece had earned Kerri a barrage of abuse, including the couple taking great delight in egging her flat. Their love was rekindled by their hatred of her. She was used to this type of abuse. People sent threatening tweets about how they were going to rape/shoot/stab her and her loved ones. Verbal abuse in the street and online trolls are manageable, but Kerri was terrified when a creepy guy started following her to work. One day he wasn't there any more and she guessed that Donna had finally scared him off.

Kerri's career had been going down the toilet for a while. If it wasn't for Donna having her back, she probably would have lost her job years ago. Kerri was sick of writing up crappy community stories, and now she was getting the worst of those stories thanks to her latest seizure. She wanted a big story to work on. Something she could get her teeth into. Something exciting. This want had turned into a need. They couldn't get rid of her if she got a scoop on something really big. But that kind of luck only ever happened in old Superman movies. Jimmy Olsen might have been a photographer rather than a journalist, but he screwed every opportunity up royally and she was no different.

Kerri glanced up to find she didn't recognise where she was. Her feet hadn't taken her home like they usually did when she zoned out after work. She glanced around the narrow alleyway. How had she managed to exit the tube station and slip so far off the beaten track? Better go back the way she came.

Kerri's footsteps crunched across crispy leaves as she tramped back the way she came. The wind whispered through an overhang of leafy branches above, sun glinting between the reds and browns, several leaves falling and fluttering down in the breeze. The narrow walkway quickly turned into a tunnel of shadows. Kerri clutched the strap of her handbag, elbow bent tight against the bag, fearful she might be mugged by someone hiding in the darkening corners behind large bins and flat stacks of cardboard boxes.

She glanced over her shoulder. A dark figure appeared and then disappeared. Someone had stepped out of a doorway and shrunk back into the shadows when they spotted her. Fear pushed her heart rate up and her stride a little faster. She stole another glance over her shoulder. Heavy footsteps accompanied the silhouette behind her. Her muscles tensed. It's the stalker! He'd found her. Chest tight, Kerri quickened her pace. The end of the alley was in sight, traffic moving past. Inside her head a familiar chant: *Get onto the busy street where the lights and people are. Hurry!*

The person behind her coughed. It was a man. She was right! He was after her. He'd rape her, strangle her and dump her body in one of the industrial bins. She had to get away. Kerri broke into a sprint, heart thumping against her ribcage. The cold air rushed to the back of her throat, lungs pricking like she'd breathed in icy splinters. She puffed white blooms into the crisp autumn air and ran like she was on the track chasing down Usain Bolt. Pain to her side. She winced and held onto the stitch. Slowed down. She couldn't keep going. Glanced back. The man was gone. Bent over, hands resting on her knees, she waited until the burning in her chest and pain in her side abated. She was close to the end of the alleyway. Relief washed over her.

A rusting sound beside one of the bins spiked fear back into her heart. Dread prickled up the back of her neck.

'Ruff, ruff, ruff!'

'Shit!'

Kerri fell backwards into a pile of damp boxes someone had been too lazy to flatten and shove in the recycling bin. Her handbag flew off her shoulder. A small dog was on top of her licking her face, his entire backend wiggling along with his waggy tail. She giggled.

'You frightened the life out of me, naughty doggie.'

'Yap, yap, yap.'

Kerri pushed up into a sitting position and patted the excited little pooch. 'Okay, calm down now.'

The sausage dog turned his snout left and right, licking her hand as she passed it over his soft head and ears. The dog was dirty and smelly, as though it had been rummaging through food waste bins. She checked the collar. The tag was scratched, phone number not clear. The dog's name was deeply engraved on the front side.

'Pud?' She scratched the dog behind the ear. 'That's a dumb name. Doesn't suit you at all.'

The dog woofed in agreement.

Perhaps the poor thing had been dumped?

She'd take him to Mark, and then they could take the dog to Mash's vet and have him scanned for a microchip. She tilted her head. The brown dog looked like a sausage. If Mark decided to keep him, his pets could be called Sausage and Mash. She giggled at the thought.

Sausage sniffed Kerri's blouse and then leapt off her lap. He stood in the middle of the dark alley and yapped. Kerri got to her feet and picked up her handbag, slung it over her shoulder, then scooped up a tube of lip-gloss and a notepad that had fallen out of a side pocket. Stuffing them back in the bag she crouched down to pick up the dog. He slipped through her fingers and ran off. She straightened up. The dog stopped a few feet away and yapped. She took off after him and he started running again. When she stopped, he stopped and waited. She crossed her arms.

'Do you want my help or not?'

She started off after the dog again and again he began to run. This time around some big green bins and out of sight. She hurried after him.

'Sausage … I mean, Pud!' She realised he wouldn't answer to Sausage, he wasn't answering to Pud either. 'Pud!'

The dog stood stock-still, nose pointed at the door of a towering old building.

'What is it?'

Pud stared straight at the door, unflinching. The sun had sunk; no sign of the moon or stars. The darkness thickened like a blanket thrown over the buildings above, giving the alley a black ceiling.

'Come on, Pud. Time to go.'

Kerri bent down to pick up the dog once and for all. He growled. She recoiled.

'Fine! I'm going home. Come or stay, your choice.'

The dog remained with his long snout almost touching the door. Kerri walked away, then paused. The dog hadn't moved. Maybe he lived in the building with a homeless guy and couldn't get back in? She took out her phone, tapped the torch symbol and marched back. The dog turned his head towards the shining torch-light and wagged his tail.

'I'll let you in but I'm not coming with, okay?'

Kerry pulled on the rusty handle and the battered door cringed open. The dog scampered through the opening, the clack of his unclipped nails echoed in the gloom inside. Kerri shined her torchlight after him. The place was a hollow shell; nothing to see except the back end of the dog trotting away, tail in the air. Dim light shone through high windows into what looked to Kerri like an abandoned warehouse.

Pud's bark echoed in the darkness. He yapped and yapped. Anxiety tightened around Kerri's throat. She couldn't risk going into some old building at night. What if there were gangs or rough sleepers? Druggies! What if she had a fit? No one knew where she was. The dog began to howl. She couldn't just leave him.

'Flipping heck!'

She held the phone up and slipped inside, the door clattered shut behind her. The smell was foul, like the inside of a football team's locker-room after a match. She coughed and cupped her hand over her nose. Other hand trembling, she shined her phone light around the run-down old warehouse. The light caught on the reflective eyes of a rat, resting on its back legs, twitchy nose in the air. It scurried off. The dog stopped howling.

'Pud?' Kerri called in a soft voice.

Treading lightly as she moved into the belly of the building, Kerri's senses tingled. *This is a bad idea. Dumb in fact. I should have left the damn dog.* Her phone light finally found Pud's sausage-shaped outline. He was weaving in and out of two table legs. Kerri tiptoed over to him. She pinched her nose because the rancid odour had strengthened and the stench turned her stomach.

'Pud, come on.' Fingers holding her nostrils closed, she sounded like a clown whose red nose was on too tight. 'It smells gross in here.'

The dog bowed his head and nudged something in front of him with the tip of his snout. Kerri moved the beam and the light revealed a plump foot. Muffled gasp. She lowered her hand.

'Oh my God.'

The odour worse still. She buried her nose in the crook of her elbow and slowly raised the light. Lying on the floor in a starfish position was the semi-naked body of a heavy-set male. Kerri's trembling increased. She couldn't hold the light steady; it darted over the man's Y-front underpants, which had clearly once been white, or at least grey, but were now stained red. His skin was ashen. No doubt he was dead. Kerri froze. She slowly lifted her head from the crook of her elbow.

'Come on, Pud. Let's go!'

She backed away from the bloodied body. The dog ran around in a circle, then sat down at his owner's feet and barked. Hands shaking violently, Kerri tapped her phone screen as she backed away.

'Come on, Pud, I'm calling the police.'

The dog scurried into the shadows beyond the dead man's head. Kerri couldn't hold her phone still long enough to punch in the emergency number. She tapped the wrong button and the camera screen popped up. Thoughts entered her head as she hovered her finger over the screen to close the camera. *This is my chance. This man is dead. Possibly murdered. I could break the story.*

Kerri puffed out the fear and slowly walked towards the corpse. *You can do this, Kerri. It'll save your arse. Think of the chief: she'll be impressed. You wanted a big story. This is it.*

Sharp nails on four little paws clacked against the floor, a slurping sound followed. Kerri shined the phone light up towards the sound. The dog was licking dry blood from the dead man's cheek. Kerri touched her face where the dog had previously licked her. *Eww, gross.* The dog stopped licking and sat back. Her torchlight fell on the big round face; a rush of panic sucker-punched Kerri in the chest. The corpse's face had red circles painted on his cheeks and blood smeared across his lips. Long eyelashes had been drawn on him with black marker, freckles dotted over the nose. One eye was glazed over and staring into nothingness, the other bloodstained and gouged. There were no lines of blood running down the face. The dog must have licked them off. Kerri's stomach churned like a family of eels wriggling in her gut. She checked the immediate area. There was no sign of a discarded murder weapon.

Who could have done this? The dog bounded over to the table and cocked his leg. His pee pattered loudly in the vast empty building. Kerri held up her phone and took several shots of the man's head and then stepped back to photograph the entire body. The male's bloody underpants didn't have any rips or tears. The killer must have pulled them down, done something to his genitals, then pulled the pants back up. If she were a man, she was sure she'd feel ball ache at that idea. Stabbed in the eye then stabbed in the cock? She stared at the flat front of the bloody pants. Cock cut off?

The dog yapped; Kerri turned the light on him.

'Did you eat his sausage, Sausage?'

She cringed at the mental image of the dog running around with a severed penis in its jaws.

The torchlight lit up something on the table. A note? Kerri took a deep breath and walked over to it. On the benchtop, lying flat, was a paper doll. It had on a patchwork dress. The flaps that hold the dress to the doll at the shoulders had come lose. Kerri hadn't seen a paper doll since the 90s. They were popular with her grandmother's generation and she remembered playing with some at a friend's house as a child, but now they were out of fashion, kids didn't play with them these days, did they? A cut out photo of the man's face was glued over the card-backed doll's face. The killer knew the victim. Premeditated. A lightness touched Kerri's mind. She'd seen something like this before – on an American cop show? It seemed familiar. She couldn't think straight. She snapped a photo of the paper doll and the dog.

'Right, Pud. Time to call the police and get out of here. You okay with that?'

Pud barked as if he understood. Kerri closed her eyes to gather some courage. *She shouldn't be doing this. The cops will ask to check her phone.*

She quickly emailed the photos to herself, checked the email had come through, then deleted the photos and the email app. She dialled 999.

Chapter Six

Bea's Inspiration

Beatrice cradled her coffee mug; the warmth had long since leached out of it, though with her fingerless 'typing gloves' on she hadn't noticed how icy-cold the cup had become until the rim touched her lips. She swigged the last dregs of tepid coffee and stared at the blank page on the screen. Crime fiction ideas were not coming easy. So far, she'd thought of a killer who suffocates people in their sleep and then it turns out to be the ghost of … *not crime, Bea.* Then she thought of a murderer who uses satanic rituals to raise the dead and … *that's zombies, Bea.* Arf! No matter what she dreamed up there was always some supernatural element to it. She doesn't write crime. She can't write crime. If this keeps up, she'd end up committing a crime! Strangling her poxy agent might be a good place to start. She couldn't do it. It was impossible.

Bea got up from her desk, wrapped her dressing gown around her bony frame, and tied a tighter knot in the belt around her waist. She paced around the room, listening to the rain lash the sash window which faced the bricks of the old Victorian building next door. Her bedroom was a double, rare in London. She had room for a desk and single bed and therefore didn't need to leave her bedroom except for food and the bathroom. Kerri often worked quietly in the living-room and Mike was never home; if he was, he was asleep. It was the perfect arrangement for all. Private people, they liked their space and kept out of each other's way, but right now Bea needed help. Maybe Kerri could help her?

She worked at a newspaper; she might have a few ideas about what Bea could write.

Bea reached for the door handle. Leaving her room meant a risk of small talk. She wasn't good at that, and not in the mood for it either. She reminded herself that if she didn't do this she would starve. Her savings were dwindling and everything hinged on this book being a smash hit. She held in her anxiety and left her room.

The living space was dark and quiet. Bea tuned on the free-standing lamp in the corner and its soft glow highlighted the minimal furniture in their apartment. It was open plan. Living space linked to the small dining area with a foldaway table. The kitchen was partitioned by a small wall between it and the dining area. Bea checked the clock above the kitchen bench. She'd never completely understood Roman numerals and relied on her memory of clock face number positions. The hands indicated it was 11pm.

Bea had been sitting at her desk typing and deleting paragraphs for two hours. The others must be sleeping. She hung her head and plopped down on the sagging leather couch. Kerri's laptop was closed on the coffee table. Bea wondered what she was working on. The last message Kerri had sent her was a rant about her boss being unempathetic about her epilepsy and how she was being forced to write boring community stories. As writers, they understood each other. Kerri probably couldn't help with the new book. The last report Kerri had written was about cheaters, and who wants to read a book about chav couples shagging their way through each other's family members? She could make them kill each other over it. Nah, still boring.

Shuffling footsteps on the landing, shadows passed across the light coming from under the door. Mike? He often came home late and got himself a snack, leaving a mess on the counter top. It was always him snacking at midnight. Bea knew it wasn't Kerri because Mike was the only one who ate meat. Empty ham packets and half the bread gone was definitely down to him. She'd left notes asking he clean up after himself, but it always fell on deaf ears and she'd given up on trying to change his late-night habits.

Bea walked over to the door and yanked it open, hoping to startle Mike.

'Holy hell! You tryin' to give me a heart attack, Ms Summers?'

The little old landlady, in a pink dressing gown and matching slippers, held her hand over her heart and glared at Bea through funky, red-framed glasses.

'Sorry, Mrs Williams. I heard a noise; I thought you were Mike.'

Mrs Williams was often up late at night. Like Bea, she suffered with insomnia. The landlady's wakefulness was brought on by old age, says she doesn't need to sleep for more than four hours a night because she falls asleep in the afternoon. Bea's was anxiety induced. She couldn't quiet her busy writer's mind at the best of times but when she needed to focus or had a deadline, it got worse.

Lowering a long-handled feather duster, Mrs Williams poked a shrivelled finger into her greying afro and scratched the side of her head. 'Thought I was Mike, huh? That boy is always rolling in drunk. Did you hear the latest?' She pointed the rainbow feather duster at Bea. Bea shook her head, amused. 'Besotted with a beautiful woman. An entertainer or something. It's not right. He'll come to a bad end if he doesn't buck his ideas up. You mark my words. A gay lusting after a woman? He's lost his mind! You ask me, he wants to be her. He goes out at night in a dress and a wig. I've seen it!'

Bea giggled at Mrs Williams's expressive nature: eyebrow-raising and wide-eyed outrage, accompanied by the waving of her multi-coloured duster. *A 'gay' she says. Never stopped for a minute to consider Mike might be bi or pan or trans.* Then again, the old girl must be in her late seventies, she probably doesn't know what LGBT means. Bea knew there were more letters than four, but she couldn't remember all of them. Mike liked dressing up. He was a sad clown by day and a woman by night. He was always sending

Bea pouting selfies in some club or another, and she would send back amusing GIFs. That was the extent of their friendship.

Bea gently took the duster from Mrs Williams and reached up to clear away the cobwebs in the corners of the high ceilings. 'Mike lives in Mike's world. I can never keep up with his exploits.'

'What're you doing up so late? Having trouble sleeping again?'

Bea raised herself up on tiptoes and swiped a large wispy web away with the tip of the duster. 'Struggling with the new book.'

Mrs Williams took the duster back, jumped and wiped another cobweb away. Energetic for her age. Bea reckoned it was down to the half a pint of Guinness the old girl drank each day.

'Want some tea? It'll help you sleep.' Mrs Williams shoved the duster under her arm like a cane and wagged her finger. 'You can't write good if you're not rested. The brain needs downtime just like a computer does.'

Bea yawned, hand over her mouth. 'Thanks, I'll pass. I'm feeling sleepy now anyway.'

'Okay, sweetheart. Tell that Mike when you see him that if he forgets his key once more, he can sleep outside for the night. I'm sick of him rapping on my bedroom window in the early hours.'

She bustled down the landing to catch more cobwebs.

'I'll give him the message. Goodnight.'

'Goodnight, love.'

Bea slipped back inside her flat, closed the door and dragged her weary body back to her room, turning the lamp off as she passed the couch. If only inspiration would strike. She thought about when her best ideas came to her; it was normally while she was near or in water. Maybe a shower would help? Though the noise might wake the others and she was already in her pyjamas – she'd been in them all day. Writers in her online groups often joked about PJs being their work uniform. For Bea, it was true.

Back in her room, she kicked off her slippers, threw off the dressing gown and climbed into bed. She curled up under the duvet then reached over and clicked the switch on her desk lamp. The room went black. She snatched back her arm from the slight chill in the air and wrapped both arms around her, shivering until the warmth returned to her comfy bed. Her frozen toes curled, fluffy socks not enough to keep them warm, she wished she'd made a hottie bottle. After her body stopped shivering and the chatter inside her head had died down, she finally drifted off to sleep.

***

BANG!

Bea woke with start. What was that slam? The front door? She sat bolt upright and stared into the gloom. The room was dark. It was still night. The lines and shapes in her room were not the same as when she went off to sleep. Kerri's laptop was open on the coffee table, power button flashing. Bea frowned. She was in the living room, on the couch. She shivered under the blanket, dragged it around her as she got to her feet, and shuffled over to her room.

She reached around the door frame and switched on the light. Eyes shocked, she switched it back off and with spots dancing, felt her way to the desk. Eyes not adjusted to the dark yet, she ran her hands over the desk top searching for her phone and knocked over a stack of paperbacks – a couple of them thumped on the floor. Her fingers found the cold oblong, she picked it up and the screen light illuminated her face. She squinted, and the glowing fuzziness sharpened into the numbers 12:05. She yawned. An hour's sleep wasn't enough; no wonder she felt like shit. More banging and crashing sounds. Familiar. She dragged back the curtain and looked out of the rain-soaked window, leaning close to the glass to get a glimpse of the street. A nearby streetlamp shone down on the quiet road, rain falling in diagonal showers through the shaft of light. Mrs Williams was putting the bins out. *She's a day early.* Bea checked her phone again and gawped at the date staring back at her. She hadn't slept for an hour; she'd slept for twenty-five hours! That can't be right.

Bea's toes were frozen, the carpet was spongy under foot and cold, like stepping on a wet towel left on the bathroom floor. Where were her socks? She felt around the floor for her slippers, found them and tugged them on. Then she shrugged off the blanket and took her flowery dressing gown from the peg on the back of her door, pulled it on, pocketed her phone and hurried back into the living room. It was as quiet as it had been the night before – or an hour before, who knew?

Bea turned on the lamp. The soft light touched edges and corners and brought shadows to life. Ham packet on the kitchen bench. Breadcrumbs everywhere. If she had only been asleep for an hour that would still make sense. Bea's head felt cold, that familiar chill when coming inside from the wind and rain. She reached up and touched her hair. It was damp. She looked down and realised she was wearing different pyjamas. What the fuck was going on? Had she been sleep walking? Maybe she had a fever and that's why her hair felt damp. Changed her clothes in her sleep because she was clammy? Bed sheets soaked so she'd moved to the couch?

It wasn't unusual for Bea to lose track of time. Her insomnia meant she often didn't know what time or day it was, but she'd never slept for so long before. Maybe she had the wrong day? The flashing power light on Kerri's laptop lured her back over to the coffee table. Bea sat down on the couch and tapped the spacebar. The screen lit up white. She scrolled down. Her eyes widened. Kerri wasn't working on a community news piece; this was a murder case. She got up, darted around the coffee table and over to Kerri's bedroom door. Bea spoke softly into the wood.

'Kerri, can I talk to you?'

Silence.

Bea knocked lightly. 'Kerri, please. I need help.'

Nothing.

She turned the handle and slowly opened the door. The hinges creaked and Bea cringed. Inside, her flatmate's bedroom was dark.

'Kerri?'

There was movement from Kerri's bed. Bea crept closer. She shouldn't wake her, but she was feeling weird and needed reassurance. Plus she wanted to know what Kerri was working on. She peeled back the duvet.

Woof!

'Fuck!' A dachshund jumped up and down on Kerri's bed. 'How did you get in here?'

Bea rushed to turn on the light, dog at her heels. Click. Kerri's room, which looked more like it belonged to a ten-year-old – cutesy duvet covered in stars and moons, soft toys in a row at the end of the bed – was neat and tidy expect for where the dog had been snoozing at the head of the bed. Bea bent down and stroked the super friendly mutt. He licked her hands enthusiastically. Kerri was lucky the pooch hadn't ripped her precious soft toys to bits.

'You're soooo cute, aren't you?'

Bea checked the dog's name tag.

'Pud? That's a daft name. You shouldn't be here, Mister. No pets allowed in the building.' *Unless Kerri's managed to negotiate a new agreement.* Bea straightened up. She pointed at the dog and spoke firmly. 'Stay!'

To her surprise, the dog sat down obediently. Bea turned off the light and shut the dog back in Kerri's room. It yapped for a few minutes and then went quiet. She took out her phone and typed out a message: *Found Pud. Mrs W is gonna freak on you if she finds out.*

Bea liked animals, as long as they weren't in her home pooping on the floor and being a general nuisance. The dog would have to go. Kerri didn't reply to her message. She was obviously at Mark's. Bea pocketed her phone. Mark had a studio flat somewhere in London; she guessed they didn't want a dog watching them shag. What puzzled Bea was why Kerri had left her laptop open. Maybe she'd had another fit and had to be rushed to hospital? Perhaps Mike had gone with her. Bea took her phone back out of her dressing gown pocket and typed quick: *Hope you're okay.* She clicked send.

Phone back in her pocket, Bea flopped down on the couch. She glanced at the laptop. She shouldn't invade her flatmate's privacy. Going in her room while she was out was bad enough. Bea couldn't help herself; she scrolled to the top of the open document on Kerri's laptop and read the headline aloud.

'The Paper Doll Murders.'

Bea's mind flooded with ideas before she'd even had the chance to read on. What a great title for a book!

Killer

You type fast. Hook the dirty fish. This one is married, grown children, interested in pre-pubescent boys. It's crazy how forthcoming they are with personal information. It's like they want to be caught. To cleanse themselves of responsibility. They write things like: *My wife never fucks me and is a miserable old trout and my kids have left home.* They can't abuse them any more. Many men have said similar things along the lines of they need to fuck little boys for the good of their health, or they might murder their wife or go on a rampage. *It's not my fault,* they'd confess, *they drive me to this.* They use any crackpot excuse to absolve themselves.

Advertisements on the dark web were one way of finding them; being a children's entertainer was another. You'd thought about teaching, but that's too much hard work. There'd be no time to hunt. You close the tab. Open a new one and type a message.

Really looking forward to seeing you again, Babe. Add a heart emoji, kissy face.

This new paedo was a change from the overweight middle-aged men who enquired through the dark web. In his twenties, he liked teen virgins, and being slim, flat-chested and baby-faced meant the guy was easy to lure without the promise of a child. For this type of kill you needed to groom him. It was uncomfortable work, but worth it to save another child from abuse.

A mother at a children's party had expressed he preyed on her fourteen-year-old daughter. You spoke with the daughter briefly. She opened up like the petals of a rose, dead bee inside. Princesses make girls and boys feel safe enough to talk. The girl told you his name, where he worked and that he got her drunk and raped her. She couldn't tell her mother about the rape. Losing her virginity that way was a source of shame for the poor thing. You know how that feels. The guy had done the usual things, said he loved her, brought her gifts. Kept grooming until the deed was done, then he stopped returning her texts and blocked her on social media.

Weasels like him screw underage teen girls rather than children because the girls don't usually scream rape; they think they're in love and that the love affair has ended. One reason this type prey on underage girls is because women usually turn down their advances. Slimy and sexually inept, impressing women their age or older is too challenging. Women see right through their bullshit. No one wants to have sex with a man whose hands are like creepy tentacles, touching all the wrong places. Although he prefers young girls, he will fuck an older virgin, so long as she seems like an underage girl. Sick.

To lure the insecure and socially awkward man with a virginity fetish, all you need to do is pretend to be innocent and in need of a real man to direct you in the bedroom. Play them at their own game. You don't let them fuck you. No, no, you pretend to be virginal, frightened and delicate. Intercourse is the last stage, a stage he will never experience with you or any underage girl, ever again.

Dressing up like a school girl and provocatively sucking a lollipop is a good one – cliché, sure, but it gets them going. He thinks you're a twenty-five-year-old virgin, waiting for the right man to come along. Make-up's a wonder; it can knock years off a person. First few 'dates' you gain his trust by playing hard to get. Third date requires some impressive acting. He likes to squeeze your breasts together, which is awful. He really has no idea how to arouse a woman and nor does he care. It's all about him. You give him a hand-job, but refuse access between your legs. The next date is the final stage. You've done this before, but last time things didn't go so smoothly. The wife walked in and wanted to join in. Two dolls for the price of one. It was messy. You got hurt, and swore to yourself you would never allow a meeting in a family home again. The new target has rented a hotel room. You've got your outfit. Game on.

Chapter Seven

Mike's a Drag

Bliss used to be a rundown gay bar. It was meant to be men only, but they couldn't close the doors to lesbians because for one, they were paying customers, and two, because the club owners would be seen as prejudiced, and in truth they were. Most gay men hated the idea of a vagina; the thought sickened them, but the lezbos came, even though it was clear the men didn't want 'dykes' there. People tend to think only straight men want male-only spaces, but gay men can be just as anal about this. In the 90s, the dark, seedy club was called Eden and full of pretty boys and butch guys in leather. The smell of amyl nitrite (it stank like paint thinner) was everywhere.

The club's popularity fell once the straights became more accepting of 'the gay lifestyle' and folks started mixing in more upmarket venues. The licence changed hands and Eden was renamed Bliss in around 2005. It was no longer a rave venue and a place of thumping techno, dark alcoves and topless hunks. The new owners turned it into a classy joint that catered to any persuasion, including straights who loved drag acts. Show tunes rang out from the stage until midnight, and a disco started after that. When he was feeling in the mood, Party Mike enjoyed being the centre of attention. Depressed Mike preferred the quiet corners at the back, the only negative being the couples necking in the booths, but it was a small price to pay for peace and quiet and a good G&T.

Mike glanced around and tried to imagine the way the club used to be. He hadn't frequented Eden back in the day; he'd only gone a handful of times before it changed hands. He'd been ignored by every guy he took an interest in. When the club got a makeover, he decided to give himself a makeover too. That's when Micha appeared. She always got attention from everyone, mostly because Mike had modelled the look after Uma's character in *Pulp Fiction*. Black bob and stylish clothes. He'd always wanted to be a blonde like the model/actress, but after trying on an insane number of wigs he decided it didn't suit him.

The interior of Bliss looked as if the designers had thrown a glitter bomb inside and had run out of the door, like that New Year's episode of Mr Bean where he puts a firework in a tin of paint. That, but with purply-blue glitter. Every surface and wall sparkled. It was bright, it was clean, and there wasn't a popper in sight. Classy drugs like coke were snorted in the toilets through rolled up five-pound-notes. You could lick the top of any of the toilet cisterns and get a hit. Mike sipped his sixth gin of the evening and spun the fancy beer mat on the table top. The picture of bright coloured shots on offer blended together as they whirled round.

'Mind if I sit?'

Mike didn't look up. He recognised the voice and the musky scent of knockoff perfume, probably named something like Coco Chantel. He nodded to the chair opposite him.

'What's eating you?'

A tall cocktail glass was placed on the table. Mike glanced at it. Blue liquid, little umbrella, straw, one of those new eco-friendly ones, and a neon-yellow, plastic swizzle stick. Bit pointless having an eco-straw alongside a plastic stick.

'She hasn't come back to the Square.'

Clatter of the swizzle stick against the glass.

'You're becoming obsessed.' Painted nails continued to twirl the stick around in the blue liquid.

'I thought about phoning, but it doesn't seem right to call out of the blue. Should I phone?'

'In the state you're in? No.'

'I should have said my name was Micha.' Mike swirled the clear liquid in the tumbler. The lemon and lime slices danced round, caught in the mini gin and tonic tornado. 'They asked for real names, not stage names. I should have lied.'

'Now what are you talking about?'

'The audition.'

He glanced up at Lady Vajazzle. Her pink wig, feathered eyelashes and big red lips were a smear of bright colour on a blotch of orange face. He blinked several times, but it didn't clear his vision. Painted claws rested on Mike's hand.

'Honey, you can't keep dwelling on lost opportunities. Anyway, they would have seen your real name when you gave them your bank details.'

'Don't have a bank account.'

'Paypal then. Your email address says Mike on it, right?'

'It does.'

Vajazzle pulled a compact from her clutch and started powdering her big nose.

'Even if it said Micha, you don't pass, so they'd know.'

'I do pass!' Mike scowled. Words slurring. He pointed a limp finger at his friend. 'Unlike you, you're huge … and hairy. You've got no chance of passing.'

'There's no need to be rude!' Vajazzle snapped her compact shut. 'I'm a man in drag and a fabulous one at that.' She gave a seductive pout. 'I've never wanted to be a woman. You need to do some soul-searching, my friend.'

'Not this again.' Mike gulped back the gin and slammed down the glass. 'I've told you. I'm not trans. Why would I go about my day as a man if I thought I was a woman?'

'You don't go about as a man; you dress as a sad clown, a feminine one at that.'

'Oh fuck off.'

Lady V sucked on the straw and the slurping sound from the emptiness at the bottom of the glass shot through Mike like the teeth-gritting sound of nails down a chalkboard. He cringed.

'Hi, girls.' Mike side-eyed the muscular beauty who'd rocked up to their table. 'Did you see my performance? I'm killing it tonight.'

Miss Lola flicked her long purple ponytail over her shoulder before taking a seat opposite Mike.

'Killing it?' Mike scoffed. 'You sure murdered that song.'

'Hey!'

Miss Lola scowled. Mike waved the empty glass in the air for a waitress to come over and exchange it for another gin. Lady V snatched the glass.

'For fuck's sake, Micha! No more booze. You're being a total bitch this evening.'

Miss Lola fidgeted on her seat; she hated confrontation. She leaned across the table and spoke in a low voice.

'Got some goss.'

Mike rolled his eyes and adjusted the chicken fillets in his bra. Lady V leaned across the table and whispered back.

'Spill it.'

'She was here again last night…' Mike's ears pricked up. He leaned in too. Who was Lola talking about? 'She told Bunny she was going to meet a man and needed some Dutch courage. She was dressed as a school girl. I think she might be some sort of escort. Trev even offered her a job.'

Mike sat back in a huff.

'Great! Everyone's been offered a job except me.'

Miss Lola sipped her orange juice. 'You could work here if you wanted.'

'I. Don't. Want.'

Lady Vajazzle stood up and shoved her clutch under her large gloved arm. 'That's your problem in a nutshell; you think working here is beneath you. This club is exclusive. It's more upmarket than begging in Trafalgar Square.'

'Begging, huh?' Mike slurred. He was starting to feel queasy. Drinking on an empty stomach is never a good idea. 'This club is upmarket for the punters, not the queens. I'm a customer and the customer's always right. Go get me another drink.'

'I'm not a waitress, Mike.'

Miss Lola gasped at the use of Mike's real name.

'Oh, is waitressing beneath you, Donald?'

'Fuck this shit.' Lady Vajazzle, AKA Donald, slid the empty tumbler across the table. Mike clumsily caught it before it tumbled off the edge. 'Enjoy your pity party, I don't wish to be a part of it.'

Miss Lola stood up dramatically.

'Neither do I. I'd rather hang out with Princess. She's a lot of fun, unlike the sad clown you are. Method acting doesn't suit you.'

The drag queens tottered towards the dance floor, dresses and feather boas flowing. The last act was on stage belting out a showtune, while the DJ was setting up in a corner.

'Whatever … I don't need ya. I don't need anyone.' Mike's brain wasn't firing; he had gin fog. An image of the smiling face in the newspaper ad broke through. Princess? 'Wait, Lola!' She glanced over her silk-covered shoulder. A belch escaped when Mike opened his mouth. 'Did Bunny say which hotel Princess was going to?'

'A Nobel Night. Good luck finding which one.'

She flicked her hair over her shoulder, like she always did, and disappeared into the clapping crowd who were on their feet, whooping and cheering for the last act. The racket thumped against Mike's head. He stumbled to his feet and took his jacket from the back of the chair. One arm in, the other missed the sleeve several times before he finally pulled the leather Matrix-inspired jacket on. He tugged at his wig, straightening it he hoped, but he'd probably made it more lopsided. He pushed out his fake tits and strolled towards the exit. He was going to find this Princess and wow her; she would be so impressed with him she'd give him a job and they would become best friends. BFFs. For life.

Chapter Eight

Kerri's Big Break

Kerri leaned over and kissed Mark again. Gentle, longing. Her boyfriend was the kind of *fit* that gave women a tingle between their legs when he took his shirt off. He was a builder, and though not ripped his body was firm. Having a physical job meant he was muscular without trying. Mark liked to show off his physique whenever possible and Kerri wondered if he did it to make up for not being classically handsome. Like small man syndrome, when guys who are vertically challenged get buff and act tough because they somehow feel less on account of their lack of height. Kerri and Mark's lips unlocked and he tenderly brushed a strand of hair that had fallen in front of her face, back behind her ear.

'Ready for the dragon?'

Kerri playfully slapped Mark's bare chest.

'Don't call her that, she could be listening.'

'You think she's tapped your phone?' Kerri's gaze darted to the bedside drawers, her phone's screen was blank, two ripped condom wrappers scattered beside it. An image of Mark opening one with his teeth popped into her head. Mark chuckled. 'If she was listening, she'd have got an earful last night. "Oh Mark, don't stop, that's it…"' He moaned and bit his bottom lip.

Kerri looked away. She could feel the blush in her cheeks. 'You're full of yourself.'

'You were full of me last night.'

She laughed and shook her head. 'You're a dick.' Mark opened his mouth ready to spout another innuendo. Kerri pressed her finger to his lips. 'Don't.'

Mark brushed his fingers down the back of her cheek. 'You're being paranoid, you know that, right?'

'You don't know her. She has spies everywhere.'

'Not in that warehouse.'

'No.' Kerri smiled, twinkle in her eye. She leaned across to grab her phone and Mark tickled her under the arm. 'Stop!' She laughed and fell backwards onto her side of his bed, clutching her mobile to her chest. She sat up, plumped up the pillows behind her and pulled the duvet up over her nakedness. 'What if I get into trouble with the police?'

'She'll get into trouble, not you.' Mark sat up and dug his hand down the side of the bed for the TV remote. 'It's her call to run the story or not.'

'True.' Kerri drew a pattern on the phone screen with the tip of her finger and it unlocked. She'd taken a photo of the dead man's dog and used it as her wallpaper. 'Will you at least consider keeping Sausage?'

Mark triumphantly pulled the remote from where it was wedged between the mattress and the bedside drawers.

'I haven't got time for a dog. I like cats. Cats look after themselves.'

Mash was on 'his' chair in the corner, licking his furry crotch, one fluffy white leg in the air.

'Mrs Williams doesn't allow pets. After all the poor dog's been through, I can't take him to the pound.'

'I'm not promising, but if he gets on with Mash, then maybe I'll consider it.'

Mash stopped licking, lowered his leg, and glared at them, as though he knew they were agreeing to something he would hate.

'Thank you!' Kerry threw her arms around her boyfriend and kissed him all over his face.

Mark laughed. 'All right, crazy girl.' He gazed into her eyes. 'If you really want to thank me there are better ways.' He winked.

Kerri tossed her phone to the end of the bed in mock outrage. 'I serviced you last night, twice.'

'It's a new day.'

'You're an animal.'

She picked up a pillow and whacked him in the face with it. He pretended to play dead, head lolling, tongue out. She straddled him and patted his cheek. 'Stop mucking about.'

He roared and shook her shoulders. She screamed, rolled onto her side and scampered down the bed. He grabbed her foot to stop her. She slapped his hand away. 'You git! Don't do that. I'm still a bit shaken up. I've never seen a dead body before.'

She sat on the end of the bed, legs dangling over the side. She felt Mark move close behind her.

'Sorry, babe, let me make it up to you.' Hair swept aside, kisses trailed down her neck. Hands under her arms, cupping her breasts. She dropped her head back. His soft lips met hers. She had time before work to let him make it up to her.

***

Stepping off the tube, make-up perfectly applied, hair blow-dried and clipped back, suit ironed, killer heels shiny; Kerri felt like she could take on the world. She was ready for anything. Confidence coursed through her. She held her head high.

The sensuous morning sex and intense orgasm she'd not been expecting had left her feeling relaxed, refreshed and fucking fantastic. She glanced around as she joined the queue for the escalator, and one after another men's hungry eyes met with hers. It was as if her aura had changed and she was giving off a 'come shag me' vibe like a cat on heat.

She stepped onto the escalator and glanced across at the people travelling downwards. Sandwiched between tourists on the descending stairs, a young man half her age was checking her out. She winked. He returned her cheekiness by winking back. She glanced over her shoulder. He was still looking at her, dopey grin on his boyish face. She lit up inside. If she'd been single, he'd have been in trouble, that eighteen-year-old hottie wouldn't have known what had hit him.

After finding the corpse in the warehouse, the police had taken her to the station for questioning and then sent on her way. As she'd suspected, they checked her phone. What was unexpected was that they allowed her to take the dog. The dead man had no relatives to collect the pooch, and when Kerri offered to take care of it she sensed relief from the officer in charge.

She stepped off the escalator and shuffled forwards with the crowd. A man the size of a mountain was in front of her blocking her view of the exit. Before she knew it, he was through the gate and she was jostled forwards by commuters behind her. She tapped her card on the yellow circle; it beeped and the shutters opened for her to pass through. As she strutted towards daylight, Kerri wondered whether she should have called the boss and given her the story right away. She had checked it wasn't online, and as she passed the newsagents a quick scan of the newspaper headlines confirmed that the police probably hadn't yet released any information. She had the scoop.

Her phone buzzed in her pocket. She pulled it out and found her notifications had piled up. She kept her phone on silent for work and always forgot to turn the volume back up again. On top of this, Mark's place was notorious for being a blackhole where Wi-Fi signals go to die. Sometimes she could get a weak signal if she sat up on the kitchen bench and leaned in close to the window. Kerri often missed important messages and phone calls and sometimes blamed her failure to respond on her epilepsy. There was a message from Bea. She'd found Sausage. Kerri quickly typed back that she was fine and taking the dog over to Mark later.

By the time she'd got home on that night it was late and everyone was asleep. She'd managed to keep the dog quiet in her room, but she couldn't take it to Mark without buttering him up first. She wrote up her story the next day and emailed it to herself. Then left the dog in her room with food (some of Mike's hotdogs she'd cooked up; she hoped he wouldn't notice they were missing), a bowl of water and a litter tray she'd made out of a shallow cardboard box, using dirt from several of Bea's pot plants.

The plants were pretty much dead, Bea never watered them. Kerri had pointed to the tray and told the dog to use it if he got desperate. Having never had a pet, she wasn't sure if the dog would go in the tray or if that was just a cat thing. She'd get some dog food, a new collar and tag and take the dog to Mark's after work. He'd managed to get the day off after she'd called him to tell him what happened. He'd hoped she would stay home with him. He'd planned a day in bed watching movies and shagging. It was so hard to get dressed and leave, but he understood that she had to go to work. The story was too big to wait.

Outside the station the air was crisp and wintery, as if it wanted to snow but couldn't manage it. Kerri strolled at a brisk pace, teeth chattering. She'd made it to work with five minutes to spare. The warmth inside the building thawed her frozen fingers, making them tingle. Strutting down the corridor, feeling back in her fingers and toes, Kerri's gaze trailed over the front pages in frames on the magnolia walls. What was she going to say to her boss? This was her chance, her big break. She must not screw it up.

She shouldered through the office door and strolled past her colleagues hard at work at their desks. Some with headsets on were talking in low voices while others were typing fast, nails clicking against keyboards. Donna stood up when Kerri approached. Always elegant, always beautiful. Today she had on a red suit with matching lipstick. She handed Kerri a hot cup of takeaway coffee, patted her on the back and whispered, 'You got this, Queen.'

Kerri smiled at her friend.

'Thanks.'

She'd phoned Donna straight after she'd got off the phone to the police. Donna had advised Kerri to write the story and then email the boss for a meeting. Donna had never steered her wrong and she'd felt sure her advice was correct – until this moment. The confidence Kerri had felt in the underground station faded as she approached the dragon's door. She took a deep breath and knocked three times.

'It's Kerri.'

The boss's voice boomed from the other side of the wood. 'Come in, Kerri.'

Kerri puffed out her nervousness and pushed down the door handle. The minimalistic office smelled of vanilla scented candles. The editor-in-chief was sitting behind her large oak desk, arms crossed over her broad frame. She wore a Sari-inspired suit of the brightest green and yellow, gold stars peppered across the flowing material draped over her arms. In her forties, British born with Indian heritage, Prachi didn't take shit from anyone. She had striking, intense features: high cheekbones, with dark eyes as black as onyx. She was a woman who could cut you down to size with a single glance. Kerri felt uneasy, her legs had turned soft like noodles. She was terrified of this woman, more terrified now than she had been in the warehouse with the dead guy.

'Good morning, Prachi.' Kerri's words jittered from her like she was still out in the cold; somehow her boss's office felt like it was in the middle of the arctic, despite the heat coming from the radiator. 'Thank you for seeing me.'

The boss held out her hand and gestured to the chair opposite her. 'Take a seat.' Kerri placed her coffee on a round leather mat on the desk, removed her coat, hung it over the back of the chair and sat down. The boss stared at her with unflinching authority. 'What's so urgent I had to cancel an important meeting this morning? Let's have it.'

Kerri took a sip of coffee, then cradled the warm cup on the desk in front of her with both hands.

'The night before last I was at the scene of a murder.'

The dragon raised her eyebrows, her face softened with intrigue then quickly turned back to stone. An image popped into Kerri's head of her boss breathing fire like a flamethrower and burning her to a crisp.

'Why didn't you give this information to Sean straight away?'

She didn't ask for any details, didn't ask if Kerri was okay. She had a one-track mind. The story was everything.

'I wanted to write it myself.'

'And have you?'

Kerri nodded.

'Where is it?'

'In your inbox.'

The editor-in-chief lifted the screen of her laptop and clicked through with the mouse. She rested her elbow on the desk and her chin on her knuckle. Kerri watched her boss's eyes dart from left to right. Three minutes passed like three hours before the boss sat back in her chair and folded her arms.

'This is good.'

Kerri's heart leapt. She suppressed a smile. *Be professional. Don't look too pleased with yourself.*

'Thank you.'

'I've emailed it to Sean to rewrite.'

The boss snapped the laptop lid shut and got up from her seat. Kerri stood too, snatching up her jacket in one hand and takeaway coffee in the other. She hurried after her boss whose garment flowed with the movement of her body as she swept towards the door.

'No, please. Sean can shadow me. Let me put my name to this. I've worked hard. I won't let you down, I promise.'

The boss's hand rested on the door handle.

'Okay, Kerri.' She pushed down on the handle. 'But if you fuck this up, you're out.'

Kerri nodded. 'I won't … screw it up. Thank you so much.'

'Get to work.' She pushed open the door, Kerri exited. 'And next time…' Kerri stopped in her tracks and glanced over her shoulder. '…Don't wait a day to bring me the story. Write the story, send it to me, then sleep. Got it?'

'Got it.' Kerri beamed.

The boss closed the door. The click of the wood kissing the frame silenced the newsroom. Kerri glanced around. Everyone was looking at her. She hurried towards Donna, everyone in the office following her with their eyes.

'Well done, kid.' Donna welcomed Kerri into her arms and she melted into her friend's embrace, breathing in her sweet perfume. 'Welcome to the big time.'

Murmuring erupted and a few colleagues got out of their seats and crowed around to ask questions. Kerri answered the verbal onslaught as best she could before Sean darted around desks and leapt over an empty chair to get to Kerri and Donna. He squeezed between the writers crowding around Kerri's work station, then shooed them back to their desks.

'Read your story.' Sean perched on the edge of Spencer's desk, squashing a giant inflatable Godzilla the twerp had won at the office summer party. 'It's pretty good.'

'Prachi said no need for you to rewrite, just help me with the edit … okay with you?'

'Suits me.' Sean played with his tie, rolling it up and unrolling it. He had a harsh frown line between his thick eyebrows which had deepened over the years, possibly caused by the stress of working long hours to keep his wife and kids in the luxury they had become accustomed too. 'I'm surprised the old bill didn't confiscate your phone.'

'Before I called them, I sent the photos to my email and then deleted the email app and the photos.'

'Clever.' He stood up and smoothed down his tie. His movements were jerky, like a kid hyped up on sugar. 'I'll send the edits over in a bit. If it's all okay, fire me an email back and we're good to go.'

Sean took off back to his desk that was tucked away in the corner of the large office space. Donna clapped Kerri on the back and muttered something about a deadline, sat down at her desk, and began typing. Kerri sunk onto her chair, the adrenaline rush petering off, the weight on her shoulders lifted. She turned on her computer and breathed a sigh of relief. She'd done it. This was what she'd always hoped for: a real story. Perhaps now she could stop writing about boring local non-news. She and Sean were working on this together. It was a big deal. She opened up her email.

A spiky-haired shadow dropped over her computer screen. 'Well, well, it seems you were in the right place at the right time.'

Ugh. Not now. Kerri kept her eyes on the monitor.

'I'm busy, Spence.'

'I know, I heard. Well done and all that.' He sidestepped to get her attention. She didn't look up. 'I'm busy myself. Got a hot date tonight, shit gonna get freaky.'

Shit? He had no idea what turned a woman on. The word 'shit' anywhere in a sentence about sex was weird, even for him. Kerri rolled her eyes. *He obviously thinks he's being impressive rather than a creepy loser.*

'Enjoy your freaky shit. I've gotta get on.'

A message appeared in Kerri's inbox from Sean. That was quick. She clicked the attachment. Spencer tilted his head this way and that, trying to read over her shoulder. Kerri ignored him. Sean's edits were good. She agreed with most of them. Except the part about the paper dolls. Sean wasn't sure they were important, but she'd researched and found two other murders where the same thing had happened, though they'd occurred years ago. Sean wanted to run with a single murder, but she was adamant it had to be a serial killer and wanted to make the piece more sensational by titling it 'The Paper Doll Murders'. Spencer leaned on Kerri's desk. His shadow darkened her screen even more.

'The Paper Doll Murders?'

'Spencer, please!'

'No problem, you're trying to concentrate, work comes first. I understand that. I had to cancel on this bird once. I told her I was married to the job. She wasn't impressed, but you know what they say: treat 'em mean, keep 'em keen.' The tension in Kerri's shoulders returned. *Ugh. Why wouldn't this jerk leave her alone?* She hated being unkind, but at some point, she was going to have to spell it out for Spencer. She wasn't interested in him romantically or as a friend and she never wanted to work with him. 'Looks like you're working on something big? Can I help? What's the story?'

She moved the monitor out of his shadow. 'I don't need any help. You can read it when it goes live this afternoon.'

'Coolio. Ping me when it's up. I'll give you a full critique, no sugar coating, I'll let you know exactly what I think of your first big piece tomorrow morning.' Kerri clenched her jaw; she didn't care what he thought. 'I can fill you in on my hot date then. Want me to get you something from the bakery for brekkie?'

'I'm not in tomorrow.' Kerri had to hit the backspace five times. He was putting her off.

'Lunch then, next time you're in. My shout.'

'You don't need to do that.'

'I insist.' He gave her an awkward pat on the back, a light tap, like a child told not to smack. 'I'll let you get on.'

With Spencer out of the way, Kerri went through the piece fast, fixing it up where Sean had suggested. He had written notes to indicate when a word wasn't quite right, or when something wasn't clear enough. Kerri felt like she was actually doing something real, something important. As clichéd as it was, this was her big break; this story could lift her career to the next level, and she would be waiting on tenterhooks for the killer to strike again. She'd never wish death on people to further her career, but if/when it happened again, she would be ready.

Chapter Nine
Bea's Video Call

She was meant to call ten minutes ago. Bea paced up and down the small living room, twisting her hair around her pen. She'd been ready to take the call ten minutes ago. Now she needed to pee. It was nerves and she knew only a trickle would come out, but the urge was there and she needed to go – but if she did Jackie might call and she'd miss the meeting … her anxiety was winning.

Third twist and the pen got stuck. She tried to tug it out, but tangles of hair were caught in the lid. The feeling she was going to wet herself took over and she dashed to the toilet, leaving the pen hanging in her hair and the door slightly open. Once on the loo, she fiddled with the knot; she couldn't talk to Jackie with a pen stuck in her hair.

She wished video calling didn't exist. Only a few years ago you could talk on the phone in your dressing gown or on the loo, but these days you had to be ready for a video chat at any moment. To think that she used to get anxious about talking on the phone – now she would give anything to go back to that.

Mike was asleep, as usual, and Kerri had taken the dog to Mark's; Kerri had left a note of apology for her and Mike under a magnet on the fridge. It was Bea's magnet: a typewriter with 'One Word After Another' written on the paper sticking out of the top of it. It was meant to be inspirational, but all she could think of was the writer who'd said those words and how much she was meant to have the great success he had and how much that hadn't fucking happened. She strained, but the pee wouldn't come out.

The pen did. She threw it across the tiled floor and sat with her head in her hands, teetering on the edge of the toilet seat. Mike was a frustrated performer; she was a frustrated writer and Kerri used to be a frustrated journo. Perhaps there was hope for her yet – or perhaps she was a hack riding on Kerri's success? She hadn't told her what she was doing; she probably should have, but somehow Bea knew Kerri would disapprove of her writing a book based on her news piece.

As for Mike, he wasn't interested in her anxieties. He'd said, 'Write whatever you like, girl. Authors steal stuff all the time. Look how much that wizard woman stole from mythology.' Bea had shaken her head at the words 'wizard woman', but he was on the right track for a change; a lot of mythology was used in those children's books and that's what made them so great. With regards to the note Kerri had left for them, Mike hadn't even noticed the pup was in the flat. He'd sent Bea a text which read: *WTF is Kerri on? Dog in her room? So she woke up next to some minger. Why is she apologising to us for that? Did you hear them fucking?* Shocked face emoji.

The note from Kerri had read: *Dear Bea and Mike, sorry about the dog in my room. Thanks for not telling Mrs W. Hugs, Kerri xx.*

Bea had almost choked on her coffee laughing when she read Mike's message. She'd explained to him about the sausage dog in Kerri's room, but was typing fast and had accidently left off the word 'dog'. This made things worse because when Mike finally replied he pinged her back with: *You found a sausage in Kerri's room and she's taken it to her boyfriend? WTAF Bea? Have you both gone nuts!*

The unmistakable sound of a video call rang out from her laptop in the living-room.

'Shit!'

Bea pulled up her knickers and washed her hands. She darted out of the bathroom and combed her wet fingers through her hair, sweeping it off her face. She hurried over to the couch, sat down and positioned herself so that her face was angled just right in the natural light in order to hide the suitcases under her eyes. She took a deep breath and clicked to accept the call. Her face popped up in the corner of her screen in a small box while the rest of the screen was filled with her agent's ruby-red lips.

'Just a minute, Doll.' Jackie adjusted her screen and sat back. The little black dress, low cut, her ample cleavage bulging, was a contrast to the rustic kitchen. Bea's eyes wandered behind Jackie's head, desperate to get a better look at her house. She spied a huge bouquet of roses in an elaborate vase on the kitchen bench behind her agent, a four-oven Aga and exposed beams above. This woman had money, a lot of it. 'That's better.' Jackie smiled broadly. 'Now, I'm gonna get right to it, okay with you?'

Bea nodded. 'Sure.'

'I read your synopsis and sample chapters…' Anxiety wrapped its wicked hand around Bea's windpipe and squeezed. '…And I didn't like it much.'

Bea's face fell. Her emotions bubbled to the surface. She willed herself not to cry. Her gaze dropped to the floor. She'd failed.

'I told you I couldn't write crime…'

'Bea, look at me.' Bea lifted her head and locked eyes with her agent. Jackie leaned forward. 'It's true, I didn't like it much… I fucking loved it!'

'Wait, what?'

'It's bloody brilliant, Babe! Now…' She clapped her hands together. 'How quickly can you get it finished? What time frame are we talking? Do you have a word count in mind? I'm going to The London Book Fair in April and I'd like to take *The Paper Doll Murders* with me. I might not be able to call it that, of course. I assume the idea was sparked by your room-mate's article.'

'T-that's right, um … word count, I dunno…'

Jackie shook her hand in the air as if swatting away a fly. 'Never mind about the word count, message me later. When can I have the full manuscript?'

'First draft could be ready in about two months, maybe.'

'Two months, good. Get it to me before Christmas, no later. I think we could have a bidding war on our hands.'

'Okay.'

'Great, I gotta go, Babes, lunch date with a hot man. A new author I hope to sign. He'll get some extra benefits in his contract if he's keen.' She winked. Bea nodded, bewildered. 'Chat soon.' She blew some kisses. 'Ciao, darling.'

Jackie was gone and a little telephone symbol appeared on the screen signalling she had hung up. Bea didn't know how to react. Words whirled around inside her head. *Bidding war! London Book Fair!* Her agent *liked* it. She'd written something Jackie *liked*, no *loved!* Beatrice Summers was back, baby! She beamed, and the warm sunshine growing inside her shone through her face. She leapt up and did a victory dance, cowboy fashion, arm above her head swirling a fake lasso.

'Who's the man? I'm the man!'

She suddenly felt a bit silly, glad no one was around to see that moment of crazed excitement. She thought about jumping on Mike's bed and shaking him awake so he could join in with the happiness. She thought twice; he'd only be pissed off if he'd had a heavy night of drinking. No one likes to be woken when they've got a hangover.

Bea's next thought was to open a bottle of wine, but it was no fun drinking alone and she didn't even know if there was any wine in the flat. If there had been, Mike had probably already drunk it. She suddenly felt sleepy. Her insomnia had been playing up for weeks and her anxiety medication didn't seem to be working; perhaps she needed to go back to the doctor and get the dosage increased. She was taking 20mg and she didn't really want to take much more. She'd read a number of addiction horror stories online. Googling side-effects and symptoms was turning into a hobby. Then again, she felt so good that maybe she didn't need the drugs any more. Maybe that burst of energy had made her tired enough to sleep properly.

Body deflated, she slumped on the couch and her eyelids drooped. She reached forward and closed the laptop, then reached backwards and dragged the throw over herself, curling up in a ball. She plumped a cushion under her head and positioned her head in the most comfortable angle. The cushion smelled like butter. Mike had obviously been wiping his butter fingers clean on it. *All he eats is sandwiches; at least he's eating something relatively healthy* Bea thought as she drifted off to sleep.

Killer

You rummage through the drawer and check each lipstick. You're looking for a soft pink that will complete your look. Your transformation took almost an hour. Thank goodness for YouTube tutorials. The make-up tricks have taken years off you; you look angelic but you can't put the wig on yet. You hadn't thought about CCTV when the previous date for the hotel meet up was set, and in hindsight, although he cancelled and that enraged you, it was for the best. A blonde girl caught on camera would have been a problem. Prep time had been wasted, sure. Had you planned properly? No. This one could have been your undoing. Shit happens, and with what you do you have to be ready for anything and you weren't ready. He's done you a favour.

The research trip to Bliss was worth it. The staff adore you. They yell your name when you arrive. Hugs and air kisses all round. Compliments. Drag queens are such gossips. If they don't know what's going on, then nobody does. The handsome barman was helpful. He works as a waiter at the hotel you're going to. You didn't tell him you were meeting your date at his hotel; you told him it was a different Nobel Night. Can't have him putting two and two together afterwards. The young stud wore lip gloss and has been heavy-handed with the contouring. His hair tied in a bun was same colour as yours. It gave you the idea of posing as him. He'd be on shift the night of your date, half an hour after you arrive, and as long as you didn't bump into him your plan would work. The barman gave you lots of insider info on the chain of hotels. It was perfect.

Not interested in you sexually, he spoke unhindered by the master puppeteer that is a straight man's penis. He was not distracted by your boobs (push-up, padded bra aided) or the possibility of getting into your knickers – there's a distinct aura around a man trying to have a conversation with you while secretly lusting and hoping you'll change the conversation to 'Let's have sex'. It's white hot, animalistic, and sometimes you feel an urge to act on it and sometimes you do.

Your fingers find what you're looking for. The pink glittery lippy. Tug off the lid, roll up and apply. This is the best part. This lipstick has moisturiser in it and glides on silky smooth. You press your lips together and admire your reflection in the mirror. So pretty.

Your mind wanders to the people you've fucked. Who will you encounter after this kill? Most men feel violated after you've had your way with them. They never admit it, but you sense it. None ever say they felt uncomfortable. It's what they say during that gives them away. *Gentle. Ouch. That hurts. Too rough.* Toxic masculinity won't allow them to admit they don't like what you do. It's all about bravado, but really they're crying inside because you bit them, or pulled a chunk of their hair out, dug your nails in too hard, or almost strangled them to death. Sex was used against you and you'll never let that happen again. If they don't wanna play rough they shouldn't pretend they do. It's all about control. You're in control of their pain and their pleasure. It's different with women. You're gentle. It's only ever a bit of fun. A fingering in the club toilets. Married women mostly, looking for a quick thrill. Something their husbands wouldn't class as cheating.

You check the bag. Wig, stocking, ribbons, paper doll, knife. Your decorative dagger is not right for this job. A kitchen knife is best. Drop it and leave. The glint of the silver blade makes your nipples tingle. You zip up the bag and sling it over your shoulder. The anticipation of the kill is intense. You tug on your black leather gloves and almost float downstairs. As you slink towards the front door there are snoring sounds from the right. The walls are paper-thin. Asleep as always at this time of day. You could set your watch by it, if you wore one. On the other side the neighbours are fighting again. Yelling so loud you can hear every word as if they were right next to you.

'I'm so sick of your bullshit! You're never home and when you are, you're drunk or asleep. I feel like a single mother. Why do you keep doing this?'

'Whatever. You're such a miserable bitch. I'd rather be at work than here with you and those brats!'

Trouble in paradise? You smirk. Then wonder if he might be someone to put on the kill list. Nah, he's not abusing his kids; he's having an affair at work, that much is obvious.

***

You ask a stranger for the time. To make sure someone has seen you outside the hotel, hair in a bun like the barman. The business man in a Sherlock Holmes-inspired coat stops and checks his expensive gold watch. He tells you it's ten to seven. You thank him and stroll past the hotel main entrance, down a side alley, and heart beating fast you slow down and hope that someone opens the backdoor. Two cleaners lean up against the wall smoking and chatting in Polish. They throw their cigarette butts to the ground and hurry towards the backdoor. You move after them, head down. They don't look at you. The last one in actually holds the door open for you. Your heart beat slows. You're inside, but you have to keep up with the staff members. They'll have passes to get through the locked doors and you don't want to get caught where you shouldn't be.

You follow the chatty pair down white corridors with blinding lights. On the right a chef shouts instructions from a busy kitchen in the middle of service. On the left silver food trolleys line the walls. Your footsteps echo loudly, the cleaners wear flat, soundless shoes. Soon the hard floor turns to carpet and you relax a little more. You're in the main part of the hotel, near the reception desk. You search for a toilet. The cleaners disappear into a lift. The lift is beside a bar. Perfect. You strut past the desk, receptionist busy checking in a cute Asian couple in matching London tourist

T-shirts, explaining the facilities to them too loudly. You hate it when people do that. English is their second language; they're not deaf.

The bar is heaving. The murmuring coming from patrons sounds like a swarm of bees, the occasional boisterous laugh penetrating the buzz. You excuse your way through the crowds of standing drinkers and those waiting in line for the bar. Check for cameras. There's one overlooking the bar. None on the toilets. You shoulder your way into the ladies' loos and come up against a queue. You exit and try the disabled toilet. Bingo. No one in there.

Your date will be here any moment; you need to work fast. You dump the bag on the floor, remove your gloves, pocket them and pull the band from the bun, your mousy-brown hair drops down. You bend over and unzip the bag, move the paper doll to one side. Its wild eyes are unnerving, as if spying on you. You take out the hair stocking, pull it on and tuck your hair in around the side of your face and back of the neck. Then you tilt your head forwards and carefully fit the blonde wig. Straighten up and rake your fingers through the curls, adjust the front, hairline in the right place. Tie it in bunches, ribbons in bows. The blonde bombshell has arrived. The dowdy woman with mousy brown hair is gone. Your own mother wouldn't recognise you.

You put the leather gloves back on, open your jacket, and take a look at yourself in the long mirror. The door handle jiggles. You ignore it. You're not done. They can wait and piss themselves. You tug the loose school tie down a little and undo another button on the white shirt. It's a size eight, the smallest size you could fit into without it bursting at the seams. The fastened button under your breasts makes the shirt gape open, showing as much of your cleavage as possible. The skirt is short. The tights are sheer. You turn to the side and pose, knee bent. Your legs look banging. Ready to go.

When you exit the toilet, you're met with the grumpy face of a young guy in a wheelchair. You feel a pang of guilt. You never use disabled spaces, and the one time you do it's needed. You lean down to talk to him, more so his eyes are level with your breasts and he has no choice but to look down your top.

'Sorry, I was bursting.'

He smiles. 'It's fine. No problem.'

You smile sweetly and thank him for understanding. Phew! Last thing you needed was a scene. Drawing attention to yourself like that could mean the whole thing would have to be called off.

As you stride back towards the bar, pleased with yourself, you spot your date. Dressed like a 1970s pimp. The weaselly guy wears a plaid suit with a shiny silver shirt underneath, hair slicked back, he's propped up against the bar like he's a gangster.

You really don't want his creepy hands on you, but it's all part of the job. No two jobs are the same and you don't want his hands on any more young girls. This is how you are going to stop that. Think of the girls. The ones like you, who without your help will become victims of his abuse. Think of the thrill of the kill. It will all be worth it. He spots you slinking towards him and makes a face like he can't wait to devour you. You smile and wink. Hands in your jacket pockets, you move them back and push out your chest so he can get a good look at what he's in for. You wonder if the guests around you will notice the school uniform you're wearing and a few do turn their heads, but most are eyeballing Spencer's ridiculous outfit.

'You look amazing.' His arm snakes around your waist, hand straight to your arse.

'Not so bad yourself.' You lean in and kiss him on the cheek. The strong smell of cheap aftershave makes your eyes water.

'Have you had something to eat?'

'Yes.' You want to avoid the small talk and drinks at the bar; no need to drag this out. 'Shall we go?'

'You're keen. Don't you want a drink first?'

'We can order a bottle from the room, right?'

'We can indeed.' His credit card is in his hand. He flashes it at you like he's a millionaire loaded with cash. You know how much junior journalists earn. He must think you're stupid.

'What can I get you?' A pretty young barmaid with a head full of dark ringlets leans over the bar and grins. I lower my head. I don't want her to be able to identify me.

'Nothing thank you, the lady is keen to get to the room.' He pushes his credit card back into his wallet and flips it shut, hoping his movements come across as suave. You glance up and cringe at the barmaid's smirking face. You know what she's thinking. *What the fuck are you doing with this loser? Rather you than me. Enjoy your shit sex.*

Spencer leads you towards the lifts, arm firm around your waist like he's carrying a blow-up doll, pretending it's his girlfriend. He's already checked in, takes the key-card out of his suit pocket and presses it to the panel inside the lift. When the doors close, he grabs at you. Pulls you to him until your bodies are pressed tight against each other. He kisses you with what he thinks is passion, but what feels to you like a slobbery dog licking the inside of your mouth. You hate the way he kisses. He has no fucking clue. It takes all your strength not to push him away. His mouth is closed over yours. Bye bye glittery lipstick. You do your best to pretend you're into it. Moving your tongue around his, which is wriggling like a distressed eel.

Relief comes when a robotic female voice announces the floor that must be yours and the lift doors swish open. He releases you. Thankfully, there's no one waiting for the lift. With the back of your hand you discreetly wipe the wet from around your mouth. Under your jacket, under your skirt, he holds your arse cheek as he guides you towards room 418. He squeezes your buttock and then rubs his creepy hand in circles like he's polishing a bowling ball. You go over the plan in your head. Get him hot, carve him up.

He presses the card to the door, opens it, and then darts inside and deposits the card in the slot on the wall. The lights spring to life, showering the modern room in a golden glow. There's a bottle of sparkling wine in an ice bucket on the table next to the king-sized bed. Spencer goes straight for it and the cork is popped before you've thrown off your jacket and taken a seat at the end of the bed. With your jacket draped across the orange couch that resembles giant soft blocks they have in children's play areas, you unzip and drop your bag on the floor, as close as possible beside the end of the bed.

Spencer clumsily pours you a glass, froth spilling over the top. You take the flute from him and sip while he pours himself a glass. He tilts the flute, but still manages to fill the glass with three quarters of foamy white liquid. You knock back the wine, bubbles tingle on your tongue, and the sharpness of the cheap plonk hits your pallet like pennies in your mouth. You place the glass on the floor next to the bed. Legs crossed, you lean back provocatively while also trying to look unsure of yourself. You're supposed to be a virgin.

'Do you like the school girl costume, Spence?' You lean on one arm and place your hand innocently into one of your bunches, twirling your fingers around the blonde ringlets.

'I love it. Very hot. Aren't you going to take the gloves off?' He tips back the glass and the last dregs of the golden wine disappear down his throat. He takes off his hideous plaid jacket and climbs on top of you.

'It'll be more fun with them on.' You run your gloved hands up his back. 'You will be gentle, won't you? I'm worried it might hurt.'

'You're safe with me.'

He buries his face in your chest, kissing your skin, and every time his slimy lips touch you, you tense up. Hands reach up your skirt; he tugs at the top of your tights. You place your hands on his to stop him.

He lifts his head to look at you. 'I told you, you're safe. You don't have to worry.'

'It's not that.' You say as sweetly as possible. Keeping up this act is killing you. 'I want to do something special for you first.'

You force your hand to rub the firm lump between his legs.

'You've given me a hand-job before.' His rat face twists with confusion.

You reach for his belt and start undoing it.

'That's not what I want to do.' You touch your tongue on your top lip. His beady eyes fill with light.

'Oh, sure. Whatever you want.' He rolls off of you.

You sit up and open your legs. No hesitation, he steps up and unzips. Trousers drop. You realise he's going to make a lot of noise. You place your hands on the band of his boxers, then wait.

'You okay, Princess?' He cups your cheek like you're a nervous teenager. You shudder with disgust, thinking of all the young girls he's lied to and pressured. 'You know how special you are to me. I mean I think I'm falling in love with you, and you don't have to do anything that makes you uncomfortable.'

LIES!

'I want to do it but I'm worried about people hearing. What if someone complains?'

'I don't think that'll be a problem, unless you think you might be loud when I pleasure you.'

Loud? Ha! You'd have to fake it, big time!

You giggle. 'You might need to gag me.' You cup his crotch with your hands. 'Can you do something for me? I'm afraid I won't be much good if I keep worrying about people hearing us.'

'What can I do to put you at ease?'

'Maybe you could bite down on a flannel, would that be okay?'

He looks confused at first, then shrugs and pulls up his trousers. He goes to the bathroom and comes back with a flannel in his mouth, mumbling. You think he says, 'Is this better?'

You nod and flutter your eyelashes.

He stands in front of you again and drops his trousers. You pull down his boxers. He's rock-hard.

You glance up. 'Close your eyes. I can't do it if you're watching.'

He closes his eyes. Mouth full of flannel. You gently stroke him, then grasp with one hand, lean forwards, and with the other hand you reach back into your bag. You breathe heavily, close to the tip. His body tenses, anticipation peaking. Your hand finds the cold metal handle inside the bag; you grip it tight. Adrenaline rushes through your body. Your lips touch the tip, his body shudders.

Both of your hands squeeze as you drive the kitchen knife up into his scrotum. His scream is muffled. His insides gush over your hand. You let out a moan with the throb between your legs. He grabs at the pain between his legs, eyes wild. Spits the flannel. You pull the knife, stand and force your hand over his mouth.

'Shushhhh, shush, shush.'

You push him backwards onto the desk, arms flailing he knocks off the ice bucket, cubes and water shower to the floor. You plunge the knife into his stomach. The handle's slippery; you can't get a good grip on it with gloves on. His body shakes, going into shock. You whisper sweet nothings in his ear, although what you say are not words he wants to hear.

'You will never abuse another underage girl again.'

His eyes roll back. He goes limp. Dead weight. You step back, leaving the knife embedded in his lower abdomen. You help his body to the floor so it doesn't make a loud thump.

Heart still racing, you pick up the bottle of wine. Thankfully he didn't knock that over. You reach down for the glass beside the bed. You pour the last dregs from the bottle, place it back on the desk, blood smeared over the label. You sit back on the bed and admire your handiwork. You sip. Cold eyes tracing the blood trail. It might be nice to keep a few parts. You always pack a plastic bag in case this urge takes hold of you. You smile, remembering when you fed Brent's penis to a stray dog. You set down the drained glass. It's time to clean yourself up and find the perfect place to position the Spencer doll.

Chapter Ten

Mike's Desperation

The clown was sadder than usual. His performance had been flat all day because that's how he felt: like a cartoon character run over by a steamroller. He'd peeled himself off the floor of his room after finishing a bottle of pink gin the night before, then forced himself to get ready and venture out into the cold day; stomach hollow, no time for breakfast. The clink of change dropping into the bowl didn't sound like the shower of coins he was used to; it was more like the slow drip of a leaky tap. The lack of cash was not only because the weather had turned and the freezing winter months were fast approaching, contributing to a lack of tourists, but also because he really couldn't be bothered today. He was tired, hungover and beat down. He wasn't going to make the rent at this rate, and that thought made him feel even worse. Maybe he was useless and it was only a matter of time before he found himself taking shelter in a shop doorway.

Mike sat down on the grass, the National Gallery towering behind him, its pillars a grand statement in Trafalgar Square. Winter coat zipped up to the neck, messy brown hair flicked up beneath the rim of the woolly hat pulled down over his ears, the chilly air was kept away from every part of him except his hands and face, with his cheeks rosy cold. He'd managed to keep down an apple, which was all he'd had time to grab before he ran out the door in the early hours of the morning. He couldn't stomach anything else for lunch, but that seedy feeling of a booze-soaked system wasn't going to go away until he ate something substantial. He stared at the gum-speckled ground while sipping water from a plastic bottle, and his mind made a comparison between the gum and his life. Chewed up, spat out, then trampled on. He was a drunk clown out in the cold – a puppet performing for pennies. Was that really going to be his legacy? His contribution to the world?

The cool water slid down his throat and gave his body a surge of wellness. Soon he'd pee the alcohol out of his system and after that he'd feel much better. Mike pondered on his actions after insulting his friends and leaving the club. He'd asked at the reception desk of all the Noble Nights in the immediate area whether the beautiful blonde in his newspaper clipping had checked in, but none remembered seeing her. Feelings of ambivalence were having a tug of war in Mike's psyche. Part of him had wanted her to show and the other part was afraid of meeting her. What would he have said to her? *Hi, you don't know me, but I came across your advert in the paper and I want to work with you* … what was he thinking? That would have come across as seriously creepy. If she didn't come back to the Square, he couldn't befriend her, and the chances of her wanting him as a business partner would be slim. Maybe he could go it alone? Then he would be in direct competition with Princess and that would not go down well at Bliss. Plus, she'd built a client base and he had nothing. He didn't want to be beaten before he'd started.

'Penny for your thoughts.'

Bat sat down beside him, limp cheese and pickle sandwich in his plump hand. Mike almost heaved at the sight of the sliver of sweaty cheese and the pickle-stained bread. He put down the empty bottle and held out his hand. Bat glanced down and frowned.

'Are you gonna give me a penny for my thoughts or not?'

Bat huffed, reached into the pocket of his navy puffer jacket, fished for a penny and then dropped a shiny copper into Mike's palm. Mike closed his fingers and shoved his fist into his pocket. He was going to need every penny he could get. He went back to staring at the ground. Bat bit off the corner of his triangular sandwich and started mumbling, bits of bread flying out from between his lips. Mike turned his head to glare at the fake superhero. Bat swallowed. 'Well?'

'Well, what?' Mike gave his attention back to the ground, where an empty crisp packet tumbled along in the wind. Why was everything reminding him of how shit his life was? How shit he was!

'What's eating you up?'

'Winter blues, I guess.' Mike lied. There was no way he was opening up to this joker. Even if he wanted to have a heart to heart, which he didn't, it wouldn't be with Bat-brain.

'Hi, Batman.'

Mike and Bat turned their heads at the same time towards the source of the voice. Blocking the watery sunlight, a girl no more than sixteen years old was smiling back at them. Dressed in a long coat almost touching the ground and gold sequin bobble hat, the youngster smiled down at Bat, doe eyes sparkling.

'Hey, sweetheart, what're you doin' here?' He beamed.

'I came to say hi, silly.' She nudged Bat with her elbow and he chuckled.

'Right. Right. You okay? Studying hard?'

She took a seat next to the overweight performer, linked her arm with his, and rested her head on his shoulder. If Mike could have raised his eyebrows any higher they'd have disappeared into his hairline never to return.

The young girl fluttered her eyelashes at the Bat. 'I'm trying, but school is so hard. Mum says I need to find a man to take care of me because I'll never pass my exams.'

Bat crammed the last corner of cheese and pickle sandwich into his mouth and patted the bobble on the girl's head.

'You're a smart cookie,' he mumbled through a mouthful of bread and cheese. 'You'll smash ya exams, trust me.'

'Thanks.' She sprang to her feet. 'I'd better go, I was going to stop at the bakery, but Mum's skint again.'

'We can't have you going hungry. You need brain food.' Bat reached into his pocket and pulled out a fiver. ''Ere you go, darlin'. Get yourself some lunch.' He pressed the note into her gloved hand.

She shook her head. 'I can't accept that.' But Mike noted the small head shake wasn't much of a protest.

'I insist.' Bat grinned from ear to ear.

'You're like a real superhero, you know that. Thank you for always saving me.'

'Anytime, sweetie.'

She waved and blew a kiss to Bat as she hurried away towards the road leading to the bakery. He blew a kiss back. Mike shuddered. That awkward exchange made him feel as if ants were crawling all over him.

'She'd have to be on top; you'd crush her otherwise.'

'*What?*' Bat tore his gaze from the girl walking away. 'Are you tryin' to say I want to … God no! Get your mind out the gutter. That's Alisha. She knows my daughter; she wants me to teach her to drive, that's all.'

'She wants you to leave your wife and take care of her.'

Bat's plain moon face twisted into a scowl. 'For fuck's sake, Mike!'

Mike stood and pocketed the empty plastic bottle. No bins in Central London; they attract bombs. 'You own your house, right?'

'Yeah, so?'

'She wants it.'

'Jesus!' Bat took a bottle of lemonade from the carrier bag beside him. He eased off the twist cap which hissed. He swigged, then belched loudly and replaced the bottle cap. 'I know you're having a bad day so I'm gonna let that slide.'

'She's looking for a sugar daddy. I've seen her type before.' Mike strolled past Bat, who got up with some effort to follow after him. 'She wants to have a baby with an older man so she can get out of an awful home life. Why else would she be making eyes at you? I mean, look at you!' Bat rummaged in his lunch bag as they walked. 'No young girl would ever be attracted to that.' Mike poked Bat's beer gut.

Bat smacked Mike's hand away. 'You're really fucking mean, you know that!'

'And you're really fucking dense. Trouble in your marriage, Bat?'

Bat pulled a cream bun out of the bag. 'I'm not taking this abuse from you.'

Mike weaved through the swarms of people moving at a fast pace past the Gallery. Having had lunch in one of the many eateries in the capital, people were hurrying back to their office jobs or to the next tourist attraction. He glanced over his shoulder at Bat who was unsuccessfully ducking out of the way of some tourists taking selfies with their fingers in peace signs. 'Entertaining jailbait will only lead to worse abuse than anything I can dish out.'

'You're not the only one who has a hard life, you know.' Bat struggled to keep up with Mike as he cut through the crowd. He turned his body to the side to squeeze through gaps in the people, but couldn't get through. 'You're alone because you choose to be. I'm alone even though I'm married. Do you have any idea how that feels? To have someone and not have them at the same time?'

Mike yelled back to Bat who was panting with the exertion of keeping up with the sad clown. 'Then fix your marriage.'

'If it was that simple, don't you think I'd have done it by now?'

'It *is* that fucking simple.' Mike lifted the waterproof cover off his box of props and took out his pointy hat. He took off his coat and placed it in his prop box. Misty rain swept across the grey Square and he was glad he'd remembered to wear his thermals.

Bat arrived next to him and under his mini-marquee he began readying himself for his afternoon performance. Coat off, bat mask on. Mask firmly in place he rounded on Mike. 'Go on then, smart arse. What am I doing wrong?'

'You've forgotten the woman you married and why you hooked up with her all those years ago.' Bat blinked, his eyelids painted black to match the mask. 'Eyes never change. I challenge you to look into your wife's eyes and see that twenty-year-old beauty you used to lust after. Her body might have been ruined by bearing children – your children, I might add – but she's still the woman you fell in love with.'

The lower half of Bat's face seemed to soften. Mike frowned. Why had he said those kind things? He didn't even like the man. He had to remedy this: he couldn't have Fatty-Boom-Batty thinking they were friends or anything.

'You ogle a girl young enough to be your granddaughter, yet you expect your wife to treat you like you're an Adonis, right?' Mike didn't wait for an answer. He plumped the ruff at his neck. 'You haven't carried and birthed any children, yet your body is a wreck; you look as if you're permanently preggers, yet you think your wife should still find you attractive. Double standards.' The corners of Bat's lips turned down, Mike felt a pinprick of guilt pierce the inside of his stomach. He softened his tone. 'Make her feel special again and she'll repay your efforts tenfold, trust me.'

'Permanently preggers, really?' Bat glanced down at his large belly. He could only just see the tip of his soft superhero boots.

'Have you looked in a mirror lately?' Mike took hold of his hand mirror from a small make-up bag in the prop box and reapplied his black lippy that had rubbed off at lunch.

Bat's hands were on his wide hips. 'Let me get this straight. I'm to take marriage advice from someone who has a) never been married and b) is one of them a-sexuals. You never show interest in women. What makes you the authority on them?'

A-sexual? He went for that over gay? Does he even know what that means?

'I live with women.' Mike smacked his lips together and put away the mirror. 'They aren't aliens.' Although Mike was starting to think Bat was. 'They have the same emotions and needs as you and me. I'm pretty sure you don't know your wife's needs or wants, but I'd wager she knows yours, and because you can't be bothered to find out what makes her tick these days, she can't be arsed to give you what you need. I've seen it many times. Try a little tenderness.'

Bat opened his mouth. Mike held up his hand. 'Don't start singing that song, and don't sing to your wife either. Your singing sounds like a rat stuck in a drainpipe. Serenade your wife and you'll definitely end up divorced.'

'Fine, O wise one.' Bat bowed regally. 'What should I do?'

Mike checked off a list on his fingers. 'Chocolates. Bubble bath. Candles. Massage. Sex. Concentrating on her pleasure, not yours. Got it?'

'Anything else?' Bat crossed his arms over his chest, resting them on his gut.

'Get in shape. Go out places. Take an interest in each other's hobbies. Be as you were when you first met. Pretend you're trying to woo her. She doesn't want you any more; make her want you. Show her why she wanted you in the first place.' Mike's backside was cold and numb from sitting on the wall. He discreetly felt it to make sure it wasn't also damp. A big damp patch on your arse isn't a good look. 'Penny for my thoughts, huh! I should be charging an hourly rate for this. Maybe giving out relationship advice could be my new career.'

'It's called a marriage counsellor.' Bat got into position. Tourists were starting to gather around other performers.

Mike took up his clear umbrella. The rain was wispy, but he had a feeling it might chuck it down any minute. 'Well, they're not doing a very good job, are they? The divorce rate is through the roof.'

'Speaking of jobs, how did the big audition go?'

Mike opened his umbrella. 'They offered me the part, but I turned it down,' he lied.

Bat fiddled with his belt. 'Why?'

'Not enough money, and anyway, Princess said she wants me to join forces with her. I just have to sort out the contract and all that. I'm going to be Belle.'

'*You? Belle?*' Bat chuckled and held his wobbling belly like Father Christmas. 'But you're a dude.'

'I'm a professional performer, unlike you. It's my job to be able to act any role.' Mike raised the umbrella over his head and struck an arabesque, then lowered his back leg, toe of his ballet slipper pointed against the hard ground. He was ready. He glanced over at Bat. 'The only role you're expert in is a sausage roll.'

'You're hilarious. You should do comedy.'

Bat struck a power pose, standing as if he were a wall of muscle and about to save the day.

Mike tilted his chin into his neck ruffles like always and whispered. 'Show time.'

As the rain swept in icy sheets across the Square, the performers outside the towering grey Gallery kept their smiles plastered to their faces and played their parts as if it was a balmy summer's day. The conversation with Bat had actually perked Mike up a bit; he remembered why he loved to perform and why it was important he did not pursue a career in marriage counselling. He would die inside if he had to sit in an office, listening to people moan about dumb problems that weren't really problems at all. Being homeless and hungry was a problem. With basic needs met, many people just get bored and start a war with their significant other. In his opinion this was a bit pathetic.

Mike twirled and danced. Sad clown and then happy. He told a story with his movements, and while adult tourists admired his grace, Batman was treated quite differently. Both had their fair share of abuse every now and again, but children loved Bat and were pretty uninterested in Mike's interpretation of Pierrot. Bat would encourage people to take selfies with him and he'd crack jokes that the adults would laugh at, but which would go over the kids' heads. When small children asked why he was so fat he said the Joker had hit him with his latest weapon: The Balloon-Belly Gun. It made him blow up like a balloon! He would then point to people in the crowd who were the same stamp as himself and whisper, 'Looks like the Joker got hit too!' Then he would tell the little ones not to worry. Alfred was busy working on a remedy in the Batcave.

Mike found himself smiling when the children giggled. He curtsied when a stack of pound coins clattered into the bowl, dropped by a cheery woman with blindingly white teeth carrying a stars and stripes bag with several motivational badges pinned to it. Mike lifted his head and was about to begin his next routine when he spotted a head of blonde ringlets bounce into the crowd. It was her!

'Look after my prop box, will ya.'

Mike threw his pointy hat into the box and hurried towards the crowd, holding his umbrella high above his head so as not to poke anyone in the eye.

'Where are you going?'

Mike ignored Bat and yelled at the top of his voice, 'Princess! Wait! I need to talk to you.'

He pushed and barged his way through people milling around like a lost herd of cows. Rain pattered onto the umbrella, and when he reached the crossing the wind turned the clear plastic and silver spokes inside out. Mike battled to keep hold of the thin metal pole, the gusts dragging him along. His eyes searched the crowds crossing the traffic-packed road. There! Blonde head sticking out in the mass of winter hats, umbrellas and brunettes. He quickly joined the mass migration before the green 'walk' figure turned to a red 'stop'. The wind ripped the brolly from his hand and whisked it up towards the ashy clouds.

Once on the other side of the road, Mike leaned forwards and grabbed the anorak-covered arm of the blonde woman, spinning her around on the spot. The startled expression on the young Asian tourist's face was enough to tell Mike the words she had spoken in a language he didn't understand meant she was seriously cross he had man-handled her.

'My apologies.' He put his hands together in prayer and dipped his head, hoping it was the right thing to do. He had little knowledge of different cultures and customs, but he had seen Japanese people greet each other this way. Fingers crossed it would mean sorry too. With a heavy heart, he allowed people to push him along the road and past Charing Cross station. The crowd thickened and stopped moving; blue lights flashed up ahead. The intermittent rain was enough to soak his white costume to his skin and plaster his mop of hair to his face. His make-up would begin to run if it rained any harder. He stood on tiptoes and craned his neck over the crowd. Police officers were ushering people away from the cordoned off road.

'Mike?' Mike frowned at the broad man shuffling through the bodies towards him, black umbrella held over his silvery-grey short back and sides. He had a charming look about him and a cheeky smile, but Mike couldn't place the middle-aged guy.

'Don't give me those eyes. I don't look that different in my civilian clothes.'

People squeezed past the pair as Mike continued to stare. 'Donald?'

'Took long enough for the penny to drop. Why haven't you been back to the club? Afraid we're still mad at you for being a prick?'

'Yeah, sorry about that. Truth is I've been busy. Auditions and stuff.' Mike pulled at a black bobble on his damp costume. 'Working loads too.'

'Forget it. We all knew it was the drink talking. Anyway, did you hear what happened?'

Donald tilted his head towards the police who were fighting a losing battle trying to get people to move along.

'Someone was killed.'

Mikes eyes widened. 'Killed? Who was killed? How?' Mike was enthralled. This was huge. 'Was it a lift malfunction or something?'

'Do you know Devan? He works behind the bar at Bliss.'

Mike's hands shot to his mouth to cover a gasp. 'Oh my God! Not Devan!'

'No, no, Devan's fine, he's not the dead guy.' Mike let out a sigh of relief. An elderly lady with a rain-speckled, clear plastic cover tied over her white curls was listening in. Donald lowered his voice. 'Devan was taken in for questioning. Trev had to show the police security camera footage of him working behind the bar the night it happened.'

'Do you know who was killed?'

Donald shook his head. 'No one does.'

Mike leaned closer to Donald, not only because he wanted to hear every word clearly, but also to shelter under his friend's large umbrella. The rain was now coming down in buckets, and Mike was beginning to shiver, his damp clothes sending a chill through to his bones. 'What happened to them?'

Donald lowered his voice further. 'Butchered. Insides ripped out.'

Chapter Eleven

Kerri's Fate

The distinctive sugary-sweet voice of the blonde morning presenter rang out from Donna's phone: *When you found him in the warehouse, how did you feel? I mean, I would have been completely freaked out, but were you calm or a bit terrified?*

Kerri snatched at the mobile in her friend's hand, but Donna was too quick. She leaned away and the team of workers huddled around her moved their heads in order to keep their eyes on the screen. The day before her trip to the BBC Television Centre, Kerri had been briefed by her boss on what not to say, but sitting on the breakfast show sofa made her feel as if she was going to vomit out all the things that Prachi had said she shouldn't, like when someone says don't look and you immediately do. Kerri's jittery voice rang out: *I was terrified at first and then I realised I had to calm down because I had a job to do.*

The silver fox co-presenter spoke next: *And that job was to get the story to the people at any cost, right?*

Kerri's voice: *No, not at any cost. I first called the police* [lies], *but because it was an important story and since I was a journalist and at the scene of the crime, I felt I should be the one to tell the public what I experienced. That way the information was first-hand.*

Kerri cringed at the sound of her voice on TV. Was it really that high-pitched and squeaky?

The blonde bombshell spoke again: *Did you not want to run away when you saw his eye was gouged out?*

Silver fox: *Run away? It's not like he's suddenly going to grab her leg like some sort of zombie, is it?*

Blonde bombshell: *Yeah I know, but it's still awful finding a corpse.*

Silver Fox: *I suppose. Anyway, let's get to the Paper Doll Murder bit. In your article you mention that this has happened before, to two other victims in fact, and that you think it might be the work of a serial killer.*

Blonde Bombshell: *The police haven't confirmed that.*

The two presenters begin to bicker and Kerri remembered being amused at the time as well as slightly uncomfortable, like a child listening to their parents having an argument. Still, she didn't want to hear any more of her television interview. Her colleagues had seen it before, so why did they insist on watching it over and over? Kerri grabbed for the phone again. This time she swiped it and turned off the video.

'Ruuuude!' Donna held her hand out for Kerri to give back her phone.

'Promise you won't watch it again, it's embarrassing.'

Donna smiled. 'I promise not to watch it at work.'

Kerri placed the phone on Donna's palm, then reached into her jacket pocket for her own phone. No notifications since yesterday. That was odd. She checked the Wi-Fi symbol. No bars. She tapped and the symbol lit up. Her phone buzzed like a hive of angry bees lived inside it. Notifications pinged one after another. The door to the editor-in-chief's office sprang open.

'Parks!' Prachi shouted out, her head peeking round the doorframe.

The entire office turned their heads towards Kerri, all except Spencer who wasn't at his desk. Kerri had no idea why the boss had just shouted her last name out. Though she wasn't keen to find out, her feet started moving towards the back of the room before her brain could engage.

The boss held the door open for Kerri and once she'd ducked inside, she slammed the door shut and ordered her to take a seat. Kerri sat. The boss sat on the opposite side of the desk. She was dressed in her usual sari-inspired look, but something was different. Prachi moved her coffee cup to one side of the desk and back again. Twitchy. Not herself.

'What I am about to tell you cannot be repeated. Are we clear?' Kerri nodded, a seed of worry growing in the pit of her stomach. Prachi puffed out her tension. 'Spencer is dead.'

The seed of worry in Kerri's stomach sprouted. '*What?*'

'The police are coming to talk to everyone … Spencer was murdered in a hotel room.' Kerri clamped her hands over her mouth. She hated Spencer's guts, but couldn't help feeling sorry for him. Tears collected in her eyes. 'We're not going to get the scoop on this, but you are going to write about it.'

Kerri shook her head and spoke into her hands. 'I can't.'

'I know it's hard. Spencer was not the most popular person but he was still part of the team, and he died tragically.'

'Sean can do it.'

'Sean will help you, but your name was on the last piece and you've done interviews with the media. Kerri Parks is the journalist covering this story and your style can't be emulated by Sean, which is why it needs to be you who writes the piece.'

The sprout of worry inside Kerri's tum was growing into a tree. She felt nauseous.

'I don't understand. How does one piece make me the murder specialist?'

'This was another Paper Doll Murder. You persuaded Sean that we had a serial killer on our hands, and you were right.'

Blood thumped in Kerri's ears. A serial killer murdered Spencer. The worm who'd sat near her was murdered. The weasel who'd had nothing interesting about him at all had been killed. Why was he targeted? Was this psycho coming after people at the newspaper? Was she going to be next?

Kerri twiddled her hair, nerves jangled. 'How do you know this?'

'I have my sources.'

Kerri knew it; the woman had spies everywhere.

'What do I tell the police when they come?'

'Tell them whatever they want to know. This is not something I can coach you through. Now, go find some leads. I wouldn't bother with anyone in the office. Find out what he was doing at that hotel and talk to anyone connected to him outside of work, okay?'

'Okay.'

Kerri's head was swimming. The stress was too much. She could feel it coming. She slumped from the chair and hit the ground with a thump.

'Kerri!' Hurried footsteps. 'Kerri, can you hear me?'

'Prachi, the police are here … Oh shit!'

Kerri slipped further away, the voices like tiny stars way up in the sky.

'Do you know anything about epilepsy, Sean? Am I doing the right thing here?'

The tiny voices were no more than a whisper. They wanted her to come back, but she couldn't come back; the seizure had her in its grip. All she could do was wait for it to let go.

Chapter Twelve

Bea's a Hack

Mike had messaged Bea. Bea messaged Kerri. Kerri hadn't replied. The waiting was torture. Bea stared out of the coffee-shop window. Raindrops raced down the glass gathering droplet friends along the way, while beyond the window figures in raincoats passed by in a blur. The view was distorted by not only the splashes of rain but the sprayed on snowy scene. Every establishment in London was ready for the silly season, with windows elaborately decorated, each trying to 'out Christmas' the other.

Bea hadn't wanted to leave her room, but she couldn't sit at home any longer waiting for Kerri to show. Her pacing up and down was annoying Mrs Williams as it was. She'd used her broomstick to bang on the ceiling, which meant Bea's footsteps were starting to grate on the old girl's nerves.

A guide dog brushed past Bea's leg, with its owner close behind. The dog led the way to an empty table. A flustered waitress hurried over, set down a tray, and the blind man thanked her. She rushed away to serve the next customer waiting by the till. The dog sat obediently and the blind man reached down and placed a bowl of water from the tray under the table for the dog, which immediately lapped it up. Seeing the dog reminded Bea of Kerri's sausage dog. She was glad the dog was gone, but also a little sad: she had liked the little sausage and could have done with his company. Her flatmates were pretty self-involved, wrapped up in their own dramas.

A cup smashed somewhere near the tills and made Bea jump. Her anxiety was through the roof; making up fantastical stories was an escape from her dull, depressive life, but now she was under pressure to finish this book and her medication didn't seem to be working as well as it used to. The stress of writing in a new genre was getting to her. Not only that, but she was relying heavily on Kerri to provide inspiration, and without her news reports Bea would be sunk. Did that make her a hack? As long as the money comes in, does it matter?

Mike messaged Bea often, but rarely asked how the writing was going. All he wanted to do was gossip or rant about trivial things (trivial to Bea – a huge deal to Mike) happening in his life. However, the last message he sent was not the usual drag queen spite or drama on Trafalgar Square nonsense; this time, he'd been at the scene of a murder. Well, outside a hotel a guy had been stabbed to death in. Mike's message was overly dramatic as usual. Anyone would think he had been a witness to the man's sorry end. Normally, Bea would have brushed Mike's message off as embellishment, much of it caused by his constant gin drinking, but there were online articles to back up his story. Nothing from Kerri though, and since there was mention of this murder possibly being linked to the one in the warehouse, Bea wondered why Kerri had not jumped on the story. Ah, well. Maybe they weren't linked and Bea would have to carry on with her story without Kerri's articles as a guide.

She sipped the froth off her caramel latte, gently replaced the bowl-shaped coffee cup on its saucer, and tapped the laptop keyboard.

Another murder had occurred in the quiet suburban street, shocking the residents to their…

She held her finger down on the backspace. What a load of shit! She was going to fuck this up, she could feel it. No bidding war, no new bestseller, no second chance. She clicked on the Internet icon and opened her social media account. She typed another message to Kerri. *I'm getting worried. Are you okay?* Send.

Her stomach twisted. Was she really worried about Kerri's welfare, or was she more worried about getting the novel finished?

Bea stared at the screen, watching for a symbol to show up indicating that Kerri had seen her messages. Her flatmate had not been online all day. Bea side-eyed her mobile phone. She picked it up and dialled Kerri's boyfriend Mark. Kerri had given Bea his number in case she ever had a really bad seizure and Bea needed to call him. Bea drummed her fingertips on the table while the dial tone sounded in her ear. Three rings … four…

'What up?'

'Hi, Mark, it's Beatrice.'

'Beatrice?'

'Kerri's flatmate.'

'Oh, right, yeah. How're you doing?'

'I'm okay, but I'm a bit worried about Kerri. Is she with you?'

'No, she's been at work all day. Big story's just come in or something.'

'Yeah, um … So you think she's just really busy?'

'Yeah, why? You heard differently?'

'I haven't heard from her at all.' Mark was silent. Bea hated silence when she wasn't alone. 'If she calls you, can you tell her I need to talk to her urgently.'

Bea hated herself. It wasn't at all urgent.

'Sure, but now you have me worried.'

'I'm probably just being neurotic; she's a big girl and can take care of herself.'

'That's true. No worries, Bea. I'll let you know as soon as I hear from her.'

'Cheers, Mark. Speak soon.'

Bea pressed her thumb to the phone symbol. She had a terrible sinking feeling in her stomach that Kerri was in danger.

Killer

The blood stains are stubborn. You scrub and scrub, orange soap suds building in the sink, but still the stains won't come out of your shirt. A little dab of ammonia; the chemical smell wrinkles your nose. You wished you'd burned the shirt. All this scrubbing and washing is a waste of time.

The last doll has drawn a lot of attention. You want that because you want the public to know why you're hunting these monsters, but the police mustn't get too clever. You mustn't get caught. You can't rid the world of them all, but that's not your aim. The goal is not for you to keep killing, and although you don't want to stop, you know that you will eventually get caught. The goal is to protect. That is your job.

The journalist has pieced together some of the puzzle, but not enough to see the full picture. When she does and the authorities learn the connection is kiddie fiddlers, what will they do? Offer protection to those on the sex offenders list? There'd be a public outcry. By the time they've worked it out there'll be no need for paper dolls. This thought makes you sad. So does the thought of the dolls running out, you can't use just any type and there are only six rag dolls in the book and you've used four. Inside your head a vision blooms of little plastic bags marked evidence, the paper dolls inside like those in detective shows. You wonder if your first paper dolls – that disgusting, sadistic couple, who were like Fred and Rose West, but without the murdering – are in a plastic bag together, holding little paper hands.

You must engage your next target today to ensure he is dead by the end of the week. It's a lot sooner than normal, but you can't wait; the winter months make things harder. Fewer children in parks and walking home from school means fewer opportunities to snatch, and really that should increase business for you but it doesn't, instead the paedos go into hibernation. The dark web hasn't been throwing up any suitable candidates; the circles are protective and secretive. The only reason you caught your uncle was because he operated alone.

You take the shirt to the washing machine in the kitchen and stuff it inside the bowl with the other lights already in there. Your dress is laid out on the couch, flyers advertising your entertainment company in a pile next to it. Check the clock. It's almost midday, you'll have to hurry. Grab the box of detergent. Powder goes in. Turn the dial. Press the start button. The machine makes a shushing sound and then a click indicates it's about to start the washing cycle.

You pull the pretty silk dress over your head and force your arms up through the long sleeves. This dress is purple and makes you feel like Rapunzel because the wig you wear with it is a long blonde plait. You smooth down the front of the dress. It's soft, and you don't want to put the gloves on because you want to keep touching the soft material, but you must put the gloves on because finger prints are a problem. The wig goes on first. Then your winter jacket and then the gloves. You pick up the flyers. Time to leave.

***

You watch him while you give out flyers. The November sky is clear and the temperature is warmer than is usual for the time of year. Global warming has screwed the planet up so much that the seasons are a ghost of their former selves. Autumn often feeling like spring, summer sometimes like autumn, winters are warmer on the whole but freak cold snaps and snow storms occur without much warming. Sun warming your face, you forget yourself for a moment and drift into a daydream about how you will kill him. A suit bumps into you as he hurries by, he mumbles 'Excuse me,' and carries on power striding. You better keep up your act while out here in public. The target is your second to last doll and this will be the last time you can appear in Trafalgar as Princess. There will be security camera footage of you up to a certain point, but you know what to do thanks to an online 'friend' who works at the Gallery.

You smile and wave to the crowd. Two small children run over to you; you crouch to talk to them. Nearly all the small children walking across the Square with their families stop to say hello to you. Mostly little girls, but the occasional boy. The majority are more interested in superheroes and Yoda than you, though the girls take an interest in all the characters equally. You glance over at him again. Not long now.

'May I have a flyer, dear?'

Your attention is stolen by an old lady smiling up at you with false teeth that would be better suited to a horse. Does she even have them in right? Nope. They just moved around. Gross. You stare at her head. Her stripy hat resembles one of those tea cosy things – it's weird that people used to put knitted tops on teapots. You notice holes either side of her woolly hat. It *is* a tea cosy. The old girl has said something. You remember to smile sweetly.

'Excuse me?'

She pushes her teeth in and out of her mouth with her tongue, coke-bottle glasses making her eyes look as big as a possum's.

'Can I have a flyer? I love pantomimes.'

She tugs at a flyer and you almost lose the whole lot to the ground. You snatch them back. The old dear pouts. You plaster the smile on again.

'Sorry, love. I'm not in panto. I'm a children's entertainer.'

'Oh, well, I have grandchildren. Give me one and I'll pass it on to my daughter.'

You glance up to make sure he hasn't skipped off for lunch.

'Sure, okay.' You hand the old lady the flyer, knowing she will stick it to her fridge when she gets home and forget about it, but who cares? Your pretend marketing stint is almost over. 'Why don't you take the lot and give them to your friends at the WI?'

That was presumptuous of you. She might not belong to the Women's Institute. Just because she looks like a jam maker and knitting enthusiast, that doesn't mean she actually is. Perhaps she's like you and has a dark secret. She tugs the stack of flyers from your hands.

'What a good idea, I'll do just that.'

You tug one back.

'I'll keep this one, if that's okay with you?'

You curtsy, she returns your grace with a bow, then shuffles away. Beside you, he waves to the last set of tourists who take a selfie with him. The curtain drops over his tent. It's time.

Before you make a move, a young girl darts around the curtain and into the small gazebo. You step back and subtly spy on them. The girl is all over the Batman. He smiles awkwardly, but doesn't tell her to stop touching him. There's a twinkle in her eye that should not be present. Daddy issues? Her mother on drugs or drunk? The girl is gaming him, but what's worse he's letting her. Teens can be sly; they'll do everything in their power to make their lives bearable, especially those in poverty. Many youngsters in distressing situations will take the least distressing option. Just. Like. You. Did.

You take out your phone and discreetly snap a few photos of the pair. The girl says she has to go and kisses the Bat. On the lips. Click. You shove your phone away in your jacket pocket. He looks startled and tells the girl she mustn't do that. She whines about not being pretty. Classic manipulation. He tells her she is very pretty, but that he's married. She pretends she's going to cry. He gets to his feet and hugs her. You mentally calculate her age. Sixteen or seventeen. Not underage, but way too young for the Batman. He'd go younger and say he didn't know. Statutory rape waiting to happen is written all over him. You've watched how he is with young girls in the Square. Prevention is better than cure because there's no cure for what these monsters inflict. Like a severed arm, once it's gone it's gone forever.

He has his back to you and you note the smiling eyes of the girl, beautiful dark-brown, like chocolate drops in cream. Her eyes meet yours, they narrow. She's not happy you're watching her while she works him over. She breaks away and tells him she has to go. He says goodbye and reminds her that she is pretty. Wrong message, Bat. Tell her she's smart, because she is and you're thick as shit if you can't see she's doing a number on you.

The girl is gone. Bat sits down on a foldout camping stool and perches his Batman lunch box on his lap. He pulls out a squashed sandwich and unwraps the cling film. He takes great big bites like he's been starved for a week. You pop your head around the curtain.

'Like them young, eh?'

'Oh, err…' Bat wipes mayo from the corner of his mouth with the back of his meaty hand. 'No, she's just a friend.'

'Are you friends with a lot of young girls?' You flutter your long eyelashes innocently. Gently does it. Don't spook the beast.

Bat smiles and adjusts himself on the chair to face you.

'No. I ain't got many friends, truth be told.'

'What about the sad clown?' You play with your long blonde plait which is as thick as a rope. 'You two are friends, right?'

'Nah, I don't fink he really likes me much.' Bat takes another bite of his ham salad sandwich and swallows. 'He's got loads of friends. Very popular down the local nightclub. I guess you know that.'

You repress an eye-roll. Mike doesn't have any friends. They hate him down at the club.

'I know he'd be crazy to pass on your friendship.' You step inside the tent and place your hand on Bat's shoulder; he quivers at your touch. 'I can see why that young girl likes you.'

'You can?' He stares at your hand on his shoulder.

'I've been watching you.'

'You have?' His gaze doesn't move from your hand.

You read his face. He can't quite believe an attractive woman is touching him. Not a youngster the same age as his daughter, who he shouldn't be interfering with. A woman. Someone he could have an encounter with, and no one would call him out on it. No one would say he was sick. He'll take any attention from younger women he can get, preferring little girls but not wanting to give in to the paedo inside. But they all crack in the end and kids get hurt. You gaze at him longingly.

'I've got a thing for superheroes.'

'Y-you do?' His eyes dart around, searching the exposed sides of the tent where people are passing by, possibly worried his wife, or someone who knows his wife, might see you flirting with him. You nod coyly and gently slide you hand down his chubby arm.

'I know somewhere we can go.' You press the flyer to his chest. 'Call me if you fancy hooking up.'

'What?' His eyes bulge with alarm.

Shit! Too much too fast. You should have reeled him in gently; he's going to wriggle off the hook. You lean over and whisper in his ear, 'Just once, no one has to know.'

Red rises up Bat's round face. He probably wishes he hadn't removed his mask to eat lunch.

'Um … that's very kind of you, but I don't think I can.'

He touches his wedding ring which is tight around his sausage finger; if he wanted to remove it, he'd have to have it cut off. The ring, not the finger. Though judging by how tight the gold band is, piling on a few pounds over the festive season could see the finger get the chop. He won't be alive long enough for that.

You step out of the enclosure, pick up your jacket, and sling it over your arm. It's fourteen degrees and sunny, and doesn't show any sign of switching to more wintery weather.

'No pressure, just think about it.' You blow him a kiss and slink away.

Chapter Thirteen

Mike's New Job

Lady Vajazzle, AKA Donald, was standing behind Mike with her arms crossed over her tremendous bosom. Mike lowered the make-up brush and studied his friend's reflection in the lit-up dressing room mirror. He could feel her frustration bubbling over, and half expected her to grab the brush from him, and start fixing his make-up the way she'd envisioned.

'It needs to be bolder than that, Micha.'

Mike ignored her. He wasn't some exaggerated reflection of the female form; he was the female form perfected. Mike went back to making himself up. Donald tutted and the late comedian Robin Williams sprang into Mike's mind, hyper cartoon voice ringing in his ears. *Call that a makeover?* Mike drifted into a daydream involving an animated fairy godmother with the comedian/actor's voice, who had appeared from nowhere and started scribbling over Mike's face before using a powder puff on him, filling the room with powdery clouds. Mike coughed. White puffs of smoke distorted his reflection. He waved his hand in front of his face, irritated. 'There's no smoking inside!' He pointed to a peeling non-smoking sign on the dressing room wall.

'I'm not smoking, I'm vaping.' Trev, the owner of the club, puffed on an e-cigarette beside him. Mike waved the last remnants of smoke away, thankful that it at least smelled of candyfloss and not tobacco, he leaned closer to the mirror and dusted his cheeks with sparkly pink rouge.

'Ever heard of popcorn lung?'

Trev puffed on the slim black tube, blowing more white clouds from his thick lips. 'Could get hit by a bus tomorrow.'

Mike applied silky pink lippy. 'That's everyone's excuse for doing abusive things to their body.'

'And pickling the liver is a perfectly healthy choice.' Trev grinned.

Mike puckered his lips and admired his pout in the mirror. 'We all have our vices, I guess.'

'That we do. Anyway, shouldn't you be buttering me up if you want a job here?'

Mike slid off the make-up chair, smoothed down the front of his golden Belle inspired dress, and curtsied to the club owner. At over six feet tall and with arms like boulders, Trev could be mistaken for a bouncer. 'Thank you so much for this amazing opportunity, Lord Trevor. I'm truly very grateful.' Mike fluttered his false eyelashes. 'Is that enough butter for your popcorn lungs?'

Trev let out a deep throaty laugh. 'It's a good job you're pretty.'

Mike picked up the hairspray and moved his arm like he was spraying a halo around his head. The synthetic smell of the strong lacquer filled his nostrils. It was a smell he associated with the theatre, that and the musty aroma of thick stage curtains and old costumes rarely laundered.

Trev tipped his hat, allowing his wild hair a few seconds of freedom before jamming the hat back down on his frizzy locks. Mike took the hint and exited. He liked chivalry. Trev was not interested in him sexually, he knew that much, but it was nice to feel special. So many people in London walked with heads down, or barged past with sour faces. Being polite and jovial was endearing, and it was what Mike liked most about the owner of Bliss.

Lady V followed after Mike. She whispered in his ear, her hot breath tickling. 'Remember to be over the top and confident. Own the stage.'

'I don't need performance tips from you.' Mike fiddled with his wig; he couldn't have even one hair out of place.

Their footsteps echoed down the long corridor that led to the back of the stage. Lady V tapped him on the shoulder. 'I'm gonna let that go because I know you're nervous.'

Mike held the rail with one hand and hitched up his dress with the other so as not to put a heel through the netting attached to the hoop. Lady V followed him up. He turned to face his friend, and plucked a bit of white fluff from Lady V's blonde trestles.

'Thanks.' Lady V pursed her lips. Mike could tell she wasn't grateful he'd helped with her personal grooming. Her wig was of low quality, shiny, like she'd cut the hair off a hundred Barbie's to make it. Mike wore his black bob for going out and the brown shoulder-length wig for auditions. Putting on the high-quality, brown wig he was reminded of his last audition and how dreadful that had gone. He was not going to let that happen this time. He patted the pretty yellow bow in his hair for luck.

Mike took a deep breath. 'I'm ready.'

'Break a leg.' Lady V strolled to the black curtain and slipped around the side. Her footsteps, heavy in high-heels, clomped down the steps on the other side as she made her way to sit in the audience. Mike tiptoed over and peeked round the glittery black curtains. The audience consisted of Lady Vajazzle, who took a seat next to Trev, and beside him was a horse-faced woman he recognised as the manager. Beside her was a beautiful creature he had never seen before. Immaculate grooming: beard short and trimmed, eyebrows symmetrical. Strong jawline, slim but clearly athletic. He reminded Mike of an action figure wearing a Ken Doll's clothes. Fantasies danced in Mike's head. He was the beautiful Belle of the ball and action Ken was his prince come to rescue him from his rent arrears.

Trev's voice echoed around the empty club. 'We're ready for you now, Micha.'

Mike's confidence had decided to bail on him and he was left with his paranoia running the show. He couldn't perform in front of that beautiful man. Self-conscious, Mike wished he was somewhere else, anywhere else. He would rather be at the dentist having his teeth drilled, or in the hospital having an endoscopy – doctor shining a tiny torchlight up his love hole.

He glanced up at the lighting and sound box. Unfortunately, they took that as the cue and started the music. Mike took another deep breath, picked up the microphone left on a stool backstage for him and pushed through where the flimsy curtains met and out onto centre stage.

He stood tall and elegant, forcing his trembling body to move in time with the intro. He sang through his nerves, his mic hand shaking, voice cracking in places. He kept his eyes on the back of the room; he knew better than to look at the people in the audience and get put off. He twirled and sashayed across the uneven stage, the lights warming his cheeks. He was a star, a bright shiny star. He was nailing this audition.

Mike's confidence grew when the audience laughed at a cheeky gesture he'd added to the routine. Because he had to look at someone for that part, he'd safely directed it at Trev, who was smiling and nodding his head in time with the music. Feeling brave, Mike decided to ad lib a little and made his way over to the stairs. The instrumental gave him enough time to reach the floor. His gaze travelled over the group; all were smiling except the manager. She had a poker face, he couldn't read her.

When he started singing again, he felt so sure of himself he began to serenade the gorgeous creature, who smiled at him and pretended to be bashful. He walked around the chairs, singing to each person in turn. His heart raced, knowing the big finish was next, it was almost over. Mike flitted around the front of the chairs and dramatically belted out the high notes. Everyone started to clap. His spirits soared. As he stepped towards the beautiful creature, his foot snagged on something and he fell forwards. The horror of what was happening stabbed him in the heart as his face plunged towards the lap of his prince charming. Mike's face collided with the beautiful man's crotch with an almighty thump. The man shrieked with the pain of Mike's hard head colliding with his genitals.

Quick as a flash, Mike lifted his head, but his wig was stuck to the beautiful man's zipper. He pulled his head backwards and his wig came off. The man stood up, horrified. The wig dangled from his fly.

Mike apologised profusely, his face burnt red. Lady V attempted to remove the wig from the man's zipper, consoling him over his head-butted nuts. The beautiful man said he accepted Mike's apology, but Mike could tell he hadn't. He'd accidently made a new enemy before he'd even known the guy's name. Feeling overwhelmed, Mike took flight. He fled to the safety of the dressing room, Trevor hot on his heels.

Mike ignored the club owner's calls for him to wait. Once in the dressing room he quickly started undressing. He ripped off his false eyelashes threw them at the lit mirror. Then unzipped his dress, shimmied out of it and kicked it across the floor.

There was a knock at the door. 'Mike, it's Trev. Are you decent?'

Mike tossed the chicken fillets out of his bra and pulled on his shirt. He sat down in his sheer tights and started buttoning the shirt.

'Come in.'

Trevor slowly opened the door and closed it with a quiet click behind him. His sorrowful dark brown eyes emptied pity all over Mike. Last button done up, Mike slouched in the chair.

Trev leaned up against the wall. 'You know, we ask our acts to always end with the "Bliss Kiss".' His body language was soft; why wasn't he mad at Mike? Mike was mad at himself. Trev pulled out his e-cigarette and twirled it in his thick fingers. 'You've seen the Bliss Kiss. It's when the drag acts blow kisses to the audience at the end of their number … we encourage our queens to push the boat out, but kissing an audience member's crotch is pushing the boat a bit too far out, even for us.'

Mike accepted Trevor's warmth and smiled back. He couldn't hold it for the long. Inside his head he replayed what his fall might have looked like from the view of the sound and lighting box. *Bet they had a good laugh*. He pulled the stocking holding down his hair off his head and twiddled his fingers through his own brown locks, which were nowhere near as long and beautiful as his Belle wig. His gaze dropped to the floor.

'I didn't get the job though, right?'

Trev shook his head and puffed on the black stick. White smoked billowed out. 'You didn't get that job, no, but I am a staff member down.'

Mike wiped away a lone tear that had managed to escape the corner of his eye. He glanced up at Trev, white smoke all around him like a magic genie who'd just appeared from inside a lamp.

'Devan quit. The press has been hounding him after your flatmate spilled the beans about his affair.'

'What affair?' Mike was shocked. Kerri had written something about Devan's private life? Why would she do that? She's covering the murders; she hates that kind of stuff.

'He was screwing the hotel owner.' Mike could feel his eyes pop from their sockets. His mouth dropped open. 'He couldn't cope with the harassment from the press and the haters. His sugar daddy left his wife and is taking care of him until his mental state improves.'

'Holy shit!' Just like that, Mike's problems didn't seem so bad.

Trev took another drag. 'I have an opening for a barman. It's a leap of faith for me, given how much you drink. You get caught drinking the place dry or being smart to customers and you're out on your ear.'

'I appreciate the sentiment, but I don't want a job as a barman. I'm a performer, an artist.'

'You're gonna be a starving artist if you keep this up. You're getting a name for yourself. A lot of the theatre producers and writers and other bigwigs come in here, and some have mentioned this guy who keeps auditioning for female roles. I would hazard a guess it's you.'

Mike sighed. The theatre industry was close knit. Everyone knew everyone else. They'd been whispering about him behind his back. Laughing at him, probably. He could sink no lower.

'Fine, I'll take the job.' Mike reached down and picked up his jeans.

Trev pocketed his pipe. 'And…?'

Mike frowned as he pulled his jeans onto his legs, and then realised his rudeness. 'Thank you, Trev. Do I need to sign something?'

'We'll put you on a trial contract.'

Mike stood and pulled his jeans up over his thighs. He zipped up and wondered if Lady V had managed to remove his wig from the man's crotch. He thought of himself wearing the uniform of a servant. His heart sank into the pit of his stomach. 'Where do I get my uniform?'

Trev scooped the golden Belle dress up off the floor and handed it to Mike. 'Your uniform will be your favourite Princess dress.'

'Huh?' Mike took the dress, bewildered.

'Come to work as Belle, Cinders, Moana, whoever you fancy. The punters will love it.' Mikes eyes welled up. His bottom lip trembled. He clutched his Belle inspired dress to his chest. Trev gripped Mike's shoulder affectionately. 'Stay in character. It'll be our new theme. What do you think?'

Mike smiled. His heart filling up with happiness. This was perfect. Princess would come in and see what a great job he was doing at being a princess behind the bar and she would offer him a job with her and then he would have two jobs doing what he loved. Out of the cold, off the streets, and with a steady income.

'I think it's great!' Tears rolled thick and fast, running lines through Mike's make-up. 'You won't regret this, Trev. I can't fall into anyone's crotch from behind the bar, can I?'

'I should hope not.' Trev laughed deeply. 'Go home and get a good night's sleep. You start tomorrow at four.'

Chapter Fourteen

Kerri's Guilt

Inside, the warm pub was decorated with tinsel and shiny and suitably tacky paper chains that criss-crossed the ceiling of every public house this time of year. The bar area was full to bursting with Friday night revellers. Office workers and tradesmen/women boozing together, laughing loudly and being crude. Kerri's ears pricked up when a brazen man propped up at the bar in a dishevelled suit shouted, 'Oi, oi!' at a young girl in a tight red dress. She flipped him the bird and his group of ogling vultures roared with laughter. He bowed deeply as she sauntered away and he then stumbled forwards, his fellow drunks catching him before he hit the deck.

Kerri was sitting in a quieter corner, full glass of red wine on a mat in front of her, pint for Mark placed next to it. She clutched her phone tight and scrolled through the comments under her article about the latest Paper Doll murder. Some were about the horrible crimes and how people don't feel safe in London, knowing there's a serial killer on the loose. They were calling the killer a reverse Jack the Ripper who was killing men rather than women – explaining away the only female victim killed with the old clichés: she saw too much, or she might have tried to save her partner.

Before Kerri could get on and write the article, she had had to endure the police questioning. It was tricky, because when asked if she and the deceased were friends she couldn't say 'No, I hated the little turd', but she also couldn't say yes, because even though he thought she was his friend, they really weren't

116

friends in any sense of the word. Kerri had opted for friendly at work, and that was as far as it went. She told the investigator that Spencer had mentioned meeting a date and that was all she knew. Which was true.

It was clear the police didn't think anyone from the office had anything to do with Spencer's death. Kerri had missed a load of messages from Bea. Apparently, Mike had been chatting to her about Spencer's murder, but she didn't let on to him that Kerri knew the guy. Thank goodness, because Kerri was in no mood for an inquisition from Mike. She had done some digging and found that one of the barmen at Mike's favourite nightclub also worked at the hotel as a waiter. Kerri had tracked him down and he agreed to talk to her.

The rattled twenty-something was a verbal sewage pipe; he had spewed every sordid detail and even stuff that was unrelated to the murder. It was like the guy had to purge, because if he didn't it would poison him. Perhaps he thought she had a kind face and would keep his secrets, but she was a journalist and her moral code of conduct didn't extend to work. She prided herself on being a kind soul in other areas of her life, but she had not taken a solemn oath to protect the public from themselves and she would write almost anything to build her career.

Kerri's eyes traced over snarky comments about young Devan and his affair with the baby boomer who owned the chain of hotels. Her article had hit a nerve and the hotelier threatened to sue the paper. Prachi was angry. She fired Sean for signing off on it. Donna was reassigned to work with Kerri on the Paper Doll reports. The conversation with Prachi rang loud inside Kerri's head. '*Someone had to go under the bus; it wasn't going to be me so that left you or Sean.*' '*Sean's worked here over a decade though!*' '*You wanna take his place?*' Kerri went quiet. '*No.*'

Kerri felt something wet on her arm and glanced up from her phone, worried she'd spilt her drink. The wine glass was exactly where she placed it.

Woof!

She glanced down. Sausage was licking her arm.

'What are you doing here?' She scratched behind his ear and he lowered his head so she could scratch behind the other ear too.

Mark dropped down opposite her, jogging the table. She grabbed her wine glass and held it steady, but it was too late for the beer. Froth sloshed over the side of the glass and onto the mat.

'Thanks, Babe.' He took a sip, then wriggled his arms out of his jacket. He draped it over the chair back behind him. Kerri put her phone face down and picked up her glass of wine. She sipped.

'How was work?' Kerri had to raise her voice; the din wasn't so loud she had to shout, but it was loud enough that Mark, who was hard of hearing but not enough to need a hearing aid, could hear her.

Mark placed his pint back down on the sodden mat. 'Smashed out a couple of houses. Had a ruck with the plumber. Piss-taking git used my tools without asking. The apprentice is a lazy little knob. The usual, really.' He winked, and Kerri smiled when a vision of them shagging in a couple of hours popped into her mind. 'How was your day?'

Mark whistled for Sausage to lie down out of the way under the table. Dogs weren't strictly allowed in the pub, but Mark knew the owners so as long as Sausage didn't cause a fuss he could stay. Kerri took another sip of wine and explained about Sean.

Mark's attention was pulled towards the bar where the group of men were lining up shots. He threw a comment at her without taking his eyes off the bar. 'Cut throat industry, I guess.'

'It's wrong, Mark.' She waved her hand in front of his face and he picked up his pint. 'I wrote that article. Sean shouldn't have been fired.'

He sipped. Half listening to her, half wanting to see which lout was going to pass out first. 'Throw yourself on your sword then.'

Kerri allowed herself to steal a glance. 'I need my job.' A skinny apprentice in dirty overalls swayed as he got down off the barstool.

A girl of similar age hooked her arm under his and helped him to the gents' toilets where she waited outside.

Mark took a packet of pork scratchings out of his jacket pocket. 'Forgot I had these.' He tore the pack open and a long snout appeared from under the table. Sausage sniffed the air. Mark threw him a couple of scratchings. 'Stop worrying about other people and do your job. This is not your fault. You didn't know the dragon would fire him.' He shook some scratchings into his palm, then tipped them into his mouth and crunched. 'Hey.' He grinned. 'Dragon, fire him – get it?'

Kerri huffed. 'Are you going to sit there and make puns at me all evening, or can we have a serious conversation?'

'What's serious? Sean will get a new job. Like ya mate Mike did.'

'Mike did *what* now?'

'You know Donald.' Kerri's face was blank. Mark spoke slowly. 'Donald. The firm's accountant by day and drag queen by night.'

'Oh, yeah, go on.'

'He came to site today. I had a chat with him in the tea room. He said the barman you wrote about quit his job at Bliss because of a nervous breakdown.' Kerri gasped. A guilty fish swam in her stomach. Mark gulped down some beer, balanced the soggy bar mat on one of its corners, and spun it one turn. The mat flopped down. 'Mike's been given his job.'

'Mike's working behind a *bar*?'

Kerri frowned. 'Whose idea was that? He'll drink the place dry within a week.'

'I dunno about that but I say good for him. Begging on the streets is not a job.'

'Mark!'

'What?' he threw the rest of the pork scratchings to the dog.

'They're not beggars! A lot of them are really talented. Would you say that about buskers?'

'The ones that are shit, I would. Shall we order some grub or do you wanna get a takeaway?' He raised his eyebrows innocently, but there was nothing innocent about that statement. 'Get a takeaway' meant go home with a bucket of chicken wings, watch some porn, and then shag until dawn.

Kerri necked the rest of the wine. 'Let's go.'

Chapter Fifteen

Bea's Deadline

At her desk, slumped over her closed laptop, Bea closed her eyes to the brightness of the writing lamp shining down over the pens and papers sprawled around her. The side of her face lying heavy on the cold surface of the MacBook, Bea tried to empty her mind. Her body ached; her joints were stiff; her bones weary. She felt as if she hadn't slept in a month, and yet she also felt like all she did was sleep. It was a strange sensation. Sometimes she knew exactly what was going on, but other times she was all over the place. Her medication was keeping her depression and anxiety at a manageable level, but she was becoming extremely forgetful and losing track of time. Sometimes she'd forget which day it was. She put it down to working too hard. She was stressed, and being cooped up inside most of the time was not good for her health.

Bea felt around the desk until her fingers found a sharp edge and she turned off the lamp. Darkness swallowed the room. She opened her eyes to a black wall. She could see nothing. Bea stretched her legs out under the desk; her calf muscles were knotted tight. Maybe she should try the gym? Her next thought was of mental illness; it often stopped her from doing things. She'd end up going to the gym once a month or not at all. Good intentions are a waste of money. It would be a different story if Bea had someone to go with, someone who would help encourage her to keep at it. Alas, she was the definition of 'Billy no mates', unless she counted her flatmates and Mrs Williams, but they weren't exactly her friends. She didn't see another living soul from one day to the next. Bea's online community was everything. They supported her when her career went tits up, coached her through her depression – many had been depressed, or were going through the agony themselves – and because they lived all over the world there was always someone to talk to on social media, day or night. Experts say social media can be a source of anxiety; people reading negative news or trying to keep up with others who only show their privilege to the online world, never the shit bits of their reality. But even though it could sometimes be an energy suck, Bea needed it. It was a lighthouse, helping her navigate the dark sea of loneliness.

Bea's recent wave of anxiety had been caused by her agent. Jackie had been on her back like a lion tamer cracking the whip. Bea was almost there; the novel would be complete in a matter of weeks, but her agent couldn't wait. She'd 'put the feelers out', and instead of taking the book to the London Book Fair next year, she reckoned she could get a pre-emptive deal with a quick release date. The last thing Bea wanted to do was rush, but she also needed money. Mike was again lagging behind with his share of the rent, leaving her and Kerri to pick up the slack. She wouldn't mind, but he didn't pay as much as they did anyway. He had the smallest room and so paid the least.

If Bea were honest with herself, it wasn't just deadlines and money worries stressing her out. She'd been having nightmares, waking up drenched in sweat. Reading Kerri's latest article about the death of her colleague and then asking Kerri for a little more info had been a mistake. It was too violent. Reading one part of Kerri's message sent her stomach acid into a raging river mode. There was speculation that the victim's intestine had been removed. Why would the killer do that? The one before Spencer had been discovered by Kerri. She had later found out that the blood on the corpse's underpants was because his penis had been mutilated. That and the gouged eye was bad enough, but keeping someone's gastrointestinal tract? That was really nasty.

Bea should have opted to make it all up, but because she'd based the book on these true events she now had to follow through. The idea of a killer so close to home, and both her and her flatmate writing about it, tipped paranoia into the mix. Bea worried that the murderer would come after her when the book was published, angry she'd written it, and then Bea would become the fifth paper doll. She hoped like hell that the police found the killer soon. Then no one else would die, she could make up the ending, and get rid of the manuscript to her pest of an agent.

A flash of light illuminated the curtains. Lightning? Bea lifted her head. Another flash. Normally she could hear traffic outside. She concentrated on listening for the crackle of thunder. Nothing. Silence. Not even a bus trundling past. The light flashed behind the curtains again. A silent light. Aliens? Like the ones she wrote about in the Young Adult supernatural novels. Bea got up from the desk and went to the window. She stood completely still. Chest tight. Panic clutching her heart.

Slowly, she peeled back the curtain. The light flashed again then flickered; it was coming from the lamppost. Bea sighed with relief and was about to shut the curtains when something caught her eye. Flurries of white fluttered down, illuminated every few seconds by the faulty street light. She moved the curtain behind her, leaned close to the glass and watched the pretty white specks dance to the ground. A chill sneaked through the gaps in the window frame, but although it made her shiver, she was warm enough with her dressing gown wrapped tight around her. The empty London streets were soon speckled with snowflakes.

Bang! Bang! Bang!

'Jesus!' Bea clutched the front of her dressing gown and turned her head towards the knocking sound.

'Kerri! Bea!' A muffled shriek travelled to Bea's ears from behind the front door. It was Mrs Williams. 'Come and see. It's snowing!'

Bea grabbed her scarf and gloves from the chest of drawers. She wrapped the knitted rainbow around her neck – Mrs Williams had made it for her when she'd said she didn't own a scarf – and pulled on her black gloves. She dashed out of her bedroom, kicked off her slippers and tugged on her boots, which she kept on a shoe rack at the door.

'Coming, Mrs Williams!' she shouted, zipping up her ankle boots.

Door open. Mrs Williams was wearing a baby-pink winter coat, pink hat with a canary yellow bobble on top, pink and yellow striped scarf wrapped around her neck several times with matching pink and yellow polka-dot wellies. Bea couldn't see her mouth for the scarf, but her big eyes smiled behind her thick glasses. Bea's landlady resembled Mr Blobby after having his head punched down into his neck.

'You didn't call for Mike.' Bea tugged on her coat and closed the door behind her.

Mrs Williams pulled down the scarf with one finger to free her mouth. 'How can Mike see anything if he's blind drunk?'

Bea chuckled as she followed the eccentric old dear down the landing. 'The first snow of the season! It's exciting, isn't it?'

'Sure is, that's why I called for you girls.' Mrs Williams waddled towards the stairs. How many layers did she have on under that coat? 'Where's Kerri?'

'At Mark's.'

'She spends more time at that Mark's than she does here.' Bea paused at the top of the stairs while the Mrs Blobby carefully took one step at a time. 'Why doesn't she move in with him?'

'She thinks it's too soon. He's divorced. They don't want to ruin things, I guess.'

'In my day, you had to get married first and there was no getting divorced. 'Till death do us part'. You had to choose wisely. Thankfully, I did, didn't I, Des.' When she reached the bottom step, she pressed her hand to an oak wood-framed photo on the wall of a white bearded old man. 'He was a good man.'

Mrs Williams waddled over to the main door. In the entrance hall corner was a naked Christmas tree.

'Putting up the tree already?'

'It takes me so long to decorate the blasted thing these days. This way, by the time the twelfth comes around the tree will be done.'

'I could always help.'

Mrs Williams began unlocking the bolts on the front door, from top to bottom. 'No, no,' she strained. 'I can manage just fine.'

Bea reached out to help with the bolts, but quickly withdrew; she knew better than to interfere. Mrs Williams was quite capable. She pulled the door open and the outside security light shone a halo over the snowy front steps. Bea drank in the view. The faulty streetlamp had died, but the ones across the road lit up the wintery scene like something out of a dream. Most windows in the Victorian terraced houses were dark. White collected on roofs, window ledges, gates, fences and tops of wheelie bins. Cars were blanketed, the roads undisturbed. That was until an empty red double-decker rolled past slowly so as not to skid. The roads didn't look as if they'd been gritted. No one had been expecting the snow fall. They watched the pretty scene in silence. Clouds plumed from between Bea's lips as her teeth chattered.

Mrs Williams shivered and rubbed her hands together. 'Brrr. Want some of my special cocoa tea?'

'That would be lovely. D'you want some help?'

'No, no.' She was already half way to the door. 'You enjoy the peacefulness. I won't be long.'

Mrs Williams returned in a matter of minutes; she must have had it all ready to go. She handed Bea a hot mug of cocoa tea. The steam carried the scent of cinnamon and nutmeg. Bea sipped, and the hot velvety chocolate spread through her body like a warm hug.

Mrs Williams slurped her chocolate tea and peered around the door frame. She leaned out a little further.

'What is it?' Bea leaned out with her.

'Did you put Christmas lights up at the front window?'

Bea shook her head. 'No.'

'Do you think Kerri or Mike would have?'

'It's unlikely.'

'Well, I didn't put them up.'

Bea placed her hot cocoa tea on the step and held onto the hand rail. She carefully ventured out into the elements, snow instantly collecting on her eyelashes and sticking to her hair. Her boots crumped over the snow dusted front lawn, and as she approached the window, Bea pulled her scarf over her nose when a nasty smell like rotting meat hit her nostrils. The bins should have been emptied. Perhaps there was a dead fox somewhere around.

She stepped closer to the string of fairy lights hanging across the middle of the window, and a shiver ran through her body. The coloured lights were strung around something brown and bobbly. Bea froze, as if the weather had turned her body to ice but what had really made her blood run cold was the grizzly realisation that she was looking at a string of intestines with Christmas lights wrapped around them.

Killer

Bat doesn't call you. He texts. You dropped your phone while hiding the ammonia in the bathroom and it hits the tiled floor with an ominous clack. Sure enough, a long hairline crack has spread across the screen. Still usable, you won't have to bother going through the rigmarole of getting a new one. Good. If it works, it stays. Plus those kinds of purchases are traceable. You don't want to give the old bill any extra help in finding you.

The text you get from Bat is cryptic.

I would like to meet to discuss the thing we were talking about at work. I can do tomorrow afternoon. Where will we meet?

You text back: *The art gallery. 3pm.*

He replies: *See you then.*

***

Inside the Gallery it's quiet. Two tourists stare down at a map, each with one foot on the first step of the grand staircase leading up to the rooms filled with decorative gold frames holding fine art from a time long forgotten. Tourists come to London all year round, but the numbers visiting art galleries and museums have dwindled. Which is surprising because entry to most art galleries and museums is free. Almost everything else costs. You have to pay to use the toilet in some train stations. It used to be a penny; now it's thirty pence. Soon they'll start charging people to sit. Want to sit on a bench in Central London? Place a pound in the slot and the spikes will lower. Only for ten minutes, though. Sit any longer and risk being impaled. You smile to yourself: actually, that's a rather fun idea.

Under your jacket, you wear a shirt and tie, your trousers similar to the staff at the Gallery. Not in the slightest bit sexy, but you'll pop a couple of buttons like you did with the school uniform. That should be enough. He probably hasn't had sex in years; the sight of breasts in a push-up bra might be enough for him to cream his pants.

No weapons this time. You can't get past security with a blade in your bag. You didn't bring a bag for that reason. You'll have to improvise. Your friend who works here isn't on shift today. She's left her wallet at the desk and told staff you were coming for it. The drowsy-eyed receptionist tossed you the wallet with all the enthusiasm of a teenager getting out of bed before noon, and sloped off to 'help' an elderly couple who'd appeared beside you, shaking out wet umbrellas.

Inside the purple leather purse you find her pass as promised. You now have access to nearly every part of the building. The 'friend' is obsessed with drama, and wants all the details of your sexual encounter once the deed is done. She thinks you're meeting some Greek God with rippling muscles. Ha! You've already blocked the bitch on social media.

You tap your foot impatiently, check your phone: it's ten past three. He's chickened out. You watch as a handful of tourists drip through the front doors. *There he is!* He's wearing a black fedora, dark sunglasses and a trench coat. He glances around sheepishly, like he's part of a terrorist organisation plotting to blow up the Gallery. Your heels clack across the marble floor as you strut over to him. You link your arm with his.

'Nice to see you again.'

He unhooks his arm from yours and skulks towards the staircase. You follow. He whispers. 'We can't let anyone see us together.'

'Are we role-playing? You're a spy and I'm the femme fatale?'

'No!' The Bat is twitchy. 'I can't have my wife find out. It would break her heart.'

You clench your fists. *Then why are you doing it, you nasty piece of shit!*

The actress in you takes control. 'I understand; don't worry; she'll never find out.'

She will, you smirk to yourself, *when she's crying over your bloated corpse.*

Bat hurries up the steps. You allow him this moment of panic. At the top, several rooms around you, he pulls you into a corner. Breath hot on your neck, he whispers in your ear. 'God you smell good. Where to?'

You cup the side of his face with your gloved hand. 'Somewhere secret.' One hand on the wall beside your head, he takes off his glasses with the other, leans in and kisses you. Gentle, tender, like the first kiss from a long-lost lover. He's not thinking of you. People don't kiss fuck buddies like that. They thrust their tongue down your throat and tear at your clothes like a starving animal. His kiss is of longing. You get a sinking feeling in the pit of your stomach. He's making you feel bad. You grab his hand, push it under your jacket and press it to your breast. Will he lose himself and undo your shirt buttons? Nope. He moves his hand, runs both hands around your lower back and over your backside. He kisses you again. Sensual. You close your eyes, tingling all over like you're one of those virginal teens in American movies being kissed for the first time by your high school sweetheart. You almost enjoy it. No way! You open your eyes and pull back, lips unlocking.

'Come on.' You shrug off the jacket and tuck it under your arm, then dart past and tug him along by the hand. You make your way to where she told you to go: an unused store room. Apparently it needs cleaning out, but no one's got around to it yet. He hurries to keep up, panting a bit.

'Where are we going?'

You don't answer, you're almost there. Two security doors later and a flight of narrow steps, and you lead the Bat into the dark room. Inside it smells like old paint and mouldy fabric. He turns on the light. Your eyes adjust. The store room is no bigger than a classroom. Cobwebs own the corners and crevasses; dust mites own the rest. There's broken frames and rusty tins, and clutter stacked up around the walls. You drape your jacket over a stack of faded theatre style chairs and loosen the tie, provocatively pulling it from around your neck. He wrings his hands nervously. Doesn't approach. You approach him. He looks at you longingly, stares at your breasts with hungry eyes. Then he stares at the floor, hangdog.

'I'm sorry, I dunno what I was thinking. I can't do this.'

You lean up against a rickety old bench, tie held taught in your hands. 'I'm not young enough for you? Is that it?'

'Young enough?' He frowns, takes off his hat and turns the rim over in his hands like a learner driver feeding a steering wheel.

You twist the tie in your hands, angry he's backing out. 'It's that young girl. You don't want me because I'm old. You like them young.'

'What? No. You've got it all wrong. I think you're beautiful. You're not old. How old are you?'

'If it's not my age, then why don't you want me?'

'I do, I want you so bad, but I love my wife. I thought I could do this, but I can't.'

'I can't say I'm not disappointed. How about one last kiss? You've already kissed me twice. What can it hurt?'

'I don't think I should.'

You're not buying this act. What's he playing at? He wants to fuck you. His eyes are all over you. It's only a matter of time before he hurts that young girl or uses her to get to a younger sibling. You have to stop him.

'Come on. One little kiss and I'll take you back down to reception, like nothing happened.'

He takes a step back towards the door. He's totally lost his nerve. 'Nothing did happen.'

Spite rises up your throat. He won't fuck you because he likes prepubescent girls. He thought younger than his wife would do it for him, and after kissing you he's realised it won't.

'Shall we ask your wife if she thinks kissing me is nothing?'

His beady eyes turn wild. You wrap the tie tighter around each fist. He turns to flee, hand on the door. You lunge. Knee to the back of his. He buckles. Falls down on one knee. You throw the tie over his head and pull back with all your strength. It catches around his throat. He chokes and splutters and tries to throw you off. You grit your teeth and pull harder. He scratches at the tie, his round face reddening. He gasps for air. You put your foot on his back, dig your heel in, lean back and grunt.

'Hurry up and die!' As if obeying your command, the Bat's body goes limp and slumps into the foetal position. You lie on top of his warm corpse, panting, tie loose in your gloved hands. You roll off the lump of a man and dust yourself down. Do your shirt buttons up. Re-tie the tie, which is now stretched out of shape and hangs limp over your chest. You pick up your jacket, slip it over your arms, and pat the breast pocket where the paper doll is concealed.

You tug one of the least broken frames out from behind a stack up against the back wall. The front ones fall and clack against the dusty floor. You place it in the middle of the room, then take out the doll and place it inside the decorative frame. You chose a photo you'd snapped of the Bat. One of him with his Bat mask on. Big smile on his lips.

A crackle comes from the bench. Grainy voice. *Ian? Ian come back. Over.* You walk over to the bench and find a walkie-talkie lying in the dust. Someone was in here, left this behind. Too much beer and curry last night, did they get a sudden urge for the toilet? You'd better move fast. You stride back, step over the body and open the door; it collides with his fat head. You push it wide enough that you can fit through. You slip out of the room.

RIP Dark Knight.

Chapter Sixteen

Mike's Only Friend

Mike floundered in the shop. He'd already bought a special gift, but wasn't sure whether to give it. It wasn't something people normally brought. Normal people brought chocolates or flowers. He checked the shelf and picked up a box of Favourites. They were on special. Thanks to his new job he had the money for flowers and chocolates, but getting both would mean less gin for him later. He settled on chocolates. Given the circumstances he should show a little compassion. Visiting with a gift was compassionate, even if he did end up eating it.

He paid for the chocolates and made his way through the white labyrinthine corridors at a brisk pace. He'd never liked hospitals. They were places where people came to be either sick or dead. He wasn't keen on the sick or the dead, or the germs that could make him sick or dead. He gave a wide berth to a grey-skinned patient in a wheelchair, head lolled to one side, drooling on his shoulder. An exhausted porter rolled him along. A zombie pushing a zombie. Mike should have worn a surgical mask; he risked being infected. He held his throat. Was it closing up? Sore? Why had he come here?

Mike checked the note scribbled on his hand. This was why. CCU ward, St Thomas' Hospital. She had called and asked him to come. He didn't remember giving out his phone number, but he must have done so. How else would she have got it? He pushed through the double doors and marched up to the secure door. He held the box of chocs under his arm, pressed the coms button, and pumped hand-sanitiser into his palm. He rubbed his hands together and the cool gel sunk into his skin. A female voice said hello through the speaker. 'Hello, Mike Gloss, I'm visiting a friend.' A grim buzzer sounded like he'd got the question wrong on a game show and the door clicked open. He shouldered his way through and into the ward.

The warmth of radiators on full blast hit him like he'd stepped off an air-conditioned aeroplane and into a desert. The beeping of heart monitors and the strange sterile smell gave Mike a foreboding feeling, a hot panic – similar to hiding under a duvet as a youngster before your lover's parent walks into the bedroom and almost catches you doing naughties. He shouldn't be here. This was a mistake.

Mike scanned the beds. Several people tucked up tight under hospital issue blankets were fast asleep, vertical blinds closed to the winter sunshine. At the very end of the ward, oxygen mask over his nose and mouth, hooked up to a monitor, drip in his hand, was Bat. He slowly raised the hand with the needle taped down, as frail as an elderly man. Mike quietly made his way past snorers and mouth breathers. There were six hospital beds, three on each side. When he arrived at his friend's bed he was lost for words. Bat looked like the living dead. Mike said the first thing that popped into his head.

'I was going to get flowers…'

Bat's breath fogged the clear plastic oxygen mask. 'It's fine. Flowers aren't allowed anyway.'

Mike glanced around. Not a posy in sight. He placed the chocolates on the bedside table. 'Got you some Favourites.'

Bat's face was gaunt, his skin worn out like pastry rolled so thin it was almost see-through. He smiled sleepily at Mike.

'Thanks, but I'm keeping away from sugar. Got orders from the Mrs.'

Mike sat down in the chair next to Bat's bed. He felt guilty about the chocolates. Perhaps he should give him the other gift? The real one. The one he had bought especially. Bat propped himself up higher on the pillows, causing the hospital bed to shudder under the strain of his heavy frame. He pulled the mask down and let it hang around his double chin.

'You look different without the make-up. Who do you remind me of?'

Usually Mike would reply with a smart-arse comment, but there was no fun in taking the piss out of a sick man. Mike crossed his legs and linked his fingers over his knee.

'A handsome celebrity?' He turned his head to show off his profile, nose in the air.

Bat chucked. 'I don't think so.'

Mike shot Bat a playful scowl. Then plastered on his serious face. 'So, what happened?'

'Didn't she tell ya?'

'She said you were attacked and asked me to come to the hospital.'

'Attacked … God love her.' Bat took a deep breath. 'I was strangled with a neck tie and left for dead.'

A cold chill snaked down the back of Mike's shirt, like someone had opened a window and let in a draught.

'*What!*'

'What saved me was I blacked out from shock. When I come to, and the ambulance crew were sorting me out like, I had a heart attack and wound up in 'ere.'

Bat placed the mask back over his nose and mouth and went silent, concentrating on breathing. *Probably worried talking about it might cause another cardiac arrest.* Mike spied an elderly lady in the corner with her eyes open. Bed covers held up to her chin, little wrinkled fingers clutching the white sheet folded over at the top. She was listening to them with interest.

'Where was this? Did you see who it was?'

Bat nodded darkly. He pulled down the mask.

'It was at the Gallery and it was one of your friends.'

Mike's cheeks burned. *One of his friends? Who? He didn't have any friends!*

'Not Donald!'

Bat shook his head, then blinked several times and leaned back. He rested his head on the plump pillows propped up behind him and closed his eyes, as if trying to block the memory. He opened them again and looked at Mike with a cold stare.

'It was Princess.'

Mike felt the colour drain from his face.

'Princess? From the Square?'

'Yep. Your bestest buddy.'

Mike picked up the box of Favourites and tore off the top. He unwrapped and shoved several mini chocolate bars into his mouth, one after the other. Bat fell back exhausted. He placed the mask over his nose and mouth.

'Why would she do that?' Mike couldn't make sense of it. What did she have against Bat? 'Was it that footage you took of her? Did she find it online and get mad or something?'

Bat shook his head slowly. Mike knew he was holding something back.

'Sorry, mate.' His voice was muffled by the mask. 'The police have been questioning me a lot … well, as much as the docs will allow. It's hard to keep going over it.'

Mike screwed the foil chocolate wrappers up and shoved them back inside the box. The granny across the way was still listening, only now she was pretending to knit. Every time Mike glanced over at her she started clicking needles.

Bat yawned.

'Do you want me to go, so you can get some sleep?' Mike's head was spinning. *Princess tried to strangle Bat to death with a neck tie?*

Bat pulled down the mask. 'No, no, please stay. Tammy has been up with my daughter, but I had to send them home to rest; they hadn't slept. I'd like it if you stayed a bit longer. I know hospitals have security, but I don't feel safe without someone I trust here. I feel like she might come back and finish the job.'

'Did you tell the police I knew her? Because I really don't.' Self-preservation kicked in and Mike's voice raised an octave. 'She's not my friend. I don't know her.'

'But you said she hangs out at the club with you.'

'I lied. I've never even met her.' He looked down at his hands. 'I haven't got any friends.'

'I'm your friend, Mike.'

Water welled in Mike's eyes; he couldn't stop the tears from falling.

'Yes, you are.' He patted Bat's big hand and sniffed. 'My only friend. I'm sorry for teasing you over the years.'

'It's just a bit of banter, no big deal. You can relax; I didn't mention you to the police. No point. I told them I met her in the Square, that she was a performer and I didn't know her real name. I told them she wanted hints on how to make more tips and that I'd agreed to meet her. Showed them the text messages.'

'Thank you for keeping me out of it.' Mike wrung his hands. He felt an urge to do something out of character, something kind that he didn't want to do but felt compelled to do. 'Want a hug?'

Bat's eyebrows raised, pushing wrinkly lines up his forehead. He laughed. 'I'm too manly for that shit.'

Mike got to his feet and put his arms around Bat's neck, giving him a quick squeeze, and then patted him on his balding head. He sat back down and side-eyed the box of chocolates. It would be rude to eat any more. Bat's eyes misted over.

'I can still smell her perfume.' His voice was soft, fragile. 'It's like she's all over me. I can't stop thinking about her. She torments me in my dreams and stalks my mind while I'm awake – know what I mean?' Mike nodded. He knew exactly. She had been doing that to him for a while and he had never had an encounter with her. 'My wife doesn't know what to think. I should have taken your advice instead of meeting up with Princess. I hope I can still save my marriage.'

'You didn't do anything wrong. Your wife can hardly be mad at you for meeting up with a work associate. Would she be mad if you had been meeting me?'

Bat's dull eyes were like that of a puppy who'd shredded its owners' slippers while they were out. 'It wasn't as innocent as all that. She told me she wanted me. When I refused to sleep with her, she turned violent.'

Mike's mouth hung open at first, but then he couldn't stop the smirk from creeping across his lips. 'She wanted to have *sex* with you?'

Bat scowled. 'Is that so hard to believe?'

Mike shifted on his seat. Uncomfortable with the little white lie he was going to have to tell Bat to keep things polite, the embarrassment of it all burned his cheeks. That, or it was getting way too hot on the ward. It was all a bit much to take on board. He opted for changing the subject.

'Do the police know who she is? Where she is?'

'If they do, they haven't told me.'

Mike gasped when a horrible thought entered his mind.

'What is it?' Bat's eyes widened.

'My flatmate is covering this serial killer story, you don't think it's her, do you?'

'A female serial killer? Pull the other one.'

'There have been loads of female killers; they're just not sensationalised by the media.'

Mike tugged his phone from his jeans pocket. He typed 'Paper Doll Murders' into the search engine. A string of reports sprang up. He scrolled. Three weeks ago … six days ago … ten hours ago. He clicked on the BBC News report. 'Trafalgar's Favourite Superhero Strangled by Woman Posing as Gallery Staff.' Mike's first thought was that this was not a very imaginative headline. Kerri's were much better. The information was sparse. He closed the report and clicked on one of Kerri's. It was about the guy stabbed at the hotel. Mike read the gruesome details. Yikes! To think Devan had quit work because he was traumatised by his affair going public, and look what happened to this poor git. Devan should count himself lucky.

'What are you doing?'

'I'm looking to see if any details have come out about the attempt on your life.'

Before Mike closed the article off and opened a new one, a sentence caught his eye. It had been added at a later date. *A beloved work colleague, a cherished brother and a loving son. Spencer Rodes will be missed by many.*

'Missed by many? What a load of bollocks. She hated him.'

'Hated who?'

'Spencer! The guy murdered at the Noble Night. Kerri worked with him.' He read the sentence out to Bat. 'She should have written: "An annoying little twerp, a childish bumlick and a leeching sleaze." He won't be missed.'

'Well she can't very well write that, can she?'

Kerri had never mentioned it was someone from her office who had been targeted, or had she? Perhaps he'd forgotten the finer details. If he was bored with a conversation he'd zone out, especially after a few gins. While reading, he was easily distracted and often lost track. He read some more of the gory details Kerri had made palatable for the public. He turned his phone around to show Bat.

'You got off lightly. The killer knifed this guy in the goolies.'

Bat shuddered. Mike turned the phone back to face him and continued the search.

'Here's one she's written on you … she'll probably want me to ask you for an interview at some point.'

Bat leaned closer to Mike and peered down at the phone screen. 'What does it say?'

Mike scanned the text. Kerri had more information than the BBC. How on earth had she managed that?

Mike read aloud: 'The Paper Doll Murderer strikes again, but this time, the killer met their match. Trafalgar's very own superhero survived an attack where he was strangled and left for dead. After suffering a cardiac arrest, The Batman, whose real name we can't reveal for legal purposes, is in a stable condition in hospital. Our sources confirm that a paper doll was left at the scene of the crime, but due to the ongoing investigation the chief of police has said she cannot release a statement at this time. She would remind Londoners to be vigilant and to report any suspicious activity. Why these particular victims have been targeted and what the significance of these paper dolls is remains unclear. A pattern has yet to emerge. None of the victims seem to be linked. Given the effort made to stick a photograph of the intended victim on the head of each paper doll, one would be inclined to think that the killer has some sort of game going on. We are told an unidentified female member of staff was caught on a security camera inside the National Gallery with the victim, however we cannot confirm whether or not she had anything to do with the attempt on the victim's life.'

Bat and Mike sat in silence for a moment. The room was eerily quiet except for the beeping heart monitors and the clicking of knitting needles. Bat sighed and broke the silence. 'She took me there to do me in; she had no intention of sleeping with me … am I that unattractive, Mike?' Mike locked Bat with sad eyes. The big man's bottom lip trembled. 'My wife ignores me, and then this woman tries to kill me … A serial killer, Mike. Princess is a serial killer. She wanted me dead from the get-go.'

Mike shifted nervously on his seat, a lump swelling in his throat. He had almost applied for a job with a serial killer; he could easily have been her next victim. He slumped in the chair and something pointy spiked him in the side. Mike reached into his jacket pocket. 'I almost forgot.' He pulled out two figurines and handed them to Bat. 'I saw them in a charity shop; thought they might make you smile.'

Bat took one in each hand. There was a big smile on his face as he studied the Batman action figure and a Pierrot ornament.

'You're gonna make me start blubbing. I love 'em. Thank you.' He passed them to Mike and Mike carefully placed them side by side on the bedside table.

Trolley wheels clunked over the threshold and squealed towards them. A bulky woman with a warm smile stopped at each bed to serve patients their hospital dinner on a brown tray. She pulled the trolley up next to Bat's bed. One hand on her hip, she moved Bat's portable table over his bed and lined it up in front of him.

'You gonna eat something for lunch, Mr Hero?' Bat side-eyed Mike as if to say he would rather eat a pasty covered in sand and dog hair than whatever the hospital worker had inside her food cart.

Before he could answer, a middle-aged woman swept in. Takeaway bags in hand, cheeks rosy. Mike thought of Mrs Christmas.

'I got you a sub and a salad.' She unpacked the bags onto Bat's tray. 'I know you wanted Chinese takeaway, but the doctor said to eat healthy.'

Bat groaned, but Mike could tell he was secretly happy his wife had rescued him from the hospital slop. The hospital worker gave Bat a wink and went to the bed opposite, where the old girl had shoved her knitting to one side and was sitting bolt upright, ready for lunch.

'Mike, I presume?' Bat's wife held out her stubby fingers. He shook her hand and nodded. 'Thanks for coming down.'

'No problem, anything for a friend and...' He trailed off. He didn't even know Bat's real name. The shame turned his face scarlet. '...Your husband is a good friend.'

'Did you know that he videoed that nutter on his phone? Pretty, she is. What he was doing chasing young women around like that I don't know.'

Mike's face heated up even more. 'Oh, er ... the video was for me. We do it whenever a newbie starts working our patch, especially since this one was in my spot. Your husband was looking out for me, making sure she didn't steal my work space.'

Her face softened. 'I don't believe that for a second; he's always had wandering eyes ... still, it's nice you two boys look out for each other. I just wish you'd been around when Alex decided to have a business meeting with the pretty psychopath.'

Alex. Mike felt a sparkle of sunshine light up inside him. Bat's name was Alex! Bat had paused what he was doing, chicken salad sub in his hand, mouth wide about to take a bite. 'Honey, please.'

'It's okay, I know who I married, and I also know you're a loyal soul.'

She kissed Bat on the forehead. He beamed. The heat from Mike's face moved to his heart. Warm fuzzies. Bat's got his wife back. It almost cost him his life, but perhaps now he could move forward. He'll certainly think twice about ogling young women again.

Chapter Seventeen

Kerri's Digging

K erri stared at her laptop screen. The body of text blurred and came back sharp as her tired eyes focused and unfocused. Her latest article on 'The Paper Doll Killer' had landed her in hot water. Not only with the boss, but she also had a troll infestation, which meant she'd had to shut down her social media account. Any excuse to rip someone to bits and those evil little creatures come out from under their bridges with their claws sharpened. They were going on about how Devan's affair with the hotel owner had nothing to do with the murders so why write it and ruin lives? She had written about it because it was a juicy side story that the hotel employee had offered up when she interviewed him. Anyone would think she was the one who had cheated, ruined a marriage and caused Devan to have a mental breakdown and quit his job at Bliss. The phrase 'don't shoot the messenger' came to mind.

Kerri had written the names of the victims in her notepad, along with when each was killed and how. In the late 1990s, the first paper doll murders had occurred. The victims were a married couple called Casey and Brent White. Asphyxiation was the cause of death for both. It had been concluded that a plastic bag was the murder weapon, although the bag used was never found. Brent had not only been strangled but his crotch was covered in blood, and his penis was missing. Two paper dolls in patchwork dresses, with each of the victim's photographs stuck on the heads, were left in the bedroom with them, and both of the victims' faces had been painted with red circles on the cheeks and red smeared across the lips. Some reports alleged the red paint was Brent's blood. The only other information Kerri had managed to dig up on them was that Brent was on the sick for a back injury from an accident at work. He was a postal worker and had slipped on an icy patch of pavement. Casey was a registered child minder.

The next victim had been Larry Pickles, or Larry the Lout as one media outlet had not affectionately named him. He was on and off the dole and when he did work it was as a labourer. He'd been on the sex offenders' list for an incident in the early 90s involving a twelve-year-old girl in his sister's foster care. Kerri's eyes widened when she read how Larry had been found by his elderly neighbour who was returning a cup she had borrowed with sugar in it. She had a spare key, had let herself in, and had found Larry unconscious with a gash to his stomach, salt in the wound. The girl he had been abusing was interviewed and had said she had hit him over the head with the pipe of a vacuum cleaner and had then taken to him in a rage with a pair of scissors. An image flashed inside Kerri's head of the young girl viciously clonking the big man round the back of the head. How she had the strength to fight off this abusive man was incredible. Kerri would not have been so bold at that tender age.

When Kerri had found Larry in that sorry state in the warehouse it had scared the daylights out of her. He had his own paper doll and his face had been painted with blood, the same as the Whites. Spencer had been found by a room attendant the same way: paper doll left behind, face painted with rosy cheeks and red lips like a rag doll; presumably the killer had used his blood as well.

Kerri clicked another article on Brent and Casey. Her eyeballs almost popped out of her head. She scribbled notes on the lined paper, missing the lines completely. The pair were child molesters and had been likened to Fred and Rose West, the difference being that they were not murderers who buried children under their house. They lured children to their house with promises of sweets, toys or kittens. After their death, seven victims came forward.

All three paper doll victims were sex offenders. *This could be the link.* Kerri glanced down at the next name on the list. Spencer Rodes. Spencer was a slimy toad, but he wasn't a sex offender, not as far as she knew. The last name on her list was Alex Waters. Again, not on the sex offenders' list. She tapped the nib of the ballpoint pen on the paper, speckling it with little black dots. Surely these attacks weren't random?

Kerri had trawled through Murderpedia researching female serial killers. Nearly all of them had a motive. Black widows bumping off old men for insurance pay-outs; nurses joyfully killing babies by injecting them with morphine; sexual predators hiding the bodies of their victims; mothers killing children to win a lover. Sometimes the reason was simply because they could kill and they enjoyed it, but there was almost always a pattern of abuse. Leaving a 'calling card' was something else, however. Kerri had typed 'Signature Killers' into the search engine and a string of male serial killers popped up, but not one female. The Zodiac Killer sent coded messages; The Night Stalker drew pentagrams on his victims with their lipstick; the BTK Killer, which stood for 'bind, torture, kill', sent poetry and letters taunting the police, but not one single female killer had gone on the same ego trip – until now. Perhaps equality had something to do with it? People's mindsets were changing. The Paper Doll Killer was definitely sending a message, and Kerri was going to find out what.

A thud like a bird hitting the window caused Kerri to swivel around in her seat. It had been snowing on and off for the past few days, but not really settling. It had disrupted transport services and had turned into an ugly grey sludge which piled up along kerbs and under hedges. Today it was overcast and drizzly. Maybe a bird's wings got wet and it couldn't fly and fell into the window? She hoped the poor thing wasn't hurt.

Kerri climbed over the back of the couch and went over to the window. The curtains were partially closed to prevent sunlight glaring on the laptop screen. Not that the sun was out. She threw open the beige curtains, but instead of a battered pigeon on the window ledge she found a rotten tomato, a splodge of red and little seeds stuck to the glass.

Kerri jumped with fright as an egg smashed against the window in line with her face, yellow yoke and brown shell sliding down the glass. She leaned as close to the draughty sash window as she dared and glanced down. A group of yobs were lobbing vegetables and eggs at her flat. When they saw her at the window, they rapidly fired the ammunition in their arms. Eggs, rotten tomatoes, and even the kerb sludge were pelted at her. They shouted slurs. *Homophobic bitch! Home wrecker! Gay hater!* She thought about trying to reason with them, but if she'd learned anything from online trolls these people were not to be reasoned with types. They enjoyed drama and spite, and that was what they were here for. If it wasn't pretend outrage about homophobia it would be pretend outrage about something else.

Kerri shut the curtains, went over to the kitchen bench and flicked on the kettle. Her phone vibrated on the coffee table as a call buzzed in. She reached over, slid it off the surface and accepted the call.

'Kerri Parks.'

The kettle rumbled with boiling water, steam escaping the spout. She moved away from the noise so she could hear the caller better.

'Hello, Ms Parks, my name's Maria Bell. I have some information on one of the murder victims and I wasn't sure who to call about it. A lady at the *Trafalgar Times* gave me your number. My daughter doesn't want to go to the police, but I can't read another article praising that man! People need to know the truth about him.'

'I understand completely.' Kerri's mind raced. *There was only one victim she could be talking about.* 'Could you give me your phone number in case we lose connection? Would you like me to call you back? Save your phone bill?'

'No, no. I've got unlimited minutes. My number is…'

Kerri wrote down the number on the notepad and listened carefully, jotting down notes as Maria Bell explained that Spencer had sexually interfered with her fourteen-year-old daughter. She made a cup of tea, phone on loud speaker as she listened to Maria explain that she wanted their identities protected but needed to get her story out. A new article bubbled in Kerri's mind as the women filled her in on Spencer's dirty little secret. The title hit her: 'The Link in the Paper Doll Chain'.

When Kerri had placed her phone on the coffee table and had sat down with a cup of hot tea in her hands, she could hardly believe what she'd heard. Spencer was a paedophile. *Spencer!* Someone she shared office space with was a dirty kiddie fiddler. The distressed mother had seen her article and had been given her number by Donna when she rang the office. The Internet had connected everyone across the globe – well, almost – and this had exposed all the hidden dirt and grime. The world was covered in filth, and it was her job to wade through it and hang out the dirty laundry for all to see.

She took a sip of hot tea and the steam warmed her face. Her nose started to run. She reached into her pocket for a tissue and put down the mug, which was Bea's 'No.1 Writer' written on it. She blew her nose and suddenly felt dreadful. She couldn't get sick, not now. She checked the app on her phone to make sure she was taking her meds. She'd missed two. How had that happened? Kerri propped a cushion up under her back. At least the vegetable and egg pelting had stopped. She had an idea that Mrs Williams might have gone out there to shoo the youngsters off, waving her umbrella at them like she does to teenage trick-or-treaters.

Kerri glanced back down at her notepad, her gaze transfixed on the name 'Alex Waters'. He was the odd one out. She'd researched him before she'd written her last piece, but he didn't have much of an online footprint. He was a family man and street performer. He played a superhero and seemed to be an all-round good guy. She already knew a lot about his personality because he was friends with Mike, and Mike would sometimes text her to complain about him, but really she knew her flatmate was fond of the guy. That meant Mike probably wouldn't dish any dirt on him. She needed to find something unsavoury. Anything. There were a few photos of him on the net with kids. She only needed one with his hand positioned in what could be interpreted as an inappropriate place and she could run the paedo hunter story. She trawled through photo after photo online. Nothing. He was clean.

Chapter Eighteen
Bea's Find

Bea kept her head down, nose in the book she was pretending to read, so none of the old dears cluttering up the doctor's office would speak to her. She hated coming here. The elderly smell of lavender soap and dusty attic blankets always put her on edge. She imagined the Grim Reaper would hang out in hospitals and surgeries when work was slow. Dressed in black robes, scythe in hand, eagerly waiting for someone to snuff it.

Bea wasn't keen on telling the doctor about why she was feeling anxious or what else they could do to help her. She just wanted the drugs and to get out of there. The nightmares had increased. She needed something to help her sleep peacefully, but she knew they wouldn't hand the Diazepam over without interrogating her first. She was bouncing between oversleeping and insomnia, and it was exhausting. Her manuscript was up to 65,000 words and she only needed to write about 15,000 more to complete it, but the words had stopped flowing and she had started to panic. Her brain was in overdrive.

The research had been gruesome reading. Two murdered with a plastic bag, his penis cut off. One murdered with a knife in the eyeball, penis mutilated. Another murdered with a knife to the scrotum, intestinal tract missing. The latest had been strangled with a neck tie and left for dead. Fairy lights had been strung on her landlady's window wrapped around intestines. Mrs Williams had put it down to kids mucking about. Doubtless aimed at Kerri because she got a lot of people pestering her as a journalist. Mrs Williams was probably right, but the coincidence had rattled Bea.

What if the killer was pestering Kerri? What if that psycho was reading her news reports?

Someone was murdering local people. It wasn't a story Bea had made up. It was real. Her novel wasn't fiction. It was real. They'd killed someone from Kerri's office. What if Kerri was next? The killer could be watching the flat! What if the psycho had tried to get information out of Mike's Batman friend? Then, when he wouldn't talk, she'd strangled him. Bea's thoughts turned on her and morphed into panic. Cold liquid metal was filling up her lungs and solidifying. Pressure. Weight. An elephant had sat down on her lap and leaned back. Her entire body was being crushed. Her throat started to close up. The paperback slipped from her hands. Her hand shot to her neck. She gasped for air.

'Are you okay, pet?'

Bea couldn't answer the old-timer to her right. His wrinkled face was coming in and out of focus. She blinked and kind grey eyes blinked back at her. The gent was wearing a flat cap and tweed jacket; that was all she could make out, the rest was a blur. Bea dragged down great gulps of air, but none of it was getting through. Her lungs burned cold. She fell to the floor, panting on hands and knees. She crawled slowly, like a blind new-born kitten, in the direction of reception. Her heart was palpitating like someone had their hands inside her ribcage, and was squeezing the life out of it. The old man was on his feet. She felt him beside her.

'A little help over here!' he shouted. A continuous flatline shot Bea in the ears. Tinnitus was a horrible affliction: the ringing in her ears would sometimes last for hours. The old man had his hand on her back. 'You'll be alright, love. Deep breaths.'

Black plimsolls appeared in front of Bea's face. Two nurses helped Bea to her feet, sat her in a chair and coached her to breathe through the panic attack. She did as she was told and the tightness in her chest loosened. Her lungs began to expand as normal. Dizziness and ringing in the ears petered out.

'I'm sorry.' Bea's words came out breathy. Her cheeks flushed.

One of the young nurses patted her hand. 'No need to apologise. Let's take you for a lie down. Do you think you can stand?'

Bea nodded. The nurses either side of her took an arm each and helped Bea to her feet. She thanked the old man for his kindness. He told her it was no trouble and hoped she felt better soon. The nurses led Bea towards one of the doctor's rooms. The patients waiting pretended nothing had happened, but when Bea turned her back she could feel their eyes on her, and she could almost hear the whispering when the door to the doctor's office was closed behind her.

***

Bea left the surgery an hour later with a prescription for Diazepam and an increase in the dosage for her anti-depressants. Outside in the car park, the bitter wind dragged its icy claws across her face. The trees bent and buckled as the gale bullied its way past. Bea held her woolly hat down over her ears at the expense of her frozen fingers. She couldn't risk more ringing in them or an ear infection. A cab was waiting for her in a space near the surgery entrance. The driver got out as she approached and opened the passenger door.

'Here you go, love.' Bea sank into the warm seat, thanked the cockney cabby and buckled her seatbelt. He slammed the door shut. Back in the driver's seat, he rubbed his hands together to warm them up. 'Cor, it's taters out there, innit.'

'Yeah, that wind is freezing.'

'Where too then, darling?'

Bea gave him her address and took out her phone. She hadn't been able to face her messages and they'd piled up. She had thirty notifications, and for her that was a lot. The engine roared to life and the car moved off. Bea opened Mike's messages first, leaving her agent's unread.

Beatrice baby! Guess what!? I GOT A NEW JOB!!!!! I landed a sweet gig at Bliss playing a princess while pulling pints! How cool is that? (Princess emoji. Confetti emoji. Clapping emoji).

Wake up, lazy cow!! (Cow emoji) We need to celebrate my new job! Pick up your messages.

Beeeeeeeeea!!! Why are you ignoring me? I'm hurt. I hate you. You smell. (Poop emoji)

I didn't mean that. I love you. Message me when you get this. (Heart emoji).

Bea smiled and typed back a congratulatory message. She was happy for Mike but also for her. He had a steady job and that meant no more rent arrears. She asked the cabby to stop off at the off-licence so she could pick up a bottle of gin for Mike. A little celebration with her flatmate might be just what the doctor ordered.

The cabby talked the entire journey. Bea was trying to catch up on the messages and would rather he didn't keep jabbering on about politics and the worsening traffic in London and '*the cyclists driving everyone up the wall, they don't pay road tax, do they, but they fink they own the bloody roads, don't they!*' He was a baby boomer who preferred the 'good old days', and wasn't keen on new-fangled things like gender swapping and women doing anything he considered the job of a man. Bea thought about trying to educate him, but she was too drained, and a lifetime of small-mindedness was not going to be undone in a twenty-minute cab ride.

Once at home and in the warm, Bea ran herself a bubble bath. The bathroom was tiny, but whoever had renovated the old Victorian house, splitting it into flats, had managed to squeeze a toilet, basin, bath and shower into the room. Steam wafted up from the hot water in clouds. Bea turned on the extractor fan. It was half-past five. Mike must have gone to work. The new job meant different shift patterns, although he would probably still come rolling in drunk after midnight and mess up the kitchen. Sober Mike was tidy, Drunk Mike was a mess.

She opened the airing cupboard and found empty shelves. Kerri usually folded the washing and placed it in each person's room. Towels always neatly folded and colour co-ordinated, because that's how Mike liked it, Kerri was organised chaos and would probably have just shoved the towels in the cupboard screwed up in a ball, but each of them tried to do their part to make living together a little easier, with the exception of Drunk Mike. He would always say that if you have a problem with Drunk Mike, don't take it up with Sober Mike; he would have no idea what you're talking about.

Kerri kept a clothes horse in the corner of her room. Bea opened the bedroom door which had been left ajar, reached up to turn on the light, then noticed a lump under the duvet in the middle of Kerri's bed. Not wanting to wake her – if she'd gone to bed in the afternoon it was because she'd needed it – epilepsy must be draining – Bea tugged a towel from the clothes horse and quietly closed the door.

After a soak in the hot bubble bath, easy listening 80s songs playing on her phone that was perched on the toilet lid, Bea felt almost human again. The weather had worsened and the wind was howling like wolves at the moon. After getting into her PJs and dressing gown, she tied the towel over her hair and piled it up on her head like a turban, then went to the kitchen to cook something for tea. The lights flickered. It got dark at around 4pm this time of year and outside the sky was black. Behind the curtains, a light flashed like someone taking a photo. Bea hated storms. She reminded herself that she was safe inside. If the storm had started while she was in the cab, she might have had another panic attack. She opened the fridge. The light inside was bright on her face. There wasn't much food. Half a packet of ham, a few vegetables, a pot of houmous, a couple of eggs and a yogurt.

She grabbed the pot of houmous and some crackers from the cupboard. It wasn't what she wanted to eat; a Ramen noodle bowl with plenty of prawns would have been nice, but she wasn't going out in the storm for that, and she didn't fancy beans on toast, which was the only other 'dinner' food she could find in the cupboards. She filled a glass with water from the door of the fridge, took her snack over to the coffee table, and reached for the TV remote. She rarely watched television, but Bea felt like seeing what was on the box tonight and the noise would drown out the storm. She pointed the remote at the TV and pressed the 'on' button. A crackle of thunder rolled overhead.

Voices echoed from the glowing screen on the wall. Bea flicked through the channels. News … Depressing. DIY show … dull. Quiz show … okay. Bea opened the pot of houmous and dug a sea salt and cracked pepper cracker into it. She answered the quiz questions as she munched and then contemplated whether or not to take the Diazepam. She was feeling much better; maybe she didn't need to take it, and the doctor had said only take as needed, don't overdo it.

Rain battered the roof and windows, and lightning flashed, casting shadows in the dimly lit room. Thunder groaned and grumbled. Bea picked up her phone and scrolled through her social media. She put hearts on a couple of posts, and commented on the weather posts from writer friends in the UK who were also experiencing the storm. Then she remembered she hadn't read Jackie's message.

Bea opened up the app and tapped on Jackie's heavily made up and filtered profile picture. She was glad to see it was a quick message. Jackie wrote that she was getting great feedback on Bea's sample chapters but no requests for a full manuscript yet. She explained it was early days and that soon people would see the potential and make a quick offer once they realised it was best to strike while the story was trending and the killer was still at large. Bea was relieved no one had offered on it; she hadn't finished the damn book yet, so even if they did ask for the completed manuscript, she was weeks off finishing.

She sent Jackie a quick reply and then typed 'Paper Doll Murders' into the search engine. She wasn't meant to be working – the doctor had told her to take it easy – but the panic was back in her chest now that her agent might ask for the complete manuscript, and she was nowhere near ready to hand it over. If she read a few more news articles it might give her inspiration a boost, and she'd get over the writer's block. Kerri's coverage of the latest attack had been patchy. She had more details than other media outlets, but like everyone else she'd probably want to interview the Batman guy. If people figured out the Batman's connection to Mike, it could result in online harassment. Bea couldn't take that. A flash of lightning coincided with a spark inside her mind. *The book! It'll throw the spotlight on her*! She cringed at the thought, but if she didn't write, she'd starve. Her savings were almost gone.

Bea had chosen a woman to be her serial killer and now, as it turned out, the actual killer, or whoever was thought to have strangled Mike's friend, had been seen on security footage and it was a woman. Bea had anticipated changing the character to a man once the person's identity had come out, but now it looked like she didn't need to, which was a relief.

High winds rattled the windows in their frames and Bea hugged one of the couch cushions. Kerri's notepad was on the coffee table. Bea set down her phone and picked up the notepad. She flicked through the pages. There was a note about Spencer, the third victim, and an underage girl he'd had sex with. The words 'paedophile hunter' were underlined.

'Holy shitballs!'

Bea glanced over her shoulder to make sure Kerri hadn't woken up and entered the living area. Her bedroom door was still ajar, darkness beyond it. A shiver wandered over Bea's skin. Her fictional serial killer was a female paedophile hunter! Bea read some more; she knew she shouldn't, but she couldn't help herself. Mike's friend must be called Alex Waters. He was the only one on Kerri's list who had not been named by the media. There were two question marks beside his name. Bea guessed her flatmate didn't have any dirt on him that would link him with the others. All of which Kerri had written little snippets about. All of them abusers. It was too weird. Maybe Bea had psychic powers or some shit?

BOOM!

That one made Bea jump, with the notepad flung over the back of the couch.

FLASH!

Clink. Darkness.

Bea stared at a wall of black and clutched the cushion tight. The rain thrashed against the windows as if someone were chucking buckets of pebbles at them. The wind whistled down the chimney, the fireplace blocked up and bricked over long ago. She ran her finger across her phone. It unlocked and the screen light illuminated her pale face. Bea hit the torch symbol and a tiny circle of light appeared on the coffee table in front of her.

Knock, knock, knock.

'Shit!' She clutched the front of her dressing gown, heart pounding.

'Is anyone home?' The muffled voice of Mrs Williams came from the other side of the door.

Bea got to her feet and shined the torch light at the front door. 'Coming, Mrs Williams.'

She opened the door, holding the light at an angle so as not to blind the old woman. Mrs Williams was shivering, thick-frame glasses gleaming, a wall of pitch black behind her.

'You have a torch?' She beamed.

Bea moved to one side so Mrs Williams could enter. 'It's an app on my phone.'

'What an amazing gadget that phone is.' Bea glanced down at the battery symbol. She only had 20 per cent left. Her torch wasn't going to last long. Mrs Williams stared down at the light coming from Bea's mobile. 'I'm old fashioned, I'm afraid. I don't have one of them smart phones. My phone's one of those dumb ones. I couldn't find the torch in the dark and I'm out of candles. Wouldn't have some I can borrow, would you?'

'I think there's some in the kitchen drawer. Do you have some matches?' Bea shined the light at the kitchen bench. Mrs Williams shuffled after her.

'I have matches in my pocket. I keep some in a basket by the door. Oh it's lovely and warm in here. Have you finished that new book yet?'

Bea dreaded this question. She was constantly asked the same thing online and she always replied with 'Not yet'.

'Almost.'

'Oh goody. I'm looking forward to reading it. I couldn't get on with your other ones – aliens and what not, and I know you won't tell anyone what this new one is about, but I bet I'll like it.'

Alarm bells rang in Bea's head. She couldn't let her dear sweet neighbour read her new gory serial killer novel. It might scare her. She hadn't anticipated that Mrs Williams would want to read the new one after she'd blatantly said how much she'd disliked her Young Adult series. Bea decided not to acknowledge her last comment. She opened the drawer and took out two tapered candles. 'Here you go.' She handed them to Mrs Williams.

'Thanks, my dear.' Mrs Williams shoved a candle in each pocket of her cardigan.

'How did you get up here in the dark?'

'The Christmas tree lights.' She shuffled back towards the door.

Bea angled the phone so the torch would light the old lady's way. 'Aren't the lights plugged into the wall?'

Mrs Williams was already out of the door and half way along the landing. 'The little tree lights use batteries.'

Bea peered around the door frame and, sure enough, a tiny tree, no more than two-foot-tall, was lit up in white lights at the end of the landing.

'Be careful going down those stairs,' she yelled as the little old lady disappeared into the darkness.

'I will. Thanks, honey.'

Bea closed the door and glanced back down at her phone: 17 per cent. She'd given Mrs Williams the last of the candles, but she knew Mike had some scented ones in his room. She could often smell them. Vanilla and peach were his favourite.

Bea shined the phone light around Mike's room. It was tidy as usual. His bed didn't look as if he ever slept in it. His room was like an IKEA display. Nothing was out of place. She guessed Drunk Mike hadn't been around a lot lately. Her torch light flashed across several empty gin bottles lined up on a shelf. The sight made her feel a little guilty about buying the gin: would she be adding to his drinking problem?

Below the shelf of empty bottles was a corkboard. Pinned to it were flyers for different West End shows and a photograph of Mike dressed as his female alias, Micha, her arms around two drag queens. Bea guessed one must be Lady Vajazzle, or Donald as he was known in real life. She didn't know who the other one was. Mike had never mentioned her.

The candles in glass jars on his dresser drawers were melted down to the wick. No life left in them. She hoped he had more, otherwise she might as well take the Diazepam and go to bed early. There was not much she could do in the dark. Maybe he kept new candles in a drawer or something? She opened the top drawer of the dresser and the large oval mirror perched on the top wobbled.

The top drawer was filled with washbags and boxes of make-up. The second had books in it. Classics that Mike probably hadn't read. Bea was sure they were props to use when he wanted to impress someone intelligent. There was a pair of glasses in the drawer beside the books. Definitely props. He hadn't read the novels and he didn't wear glasses.

She opened the bottom drawer. The ring of light from her phone settled on a stack of thin magazines. Comic books? She knelt down to take a closer look. Maybe he had a rare Wonder Woman comic or something. She pulled the top one out and shined the light over the cover. It was faded. On the front was Cinderella. She flicked through. It was a book of paper dolls. She picked up the next book. The next paper doll book was Sindy, the one beneath that was Rainbow Brite, below that, She-Ra. She flicked through the Rainbow Brite book: some of the dolls and clothes inside were missing. She checked the drawer and found a plastic box. Bea peeled back the lid. There were piles of cut out paper dolls and accessories inside.

She picked one up. It was a bride. Where did he get these? A car boot sale?

CRACK!

Bea jerked with fright and dropped the paper doll back into the plastic box. The thunder crackled. She closed up the box, tucked it back where she'd found it, and replaced the thin children's books back on the stack and shut the drawer. Why did he have vintage paper doll books? The paper doll killer is a woman, Mike's a man. Mike dresses as a woman when he goes to Bliss. He'd just got a job there behind the bar, dressed as a princess.

Bea started to question how well she really knew Mike. She got up off the floor. No, no. She knew him. He was as soft as a kitten. His words about Drunk Mike rang in her head. No. Even Drunk Mike wasn't capable of being a crazed killer. He collected vintage doll books. That's all. He didn't try to strangle his annoying mate from work. Bea hurried out of Mike's room. She paused beside Kerri's: should she wake her? Tell her about this? No, she'd think Bea was reading too much into it. Being mentally ill meant people blamed everything on it. Whatever you did it was down to being mental. Like when a woman is angry it's always down to her period, whether or not she was having one at that particular moment. Bea didn't want to face that look she always got when people thought she was being paranoid. Instead she opted to take the pills. She wrote a note for Mike and left his gin on the bench before turning in for the night. It wasn't long before she had passed out in her bed. Sound asleep.

Killer

Almost caught. Have to lie low. Why didn't he die? He was dead when you left the fucker on the floor. You can't go back to the club as Princess. Not that you liked it there; it was just somewhere to go, somewhere where people admired you. The Bat will have spilled the beans. The question is, should you finish the job? They still haven't worked out you're killing evil people. They think Bat and Spencer are good guys. If they don't have a clue that you're a hunter by now, they are fucking stupid. You flick through the photos on your phone. Maybe you should help them out. Make them focus on the Bat, take some of the heat off you. You need another hit and you can't do it with pigs breathing down your neck. You were interrupted before you could play with the Bat. It wasn't enough. Worse now since you found out he survived. Dolls need to be dead. It is more than infuriating.

Ping!

A message from him. You light up inside. If the Princess can't go to the club, the club will come to the Princess. You take a sip of black coffee then type out a reply.

I have the perfect toy for you. From a Muslim family in the East End. They need the money. Interested?

Age?

Four.

Done.

Your heart races. You pick up your blade and admire it. You haven't had to sharpen it yet. It cuts through skin like a hot knife through butter. A demon fang dagger split blade. It's a thing of beauty. The hilt in the shape of curved devil's horns, the black handle is a decorative twist like several snakes wrapped around each other. It's topped with a dome and silver nipple. You hold out your arm and press the sharp point to your skin. Make a red mark. You've never cut yourself and you never will, but you are gagging to cut into someone else.

You place your right foot up on the couch, knee bent, and rub the tip of the cold handle over the outside of your knickers. It excites you. You need to lie low, but you also need to draw blood. Soon. This new client might be your last. Serial killers who leave clues always get caught in the end, but by the time you're caught they'll know why these monsters had to die. You'll be a hero. People will have to listen. Have to protect the children. Your body tingles with the idea of the Internet exploding. Everyone saying those bastards deserved what they got. You place the knife beside you on the couch, lean back, hand in your knickers.

'Time to ring the Devil's doorbell.'

You close your eyes and enjoy.

Chapter Nineteen

Mike's Snooping

The next number started with a loud trumpet introduction, followed by the sexy sound of a saxophone. From the staff room, Mike could hear every lyric sung by his friend Donald, clear and crisp, like he was singing directly to him. The walls were paper thin and the music vibrated through as if a Subwoofer was pressed up against them on the other side.

Mike sipped his sparkling water with ice and a slice of lemon. He hadn't had a drink since he started the new job. He struggled behind the bar, watching others enjoying cocktails and wine and beer and gin, but he was holding to his word and not drinking on the job. He felt good and terrible. Revitalised yet still a wreck.

He'd slept deeply, awakened late, and almost missed his shift. He was only on for four hours today, covering for one of the girls who'd twisted her ankle at a pole-dancing class. Sitting at a small plastic table, the dirty white top stained with tea and coffee mug rings, Mike twisted the cold tumbler in his hands. He couldn't decide whether to go home or stay for the disco. He was wearing his golden Belle dress and couldn't really remain in it because people would think he was working. He didn't have his black wig with him or a dress to change into. He'd come to work in jeggings, black boots and a burgundy shirt, which was okay but wasn't his usual Bliss outfit. People knew him as Micha, not Mike. Kerri had messaged him to ask for an interview with Alex, which he'd expected. Alex wasn't giving interviews to anyone else: Kerri would have the exclusive.

The staff room door swung open and crashed into the wall. 'I am outta here!'

The thirty-something barman, who had served Mike on a number of occasions, immediately started to strip off. He threw his black waistcoat into a locker and quickly unbuttoned his white shirt. Mike glanced up at him every few seconds. He didn't want to stare, but he was interested in seeing if Billy worked out or not. Mike didn't. He was scrawny and thought skinny guys with tiny muscles looked weird.

Billy had a boyish face and a cheeky grin. 'You staying on, Micha?'

'Nah.' Mike downed the rest of his water. 'I might head home.'

'That's a shame.'

Billy pulled the lemon shirt sleeve over his muscular arm.

Mike pushed his fingers into his wig and twirled a strand of hair coyly. 'Why?'

Billy sprayed deodorant before buttoning up his shirt. 'I was hoping you might come out with me.'

Mike's skin tingled. He couldn't remember the last time someone asked him out. 'Out where?'

'The local meat market…' Billy slammed the locker door shut. 'It's rainbow night, every fag and their hag will be in. It's a right laugh. Wanna come?'

'Fag?' Mike frowned. That was not a word he would ever use.

'No use being a victim; might as well own the word, like women own bitch and black people own…'

Mike raised his hand. 'I get it.'

He didn't know what to do. Billy had never shown interest in him before, but since they'd been working together things had changed. They'd had a laugh behind the bar and Mike enjoyed working with him. He wanted to go and he could actually afford to. He wasn't paid much, but when he came out from behind the bar to bring drinks to tables the volume of tips shoved in his hand was like a second income.

'Sure, okay. Let me get changed.' Mike paused. Maybe this wasn't a date; maybe it was one of those group invites and the staff didn't want to leave him out. 'Who else is going?'

'Just us.' Billy winked. 'I gotta talk to Trev first, I'll meet you out the front in ten.'

He swept out of the room. The masculine scent of his deodorant lingered in the air. Mike hurried to change out of his dress and clean the caked-up make-up off his face, fix his hair and reapply a no-make-up make-up look. He was so glad he'd left a toiletry bag in his locker.

***

The line for the club snaked around the building. Mike shivered. It was about two degrees, and although not raining or snowing, he felt frozen to the bone. Billy reached his strong arms around Mike's shoulders.

'I'll warm you up, I'm never cold.'

Mike's body tensed, the smell of Billy's body spray was intoxicating. Everyone in the line shuffled along. The tubby couple behind were wearing matching blue denim and lumberjack shirts, and in front was a hen party wearing pink feather boas and penis-shaped accessories. They were led by the hen's loud-mouthed gay bestie who wore a pink shirt and a hat in the shape of a labia. The women in their twenties and thirties squealed with excitement like teenagers at a pop concert. Mike rolled his eyes. He couldn't think of anything worse than hanging out with these bimbos.

The line moved quickly and they were soon inside the dated club foyer, thumping dance music coming from above. Billy was searched first; he went to reception and paid the entrance fee. Mike held his arms out for the pat down. He never understood why men searched the men and women searched the women. He decided it was because no one gave a shit if gays or lesbians were felt up by security staff. Pat down complete, the po-faced security guy grunted.

'ID.'

Mike was stunned. 'What?'

The stanch security guard stared at him, deadpan. 'What's your date of birth?'

He didn't look younger than twenty-one, what was this guy playing at?

Mike rattled off his date of birth. Hearing he was born in the 80s, the guy stepped aside for Mike to enter the club and signalled for the guy behind him to step up and be searched. Billy was at the cloakroom. He held out his hand for Mike's jacket.

'Everything okay?'

Mike handed over his jacket. 'I was asked for ID.'

Billy handed the jackets over to the miserable middle-aged woman in the window. She was dressed in a shiny black catsuit that hugged her love handles and podgy tummy. It looked like she'd bought new outfits hoping she'd fit into them after a few weeks of sliming club but still couldn't so she'd settled on wrapping herself up in a bin bag. Red lipstick was smudged across her thin smoker's lips and her heavy liner made her look like she had two black eyes. She gave Billy some raffle tickets. He turned to Mike and handed him one.

'Get out! You're not in your early twenties, are you?'

Mike pocketed the ticket, pushing it deep inside the back pocket of his jeggings so as not to lose it. 'He knocked fifteen years off me. Maybe he left his glasses at home.'

'Maybe he's blind.' Billy laughed.

'Hey, I look younger than my years.'

'You look early thirties, not under twenty-one.'

'Well, I'm taking it as a compliment. The guy is obviously into me.'

'He's not the only one.'

Billy stared into Mike's eyes with such intensity that Mike felt the urge to kiss him right there. His cheeks pinked. Billy linked arms with Mike. 'Don't be self-conscious. I've always thought you were hot, and I'll admit I also thought you were a bit of a prick, but that was before we worked together. I had you all wrong.'

Mike lowered his head in shame as they started up the stairs and towards the thumping music. 'No, you've got it right. I was a prick – and a drunk.'

'Does that mean you're not drinking tonight? I didn't know you were off the booze. I feel bad now, we should have gone for coffee or something.'

'I promised myself I wouldn't drink at work, and we're not at work.'

Billy grinned. 'Okay. First round is on me.'

***

It was 1am and, light as a feather, Mike drifted towards a row of black cabs. Was he drunk? Nope. Was he a little tipsy? Sure. He had managed to have a wonderful evening without getting blotto and he might have a new boyfriend; 'might' being the operative word because he really didn't know if Billy wanted to see him again. He'd said he did, but guys could be fickle: they say one thing and do another.

Mike had not drunk so much that the night ended with him giving the guy a hand-job or a blow-job or any other sexual job, usually in the disabled toilet. He had played it cool rather than rushing in too fast, only to be brushed off the next day.

Mike got into the nearest taxi. Billy had offered to walk Mike to his cab, but Mike had said it was fine. The breeze was bitter, and although Billy said he had thick skin and never felt the cold, he didn't want to do anything that might ruin the night. An awkward goodbye snog was something he wanted to avoid. Instead he pecked Billy on the cheek and walked away. Mike had stolen a peek over his shoulder and his heart had soared when he saw Billy was watching him walk away. People only do that if they really like you.

In the back of the cab spectrums of light passed over Mike's face as the driver steered them through the illuminated streets of London. Mike leaned back and fell into a daydream. A bird's-eye view of him and Billy on the dance floor, and that perfect moment, a fairy tale kiss. They'd been doing silly dances from the 80s and 90s when songs from that era came on. Then a song from an iconic movie played and Billy started dirty dancing. They were grinding on each other and lip-syncing the lyrics, big smiles. The music slowed and Billy cupped Mike's face, singing softly to him. Mike instantly felt like Baby and Billy was Johnny, gazing at him with all the love of the world in his baby blues. When Billy leaned in and his lips met Mike's, it took him back to his teen years and the first boy he'd ever kissed. The first person he'd ever trusted. That nervous excitement. Billy's soft kiss was electric, and although Mike wanted more, he'd decided not to push things. Anticipation is everything. He needed Billy to want him so badly that the sex would be mind-blowing when it finally happened. That was the key. Bed-hopping always left Mike feeling empty; the sex was dull and no one ever stuck around.

Back at his flat he searched his pockets for his key. If he'd forgotten it again Mrs Williams was going to do her nut. The last time he'd tapped on her window to let him in she'd given him a right lecture. Said it was time he grew up and took responsibility for his life. Mike's numb fingertips touched the top of the cold keys in his jacket pocket. He pulled the keyring out triumphantly and unlocked the door.

The entrance hall was dark, the old house fast asleep. The Christmas tree was up, and now it was December Mrs Williams had decorated it. Mike crept up the stairs, a little unsteady on his feet, the floorboards creaking loudly. A smaller Christmas tree was lit up on the landing, but it wasn't bright enough that he could see what he was doing, and he'd tried to open the door to his flat with the main front door key several times before finally using the right key.

The flat was cold and lifeless. He was hoping Bea might be up so he could have a girly chat about his first kiss with Billy. He was less enthusiastic about talking to Kerri; they'd never really clicked. She liked make-up and dresses, unlike Bea who was a bit of a plain Jane, but somehow, they hadn't really connected. Mike flicked the light switch and the wall lights bathed the room in a gentle glow. He sauntered over to the fridge. Opened the door, spilling light. He rubbed his hands together.

'Sandwich time!'

He took out ham, cheese and butter. With the things he needed to make his 'after-midnight sandwich' ready on the bench, he slammed the fridge door shut. There was a note on it from Bea. *The gin is for you. Congrats on the new job. Clean up the bench after you! Bea xxx*

There was a bottle of gin on the bench. He smiled and set to work making his sandwich. Butter the bread first, stick a slice of cheese onto it, ham on top of the cheese, fresh bread on top of that. Lovely. He didn't bother cutting it in half. He bit a big chunk out of it and made his way to the couch. Why was it that sandwiches tasted so good late at night and after a few drinks? He took another bite; something was missing. No pickle. He doubled back and rummaged through the fridge, then the cupboard.

'Kerri!'

He didn't care if he woke her up. The girls moaned about him making a mess in the kitchen late at night, but what about Kerri, the cheese and crackers muncher? She never put the pickle back. He had found it in her room on more than one occasion.

He put his sandwich down on the coffee table and marched over to Kerri's room. Mike threw open the door and switched the light on and off.

'Wake up pickle hog! Where is it!?'

Kerri's bed was a mess of duvet and sheets. She was at her man's flat again. Mike wondered why she didn't just move in with him. She was always over there. What was the point in paying rent for a room you rarely use?

He picked the almost empty jar of pickle up off Kerri's bedside drawers and screwed his nose up at the mess her bedroom was in. How could she live like this? There were dirty socks in balls on the floor, used cotton pads piled up next to her bed with peach foundation and black marks smeared on them, and a bottle of eye make-up remover next to the pile. The light grey carpet had cracker crumbs sprayed over it. When was the last time she'd used the vacuum cleaner?

Jar of pickle in hand, Mike was about to leave the room when he noticed Kerri's wardrobe door was open. He opened the door wider. Rows of clothes called to him. It was her fault he was in here. If she'd put the pickle back, he wouldn't be in her room snooping through her wardrobe. He smacked a teddy bear out of the way to make room and placed the jar of pickle on her chest of drawers, which was piled up high with soft toys.

He opened the other wardrobe door and started pushing clothes on coat hangers to one side.

'Gross. Hideous. She actually wears this?' He pulled out a sparkly boob tube and turned up his nose. 'Stuck in the 90s much?' He hooked it back on the rail and continued rummaging. He leaned in to get to the clothes in the far corner and tripped over his own feet, falling into the back of the wardrobe. The flimsy back panel came loose.

'Oh fuck.' Mike backed up. The one time he wasn't pissed was the one time he'd broken something belonging to one of his flatmates. He tried desperately to pull the panel back in place but it shifted sideways, making things worse. A hint of purple caught Mike's eye. There was something behind the panel.

He reached in further and pulled a dress from behind the panel. He held it up to the light. His legs went weak. Heart beating out of his chest, he threw the frock on the bed and reached back behind the panel. He pulled out a blue baby doll dress. His heart almost stopped. This dress belonged to Princess. He threw it on the bed like it was cursed and chewed his nails. What the fuck? He took a step back.

It's not what you're thinking, Mike. Stop being stupid.

Hands shaking, he reached into the back of the wardrobe once more and pulled out a blonde wig. He shrieked and threw it onto the floor like it was a filthy rodent. There had to be a simple explanation for this. There had to be. Maybe Kerri dressed up in her spare time. He did, but then he was a performer and had many costumes, not just princess dresses. He had lots of different outfits saved from amateur pantomimes and community shows he'd done years ago. Kerri had never mentioned doing anything like that.

Mike went into the living room and paced up and down. Princess wore heavy make-up, and the quality of the footage Bat had taken wasn't the best; there was no way to tell whether or not it was Kerri. He grabbed his phone out of his jacket pocket. There was a loved-up message from Billy. It was sent twenty minutes ago. Shit! He quickly typed a message back. *It was an amazing evening. I had a wonderful time. Can't wait to kiss you again. (Heart emoji. Kissy face emoji).*

Mike opened up his social media account. It took a few seconds to load which irritated him as it felt more like minutes. He flicked through Kerri's posts. Nothing strange. Her news articles had squillions of comments on them. There were photos of her and her partner, and of the guy's cat and a little dog. One of the photos was of the animals wearing Christmas hats. The dog looked happy enough, but the cat's grumpy face suggested he'd claw the next person to take a photo of him in the stupid Santa hat.

Mike studied a photo of Kerri and her buff boyfriend at the beach enjoying an ice cream, a photo of her and her friend Donna at a concert – he only knew it was Donna because she was tagged. The next one was of her and the BFF having dinner in a posh restaurant – all smiles. Kerri was a sweet girl. There was no way she could hurt another human being. But the truth was he didn't really know her all that well, not like he knew Bea. Mike sat down on the couch and scrolled back through the messages from Kerri.

Kerri: Can you grab some milk? We're out and I don't have time to go to the shop.

Mike: Sorry for the late reply. Did someone get the milk?

Kerri: I had to ask Spencer to get it, he was the only one breaking for lunch. Now he thinks I owe him. He's such a letch. I wish he would drop dead.

Nothing odd about that. Mike kept searching. He scrolled right back to older messages.

8.45 a.m. Tuesday

Mike: Ugh. Tourists are so annoying.

7.17 p.m. Tuesday

Kerri: Try working with Spencer! Some days I just wanna stab him in the eye with a fork.

6.07 a.m. Wednesday

Mike: I hear ya! Batty is driving me Batty!

7.01 a.m. Friday

Kerri: Sorry, only just seen this. Tell ya what, after I've stabbed my annoying git, I'll come down to the Square and strangle yours.

11 p.m. Saturday

Mike: Haha! Your little hands wouldn't fit around his fat neck.

Mike's blood turned to ice in his veins. She joked about strangling Bat, and Spencer is dead. He'd given her the green light to interview Bat! What if it was her and she went to the hospital to finish the job? He grabbed the gin from the bench, ran to his room and locked the door. He typed a message to Alex. He hoped he would get it before it was too late.

Chapter Twenty
Kerri's Moral Code

The office was buzzing with excitement. It was the beginning of December and for office workers the month should be renamed Drunkcember. The Christmas do had been arranged, but Kerri wasn't going. She couldn't be arsed to sit around watching people get smashed off their face and cheat on their partners. Donna never went; senior staff were forbidden to go. Also, Kerri hated doing Secret Santa; she always got a naff present. One year it was a giant pair of knickers that would fit a hippo, the next year an inflatable boyfriend (this was before Mark), and the one after that someone got her a novelty set entitled: 'Stop Smirkin' at my Murkin' with the tagline: 'Dare to Wear Body Hair'. The pack included three 70s bushes of various colours and a landing strip! Kerri's memories of the night flooded back. Her colleagues passed round the hair pieces for your foo and held them to their faces like beards. It was cringe worthy, but unlike the other presents that were bordering on offensive, Kerri could see the comedic value in such a gift.

Kerri set down her mug of tea and a coffee she'd made for Donna. She opened her emails. There was one that looked like spam; she took the risk and opened it. She could hardly believe her eyes. It was an incriminating photo of the Bat.

The connection she'd needed had, as if by magic, turned up in her inbox. Sent via the email address ForeverAPrincess90@hotmail.com, but when Kerri replied a mailer demon pinged back.

'How's it going, Super Star?' Donna was standing over her in a glorious royal blue suit, gold hoop earrings and matching gold bangles, which clattered together around her wrists. Kerri pointed to the coffee mug on her desk. Slivery-blue painted claws wrapped around it. 'Thanks, sweetie. Two sugars?' Kerri nodded. 'What we looking at?'

Now that Sean had gone Donna was her new partner in crime. She pulled up a chair beside Kerri and joined her in starting at the monitor.

'It's Alex Waters kissing a young girl.'

'She's a pretty little thing. Step-daughter?' Donna took a sip of coffee.

Kerri eyeballed her friend. 'She's kissing him on the lips.'

Donna cocked an eyebrow. 'Don't you David Beckham me!'

'What?'

'Didn't you see that photo of him kissing his daughter on the lips? People hated it. Said it was sick. I saw a father who loves his daughter.' Donna took another sip of coffee.

Kerri remembered she'd made herself a drink too. She gulped down a mouthful of tepid tea. Gross. Too much milk. She always took great care when making a hot drink for others and then neglected herself. She put the mug down next to Donna's. 'I never saw it … this girl looks to be in her late teens. Legal but still, it looks bad.'

'Gonna run with the paedo hunter story, eh?'

'I don't know if I should. I met his wife when I interviewed him the other day. She's lovely, and he didn't seem like the type.'

'There's a type?'

'Yeah. Spencer was it. It was pretty obvious, now I think about it.'

'Well, I certainly can't spot them. I was shocked when I read your piece on Spencer. How long until I get the new one?'

'I'm working up to it.'

'You'd better work fast. The boss is itching for another paper doll story. The hits online are in the millions. Prachi wants to milk this as much as possible.'

'I know, but the guy's a friend of Mike's; I'm not sure I should do it.'

'A journalist with a conscience is a journalist out of work.'

'True. Thanks for always supporting me, Donna.'

'Any time. I'd better get back to it.' She leaned in and Kerri got a whiff of expensive perfume, Donna whispered near her ear, her hot breath on Kerri's throat, 'I don't want the dragon breathing down my neck.'

Kerri chuckled as Donna departed. She clicked through the rest of her emails. She had one from Bea. Odd. The only time Bea had sent her an email was when she wanted an opinion on the blurb for one of her young adult novels. The subject line read: 'The Paper Doll Murders'. Did she want information on Kerri's reports? Maybe she had information for her. Kerri read the body of the email with wide eyes.

Hi Jackie, attached is the first daft. I hope you like the rest of it. I'm going into editing mode now. Let me know if there's anything glaring that you want me to fix up. Best wishes, Bea.

It was Bea's manuscript. She'd sent it to the wrong person. This email was meant for her agent. Bea's new novel was called 'The Paper Doll Murders'? Kerri had a sinking feeling in her stomach, as if the tea she'd just swallowed had turned solid as a rock. She shouldn't open the attachment. It was Bea's work, and she hadn't been asked to read it. She should just mind her own business. Kerri twisted her fingers up in her hair. If Bea had based her novel on Kerri's articles without asking if that was okay, Kerri had a right to know.

Kerri mentally blocked out the sound of typing and talking around her while she skim-read the first few chapters. Names had been changed, but it was clear Bea had used Kerri's reports as inspiration for the book. She flicked to the acknowledgements. *The cow hadn't even credited her!* She flicked back to the beginning of the manuscript. She'd written a note on the title page, but still there was no mention of Kerri. The note read: 'Based on the true story of the Paper Doll Killer.' Kerri read on, fuming. If steam could have come out of her ears it would have. How *dare* she jump on the bandwagon and try to profit from Kerri's hard work! Why hadn't she asked her if it was okay to use her work as source material? Kerri would have said yes. She might have even helped her.

Maybe she meant to send her a copy? No. The email message was for Jackie. She'd sent it to Kerri by mistake. Kerri checked the email addresses. JH@Keylit.co.uk. That didn't start with a K. How had Bea made a blunder like this? Then she realised Bea must have typed in 'key' because Key Literary was the name of her agency, then a list of emails would have dropped down, Kerri's above Jackie's. She'd definitely clicked Kerri's address by mistake.

Checking around her every so often to make sure none of her colleagues were reading over her shoulder, Kerri read as much of Bea's novel as she could in the time she was meant to be using to type up her new report outlining the connection between the victims. The novel was well-written and the murders frighteningly gory and detailed. Bea had taken Kerri's reports and wildly expanded on them. The story was told from the killer's point of point of view as well as the victims. What disturbed Kerri more than the fact Bea had failed to mention her was the intensity of the killer chapters. It read like non-fiction. Like Bea had experienced these things first-hand. *Sick.*

Nausea crept up the back of Kerri's throat. She could feel it coming. She was *not* going to have a fit. She willed herself not to feel faint. She wasn't going to pass out. No, no! She wasn't… She closed down the tabs open on the monitor, tugged on her winter coat and woolly hat, slung her heavy handbag over her shoulder and called out to Donna.

'Donna, I have to go.'

Donna glanced up from her screen. 'Everything okay?'

'I don't feel so good. I'm going home.'

'Alright, sweetheart. I'll let the boss know. Take it easy.' Donna waved her off.

Kerri waved back and hurried out of the door.

***

At home, Kerri flicked on the heating and downed two glasses of water. Feeling better, calmer, she went to talk to Bea. Knocked on her door.

'Bea? Are you home?'

No answer. Surprising. She was always in her room. Her 'Do Not Disturb the Writer' sign was hung over the door handle. It could be that she was deep in editing mode and ignoring Kerri; perhaps she had headphones on and was editing to music. Kerri turned the handle and opened the door to Bea's room.

The room was dark except for a strip of orange afternoon sunlight shining in from between a crack in the curtains. Books were piled up everywhere: on the floor, on the bed, on the desk. The journey home had cleared Kerri's head. So what if her flatmate had used her work as a source of inspiration? She might simply have forgotten to mention Kerri in the acknowledgements; it happens a lot. Fiction writers are notoriously flighty and many have mental illnesses; that described Bea perfectly. She would probably be horrified to know Kerri was cross with her.

Kerri backed towards the door. Something shiny caught her eye, tucked under Bea's pillow. Against her better judgement, Kerri went over to the bed and lifted the floral pillowcase. She gasped. Nestled in the middle of the bottom pillow, like a precious baby bird in a nest, was a shiny black and silver knife. It wasn't a kitchen knife or a letter opener; it was a decorative dagger, like something out of a fantasy computer game.

Kerri picked up the split-blade and turned it over in her hands. The razor-sharp edge sliced through her fingers.

'Ouch!' She dropped the dagger, which landed softly on the duvet.

Blood pooled on the tips of her fingers. She shoved them into her mouth and sucked. Her fingers throbbed painfully, like a paper-cut magnified by one hundred. What was a huge dagger doing under Bea's pillow? The murders flashed through Kerri's mind. *Penis chopped off. Gouged eye. Penis mutilated. Stabbed in the ball sack.* Kerri's imagination was running wild. A headline came to her: 'Failed Author Uses Killing Spree as Inspiration for her Next Bestseller'.

What if a lunatic author, disillusioned by the cruel world of publishing, decided to create their very own non-fiction story? Kerri's inner voice scolded her. *Don't be dumb. This is Bea. The sweet hermit who never comes out of her room, let alone go on a killing spree.*

Fingers still in her mouth, the metallic taste of pennies washed over her tongue. She gulped down the blood and her eyes rolled back in her head.

Blackout.

Chapter Twenty-One
Bea's Worst Nightmare

B ea's nightmares intensified after she found Mike's stash of Paper Doll books. She couldn't confront him about it, and she knew she was putting two and two together and making five, but at the back of her mind there was a nagging feeling.

Bea suffered with insomnia, and yet she sometimes slept more hours than should be humanly possible. The doctors didn't know what was wrong with her so they loaded her up with pills. She kept getting a skin-shivery feeling that there was someone watching her while she slept. Not Kerri or Mike or even Mrs Williams: someone else, someone evil. Someone who knew her more intimately than she knew herself, but who was also someone she'd never met. A stalker? Like Kerri had that time. A fan of hers? Spying and prying. Who knows?

Bea was lying on her back on the couch, staring up at the ceiling. Dreams are weird. They feel real but they're not real. They happen inside your head, but sometimes you wake up and the intensity of the dream is so strong you swear it happened or will happen. You were there: you felt all those feelings, saw all those things, smelt them, touched them, tasted them. She was feeling worse. She was worse. Maybe she should talk to someone?

Bea reached over to the coffee table and brushed her fingers over the top of her phone. She couldn't reach it without moving. She scooted over a little and stretched until her biceps groaned, and then snatched the phone before it fell.

It rang in her hand, a chirpy ringtone that was already on the phone when Bea got it; she couldn't be bothered with all the fancy ones you had to download an app for. The name 'Jackie' was on the screen. Bea took a deep breath, pressed to accept the call, and held the phone to her ear.

'Hi, Jackie.' Bea couldn't manage a cheery voice today. Jackie would have to put up with monotone.

'Hey, lovely. Long time, no speak. You like to go off the radar, eh! I'll get straight to the point. Got you a gig. You gotta be there in three hours.'

Bea swung her legs off the couch and sat up. 'Excuse me?'

'Normally publishers do this stuff, but a friend needed someone to fill in when one of her authors dropped out last minute and I said your name. Bingo, you got the gig.'

'The gig?' Bea was confused; since when was she a musician?

'Get a pen.'

Bea put down her phone and felt around the shelf under the coffee table. She found a pen and an old supermarket receipt. She clicked the lid and poised the nib on the paper, picked up the phone and held it between her ear and her shoulder. She could have put it on speaker, but old habits die hard.

'I've got a pen.'

Jackie rattled off a time and address and Bea wrote it down. She dropped the pen and held the phone to her other ear. 'What's this about?'

'You're going to Specfest.'

'Specfest? Sounds like a convention for people obsessed with collecting reading glasses.'

'It's for folks who write speculative fiction.'

'I don't write that.'

'Yeah you do, it's all the weird shit under one umbrella. You wrote those weirdo alien novels. They fall under spec-fic.'

'No, they fall under Young Adult.'

'Whatever, I got you a spot on the panel.'

'You did *what?*' A cold dread clambered over Bea's skin like a million spiders hitching a ride. 'Jackie, please don't make me do this.'

'Don't be silly, Babe. It's exposure. You've been out of the loop for a while; let's get you back in. When you get a publishing deal there'll be more panels and newspaper interviews, and all sorts. You know that.'

Bea did know that and she'd hated it the first time.

'I'm not in a good place right now, Jackie.'

'Oh no you don't; don't you use the mental illness card on me. This is your chance for a comeback. Not many authors get a second bite of the cherry. When I said I would send you, the publisher asked for a full manuscript. Sometimes these things unfold in unorthodox ways, and you just have to go with it.'

'Which publisher?'

'Let's not get into details until we have a deal, eh? Don't want to get your hopes up.'

Bea knew she wasn't going to win. Jackie did what Jackie wanted and everyone else had to fall in line.

'What's the dress code?'

'Wear something that'll keep the attention on you. Bright colour, and make sure your tits are on display.'

Bea didn't have any tits; she had small buds and was comfortable with leaving what little she did have hidden away.

'Something smart casual then.'

Her agent laughed. 'Make sure it's eye-catching. The event will be filmed.'

Bea swore under her breath.

'Beatrice, don't flake out on me now. You can do this.'

'Okay, but before you go can I ask you something?'

'Fire away.'

Anxiety burned in Bea's chest. She needed to talk to someone. Her relationship with Jackie was meant to be purely professional, but how often did her agent stick to that rule? Surely Bea could break it just this once?

'I found some vintage Paper Doll books in Mike's room.'

'The gay guy?'

Bea rolled her eyes. Was that the only way straight people knew how to describe gay people? She could have said the actor or the mime or your male flatmate.

'Yes, the gay guy. I'm concerned about it.'

'Concerned?'

Bea would have to spell it out to her.

'It's kinda weird, given there's a serial killer on the loose leaving paper dolls next to their victims, don't you think?'

'No.'

'No?'

'It's a coincidence, Bea. Me thinks your imagination is running away with you. Take a break from the manuscript. It can wait a week.'

'I've sent it to you.'

'Well great!' Jackie squealed. 'Well done on finishing it. I didn't get it. Send it again.'

'I'll re-send it before I leave. Will you be at this event?'

'God no! I can't stand the things. Boring as hell.'

Bea was stunned at the bluntness. Every time she spoke to her agent the woman had managed to shock her in some new way. Say it like it is, Jackie, don't hold back or anything. Bea started at the address she'd scribbled down. The Cinema Museum wasn't a venue she was familiar with, but the area was. She knew how to get there, so that was one thing she didn't have to worry about.

'I guess I'll go and get ready.'

'Good girl. Ciao for now.'

Bea dropped her phone arm and flopped back miserably. Why did she have to do this shit? Why couldn't she go back to the days when authors were allowed to be introverts and not expected to be seen? Roald Dahl didn't know he was born. Writing in the shed on lined paper with a pencil, someone else typing it up for him. No scary panels to do or online profiles to build up. Bea had only a few hours before she needed to be out the door, and she had no idea what the fuck she was going to wear. She dragged her reluctant body towards her bedroom. If all else failed, maybe Kerri would let her borrow that hideous sparkly boob top she'd worn to a 90s themed hen weekend. Jackie would love it if she wore that.

***

The journey to Lambeth was a struggle. It was rush hour and Bea was crammed in the corner of the tube; the woman beside her was holding on to a high handrail, her armpit in Bea's face. Stepping onto the underground train, she'd accidently brushed bottoms with a stranger. Then, when she'd squeezed though the tube, people packed in like baked beans, bags had bashed into her. Someone stood on her foot and a guy opposite her had coughed and spluttered like he had a deadly disease. He wasn't close enough to cough on her, but watching him hacking up in a confined space was enough to make Bea feel like she was getting sick.

After getting lost in the maze of housing that surrounded the water tower, Bea arrived outside the Cinema Museum with fifteen minutes to spare. The doors to the old Victorian building were lit up by floodlights either side of the arched entrance way. Bea studied the tiny bricks, stacked neatly on top of each other and decorative coving. The long windows were a grid of small squares topped with a porthole that had a cross frame through it. The arched brickwork above the glass made the windows look like little people in headdresses standing side by side. The building used to be a workhouse and home to Charlie Chaplin as a child – Bea had scanned Wikipedia before leaving home – now the building was a celebration of film and a place for creative types to gather.

Bea hurried inside; it was a little warmer in the foyer. She was directed past old cinema equipment and dummies dressed in 1950s clothes. The walls were cluttered with black and white photos and hand-painted signs. Through a door at the end of the memorabilia corridor, Bea made her way up a narrow staircase.

Inside the main room, people dressed in their finest mingled with hippy types dressed like they'd just rolled out of bed and pulled on a branded T-shirt from the floor. It made her feel a little better about the rather plain A-line skirt and cream blouse she had settled on. The crowds moved like a gaggle of geese, and Bea struggled to find a way through. She grabbed a flute of bubbles from a young helper holding a tray of glasses of sparkling wine. Bea downed it in one and then placed the glass back on the tray. She thanked the young woman with rainbow highlights who smiled politely, but Bea knew the girl was secretly judging her.

Bea read the sign on the stand and cringed. *Want to be a Success like Margaret Atwood? Our Speculative Fiction Writers Can Help.* She couldn't help, and she wasn't a success like Atwood. Anxiety levels rose up her throat. *What the fuck was she going to say to these people?*

Bea hung her coat on a rack in the corner, following the lead of others. It was stuffy and humid, despite the high ceilings, and smelled of fabric that had endured a million different alcohol stains. The walls were plastered with old movie posters and chairs were set out in rows of ten facing a tiny stage. It made Bea feel like she was back at school, a nativity about to be performed, and she hadn't learned her lines. Above, the ceilings criss-crossed with exposed high beams, and sad lamps hung down between the dark wooden planks like those in a rundown lunatic asylum.

She approached the stage where two people were already seated. A third was standing in front of them, setting down microphones and bottles of water on a small round table. The male and female seated gave Bea a cold stare as she stepped up on the stage. She smiled sweetly.

'Hello.' Bea acknowledged those seated, but spoke to the woman standing, 'I'm Beatrice Summers.'

The frail lady, draped in a black gown, 1950s-style glasses perched on her thin nose and burnt-orange lipstick running into the lines around her mouth, wore a vacant expression.

'Hello.' She gave Bea a tight smile and went back to briefing the people sitting.

Bea hovered for a moment before sidestepping into the woman's line of sight. 'I'm meant to be on a panel today. My agent sent me.'

'Oh!' A smile bloomed across the woman's orange lips. She spoke with a plumb in her mouth. 'I'm sorry, they didn't give me your name. Lovely to meet you, please take a seat. I was just briefing the other authors on what to expect from the crowd.'

Bea nodded and sat down next to a female panellist, who smiled warmly at her. The girl's legs in sheer tights were swept to the side like a posh lady riding side-saddle. She wore a blood-red flowing skirt and matching suit jacket with a black singlet underneath. The male author opposite her wore jeans and a leather jacket over a sci-fi-inspired T-shirt. Bea couldn't quite make out which fandom it was, because she could only see the middle part of the design from beneath his jacket. The male author reminded her of John Travolta in *Greece*, but not quite as handsome, possibly because he wore an expression of arrogance on his serious face.

The posh woman in the 1950s glasses was the moderator and she would field questions to them that she had prepared and then they would answer questions from the audience. Bea didn't like the idea of random questions being fired at her, but what could she do? She was there now and there was no getting out of it.

The seats filled with excited guests. Bea studied the attendees as they chatted and shuffled along the aisles, choosing where they wanted to sit. The curious thing about people sitting down without the aid of numbered seats was that they never sat in a logical way by filling up from the front row. They sat all over the place, and others had to squeeze past them, or they had to stand up and move out of their seat in order to let them pass. Bea watched on as the game of musical chairs continued. Once most people had been seated the moderator introduced herself as Julia Brambles and welcomed everyone. She then introduced the panel – in order of importance, Bea assumed.

'*New York Times* bestselling author Jake Penfold, bestselling author and award-winning screenwriter Ellen Dove and Young Adult author Beatrice Dummers.'

Beatrice's shocked face was captured forever on the camera set up in the middle aisle. Julia cleared her throat, slid her glasses down her long nose and squinted at her clipboard.

'Beg your pardon, Beatrice Summers.'

Bea was relieved Julia had corrected her mistake, but the damage had been done. The tone had been set, and the entire room now associated her with the word 'dumb'. From there, the evening went downhill fast. Bea found herself wanting to sell her soul to the devil, and for him to appear from beneath the floorboards in a shower of fire and brimstone and drag her down to hell. What she was suffering right now was worse than an eternity of sweltering heat and being jabbed in the arse repeatedly with a pitchfork.

Jake dominated the session. Man-spreading, laid back, he flipped the microphone like a pop star. His replies were so long there was barely time for Ellen to give an answer, let alone Bea.

The crowd were super impressed by him, mildly interested in what Ellen had to say, and completely switched off when Bea spoke. She fidgeted on her chair; this was meant to help her get noticed. What publisher would want to take her on after watching Jake the snake reducing her to a little mouse begging not to be swallowed up by him? She was relieved when the hour was almost up and it was time for questions from the audience. This was her chance to shine, her chance to show she knew what she was talking about. She *was* going to make a huge come back, just wait. Her name would be on everybody's lips.

'Could someone pass this lady a microphone,' Julia hustled. 'We can't quite hear her.'

A woman in her fifties with wild red hair, wearing a retro-inspired patterned dress and silver necklace in the shape of a scorpion, was standing in the second row, waiting to be handed the microphone. It whistled when a young helper placed it in the guest's hands.

'I just wanted to ask.' Her voice echoed loudly around the high ceiling. 'With regards to becoming a bestselling author like Atwood and yourself, Jake…' Bea rolled her eyes; another question for him. 'What do you think is the driving factor in that success? Is it about talent, or are there other forces at work?'

Jake answered with the usual self-important crap about being recognised as a skilled and prolific writer, and that the only way to becoming a bestseller was the way he did it, and that there were no better ways than his and blah blah. What a load of shite! Bea couldn't stay silent any more.

'If I may interject…' The look of distain on Jake's face flashed with the demon that resided inside him – the evil he kept hidden from his adoring fans. The room went silent, Bea held her head high. 'There are many different factors to becoming a successful writer, not just skill and talent as Jake would have people believe.' *Oh shit*! She'd said it now, no backing out. 'There is an element of who you know, and if you know the right people, you're more likely to get a book deal with an advance from a traditional house. The amount of marketing the house is prepared to put behind you is always a factor. There is a tiny element of luck with hitting a trend before it starts or just after a genre has become popular. There is also online fame to consider, this is why influencers get book deals and then a ghost writer is hired to write their novel. You have to work hard, you have to play hard, and you have to accept that some things won't go your way, and that your path will be different to someone as well-connected as Jake Penfold.'

Jake blinked several times, astonished Bea had been so bold. Ellen smiled. From what Bea could tell from her answers, Ellen had had to fight her way into the industry and onto this stage, and getting a start in the world of screenwriting was probably no picnic either.

Jake raised his hand with authority. 'Can I just…'

Bea cut him off. 'I'm not finished, Jake.'

'Yes, you are.' He sat up in his chair and leaned forward; the snake had reared itself up ready to attack. 'You were finished a long time ago. I'd never heard of you before you sat down in that chair. A quick search of your online profile before we began and I find out your supernatural series tanked.' Bea's skin prickled with trepidation. She should have kept her mouth shut; she was no match for him. Her eyes watered. The crowd was deathly quiet. Julia cleared her throat, ready to douse the flames, but Jake silenced her with a single hand gesture.

'Who are you to give advice to these lovely people who have paid to be here and learn about how they can become a success?' Bea shrank in her chair. 'You don't have a string of bestsellers under your belt, and you haven't put out a book in years. They can't learn how to succeed from a failed author like you.'

The stunned silence was broken by Ellen Dove's soft tones.

'Now hang on, Jake. Every writer's journey is valid.'

'The self-published all say that.' He threw up his hands, exasperated. 'Listen up, folks: self-publishing will *not* make you money! You need an agent and a traditional publisher, and to have your books optioned for film or TV. Don't listen to all these bottom-of-the-barrel writers telling you otherwise.'

'Excuse me.' Ellen's arms were crossed and her young face suddenly held a wealth of wisdom. 'I'm not self-published.'

'Oh sorry, indie, right, Ellen? That just makes you even dumber. Independent publishers take all the cash, do bugger all in the way of marketing, and you end up trying to live on the chicken feed they throw you.'

Ellen got to her feet, fists clenched. 'That's bullshit! I make a good living.'

Julia laughed nervously into the microphone. 'Okay, well, thank you authors for your interesting and intense insights. There's wine and some canapés at the back of the room, folks. Please help yourselves.'

The audience started to murmur, and some, feeling the awkwardness coming off the stage like steam from a blistering sun-heated tarmac, got straight out of their seats and headed for the safe haven at the back of the room: a table of booze and nibbles. Jake locked Ellen with a dark stare. 'If I'd have known Sarah wasn't going to be here, I wouldn't have come. The two of you are no replacement for one of her. I've had to carry this panel, and you thank me by making me look like the bad guy.'

'Y-you didn't need us to make you look bad, Jake,' Bea stuttered. 'Try looking in the mirror at the person you are.'

'*You* try looking in the mirror; your face will probably crack it.'

He got out of his seat, jumped down from the stage, and made his way through the crowd and towards the youngsters serving drinks. Disappointingly, desperate writers engaged him in conversation, their body language a dead giveaway that they were hoping if they befriended the bully he might help them bully their way to the top.

Bea sobbed silently into a tissue. She knew this panel was a bad idea. Ellen put her hand on Bea's shoulder. 'He's a self-important jerk. Don't shed tears over his vicious words.'

'Thank you, Ellen, and thanks for sticking up for me.'

'No worries, I was sticking up for me too and the millions of other writers out there. Not everyone will be an overnight success like that prick, and not everyone wants to be. They just want to write – and why should *he* be the one to decide who can play in the playground? We might be playing in the sandpit, but he's climbed right to the top of the slide and the only way is down.'

Bea smiled. 'Are you on Instagram?'

Ellen took her phone out from her inside her jacket pocket. 'Yep, what's your handle?'

Bea pocketed her tissue and got out her phone. At least she'd made a new friend.

Killer

You dance around the bedroom in your bra and knickers, 90s club music blaring from your phone resting on the bedside drawers. You slip the leopard-print top over your head; it's tight across your chest. Tug on some jeggings. You pull on brown knee-high boots and zip them up. Sadly, you don't need to wear a pretty dress for this job. He thinks you're coming with a little boy for him to play with. The client is not in the slightest bit interested in women dressed like princesses or school girls. They ordered a little brown boy, and they'll soon wish they hadn't placed that order with you.

You swipe your arm across the top of the drawers, sending soft toys flying; they flop onto the bed and some roll onto the floor. You open the drawer and take out the big bag of make-up. Unzip. Moisturiser, foundation and then concealer. You dab the concealer under your eyes; the bags are puffy and hard to cover. Check the crow's feet creeping in beside your eyes. *Stay back wrinkles, I'm not ready to be old.* Dust your face with powder. No one will ever know how old you are. Steady hand while lining your lips, then apply the metallic pink lipstick over and over. It builds up a thick, creamy layer. You lick some off, chew your bottom lip, and eat some of the cosmetic concoction. You savour the bitter taste on your tongue. Blusher comes next. Big round circles, like the ones you paint on your dolls.

The sound of someone vacuuming next door is ruining the dance music. You turn up the volume and drown out that horrible cleaning sound. Black eyeliner next, pink glittery eyeshadow. The make-up brush is soft on your eyelids; you pass it over several times, enjoying the sensation. Fake eyelashes glued on, which are sometimes fiddly but not today. You pull your blonde wig over the stocking cap, holding down your real hair. Brush out the curls a little. Hair spray halo. Gorgeous.

You pout at the mirror and flutter the long eyelashes. 'I look like Barbie.'

You scoop your coat up off the floor and throw it on. On the bed is the doll you made earlier. You fold it in half and shove it in your coat pocket. Time to go. You tap your phone screen. The device falls silent. You pocket it. Pull on your black gloves. Hang on. Where's your knife? You search the wardrobe. Not there. Think. Where did you last leave it?

You hurry to the next room. You have plenty of time, but searching for your knife could easily eat into it. You open each door and scan each room until you finally find it. Swipe it from the bed. Shove it in your pocket with the paper doll.

Out of the door, you skip down the landing and bounce down the stairs. Your footsteps thud on the strip of carpet down the middle of the floorboards. She can't hear you. She's too busy vacuuming. The droning noise cuts out.

'Kerri? Bea?'

You stand perfectly still. The old woman shuffles out into the entrance hall. She spies you at the bottom of the stairs. Busted! Hands on hips she glares through her heavy-framed glasses. 'Who are you? One of Mike's drag friends?'

'You could say that.'

'Where's Mike? He knows he can't have friends to stay.'

'Oh, I'm not staying.'

You skip past her. She lunges for you, grabbing your arm.

'Now you listen to me! He only pays rent for one person to live here. If you're living here without my knowledge, there'll be trouble. I might be old, but I ain't gonna have the Mickey taken out of me.'

You peel her fingers back. 'Let go of my arm, bitch!'

'Who're you callin' a bitch? Bitch!' She clutches the front of your coat with her other hand. She's freakishly strong for an old lady.

You grab her face and shove her head backwards. Unsteady on frail legs, she topples over and hits the floor with a thud. *That'll be a hip replacement*, you smirk. The old girl cries out in pain and crawls towards her door.

'See you, Mrs Williams.'

Before you leave, you take a moment to admire the traditionally decorated six-foot Christmas tree in the corner of the entrance hall. You wonder what happened to the fairy lights you'd strung at the window, pretty colours wrapped around Spencer's entrails. If only you could have seen her face when she found it! You reach for the door handle.

'Come into my home and insult me, will ya?' You turn to face her. 'Take this!'

Thwack. You scream and stumble sideways. Searing pain to the side of your head where the vacuum cleaner pipe hit you. All you can think of is the poetic justice of the act. You whacked your uncle with a vacuum cleaner pipe, and now someone has done the same to you. You hold the pain in your head. Your vision is awash with bright flashes and dark patches. Now you know what is meant by the phrase 'seeing stars'. You sway. The room is a boat and a sea of waves are crashing over you. The old girl is talking. Apologising? Your ears feel blocked, her voice sounds like the weird trombone noise the teacher from those Charlie Brown cartoons would make. *Pop.* Clear words rush in.

'I'm so sorry. Are you okay? I don't know what came over me. Come, I'll help you sit down.'

You steady yourself, one hand on the old girl's shoulder. Vision comes back online. You reach into your pocket. Lock eyes with the vicious bitch. Alarm rings over her face. Your evil is showing. You grip the handle tight. In one swift movement: arm back, plunge. Drive it hard. She hollers and holds your wrist, tries to force it back towards you. You grip her shoulder and pull her in close.

Twist the blade. Her glasses fall to the floor, tears escaping the corners of her lined eyes. She can't get away from the pain, yet she's not screaming at you to stop. She won't beg for her life. Tough old bird. You twist the knife again, hoping to get a reaction. She doesn't oblige. Your gaze is locked with hers. *This pain is the last thing you'll ever feel. Savour it, Mrs Williams.*

She claws at your face, tries to scratch you. Grabs a handful of blonde wig, rips it off your head. Her knees buckle. Your head throbs. You go down with her. Pull the knife and blood pumps out across her white frilly apron. Grasping the handle tight, you crawl across the floor and up the stairs. The tip of the sharp blade drags across the wall, scraping a line into it each time you move up a step. Stomach churning, you lean your back against the banister. A few seconds pass, deep breathing, nope, it's coming. You lean forward and vomit into the pot of the small Christmas tree at the top of the stairs. Bile burns up your throat and you vomit again. Your eyelids droop. Concussion can kill. You're not ending up in a coma. Stay awake!

You wipe your mouth with the back of your hand. Now there's vomit on your gloves, blood on them too, a trail of red up the carpet behind you. You pull the gloves off and shove them behind the small lit-up and now vomit-splattered tree. Keep crawling, your stomach turns like a washing machine, you don't have enough energy to puke again. You collapse back at the flat. Pull the stocking off your head. You can't lie here for long. You'll have to act quickly. A little headache isn't going to stop you.

Chapter Twenty-Two

Mike's Battle with Booze

Mike's eyes refused to open. His tongue felt furry and he could taste his bitter bad breath. How much had he had to drink last night? He held his pounding head and lifted it. His back ached. Oh, please say he hadn't got drunk at work and lost his job? Please no.

Mike gently lowered his head, careful, like his skull was as delicate as an egg shell and would break if he let it drop down fast. He rolled into the foetal position. The floor was spinning, him going around with it. He closed his eyes, but the spinning kept going. He willed it to stop. It wouldn't. Eyes still closed, he reached into his pocket for his phone. This was bad. He felt like he was dying. He needed his stomach pumped or something. He drew the symbol to unlock the phone. Opened one eye. It was dark. The phone light too bright. Mike squinted. He could barely see the numbers on the glowing screen. He dragged the tip of his finger across the screen again. It wouldn't take the pattern. Had he changed the pattern while he was drunk?

He yelled out in desperation. 'Kerri! Bea!'

Somebody help me.

Nobody came. He tapped emergency call and held the phone to his sore head. The ringing was loud; he held the phone away from his ear. A female voice answered.

Emergency, which service?

'Ambulance, please.'

He managed to tell the operator the address and that he needed help. He felt he should try to get to the front door so the emergency workers didn't have to climb the stairs. He stumbled along the landing in the dark, slumped over the banister. His feet carried him downstairs, but before he could get to the door, he fell unconscious.

Chapter Twenty-Three

Kerri's Shock

erri shivered. There was a cold draught coming from somewhere and her body felt weak, like she'd gone ten rounds with a boxer. The seizures were getting worse. She opened her eyes and blinked several times. Her head throbbed. She must have hit it on the couch when she passed out. Eyes focused. Nothing to focus on. It was dark except for a warm glow somewhere beside her. Her face was in line with the bottom of a door. The draught was coming from underneath it.

Confusion flooded Kerri's mind. She pushed herself up into a sitting position. Her eyeballs felt as if they might fall out. The light source was coming from Mrs William's six-foot Christmas tree. Twinkly white fairy lights struggled to hold back the darkness. Kerri frowned, confused. What was she doing downstairs?

She spread her fingers across the cold wooden boards, but as she pushed herself up onto her knees she felt something beside her and glanced down. Kerri's hands shot over her mouth to retain a gasp. Twinkly Christmas tree lights reflected in the lifeless brown eyes of her neighbour and landlady, Mrs Williams. She was slumped on her side, apron stained red.

'Mrs Williams,' Kerri whispered through her fingers. Shaking, she lowered her hand and tapped the dear old lady on the shoulder. 'Mrs Williams!'

Mrs Williams didn't answer. Kerri shook her shoulder, but it was like shaking a rag doll stuffed with rocks. She was dead. Kerri sat back, wrapped her arms around her knees, and rocked backwards and forwards. *The old lady was dead.* Murdered? Kerri's eyes widened. Her thoughts raced. Mrs Williams was murdered and Kerri had been left for dead beside her. The killer was in the house! The Paper Doll killer was after her!

'What am I gonna do?' Kerri whispered to herself, hugging her knees to her chest and burying her face. 'What do I do?'

Kerri flinched at the sound of the doorbell; the tune was Big Ben chiming. Kerri's joints locked with fear; she was glued to the spot. She scanned the outlines in the darkness, fearful the killer might jump out and attack her.

Bang, bang, bang, bang, bang on the front door.

'Kerri? Are you home? It's Mark.'

'Mark?' Tears of relief squeezed from the corners of Kerri's eyes. Her knight in shining armour had come to rescue her.

Kerri scrambled over to the front door on hands and knees, got to her feet, tore the door open and threw herself at Mark. His arms wrapped her and she sank into his warm embrace. The bright porch security light shone down on them and spilled across the dark entrance floor like liquid gold.

Mark squeezed Kerri tight, his strong arms made her feel safe. He rested his chin on her head. 'What's going on? We had a dinner date, remember? I've been phoning you for an hour. I was worried you'd had another seizure.'

Kerri sobbed into Mark's thick winter coat. 'We've got to get out of here. Mrs Williams is dead and the killer is in the house. She's after me, Mark. Don't let her get me.'

'Shush, it's okay. No one's after you.' He stroked her matted hair. Icy cold drops landed on Kerri's cheek. She glanced up. Snowflakes fluttered past the security light like tiny dancers competing for the spotlight. 'It's alright, I'm here now.'

'You're not listening!' Kerri pulled him away from the door. Plumes of white jittered from her lips and evaporated into the bitter winter air. 'Mrs Williams was murdered! We have to go!'

'Murdered?' Mark raced inside the house and turned on the light. Kerri peered through the doorway at her boyfriend. He knelt down beside the old woman. Mark spoke to the corpse in a soft voice, hoping to revive Kerri's landlady. It was even more real now the main light was on, or maybe it was all just a game? A murder mystery, and everyone was in on it except her. Mrs Williams was playing dead. The butler did it in the entrance hall with the knife. Kerri buried her face in her hands. She couldn't bear this.

Mark's sharp tones struck Kerri's ears. 'Call an ambulance!' She peeked through her fingers. He glared at her like she was a stupid child. 'Didn't you hear me? My phone's in the car. Call an ambulance and the police. Now!'

Kerri shook her head. 'My phone's in the flat.'

'Go get it!' Mark took off his coat and folded it into a makeshift pillow. He rested Mrs Williams head on it. 'Go now!'

Kerri turned her back. 'No.'

Woof!

Sausage was at the bottom of the steps, tethered to the railing. The dog's stubby legs lifted a few inches off the ground as he jumped to chomp snowflakes. Mark's tone changed from urgency to frustration. 'Kerri, snap out of it! You either stay down here with Mrs Williams or go upstairs and phone the emergency services. Killers don't stay behind at the scene of a crime to get caught; you know that! You've covered enough murder cases to know, and, look, there's no paper dolls. If this was your murderer, she'd have left her signature doll behind. One for you and one for Mrs Williams. This was probably some horrible accident.'

Kerri couldn't turn around; she didn't want to look at the dead body again. Sausage had spotted her. He pulled against the lead, desperate to break free so he could scamper up the outside steps and into her arms. She turned her head and screamed into the house. 'She's covered in blood, Mark! It doesn't look like an accident to me.'

'There could be any number of reasons why. She might have hurt herself in the kitchen and stumbled out here and called you, and then you had a fit and fell down beside her. Go now and make the call! Take Sausage with you if it'll make you feel better. We don't need to leave him outside now that Mrs Williams can't protest about dogs in the building.'

That last comment brought tears to Kerri's eyes. Mrs Williams couldn't do anything any more. That dear sweet old lady was dead and it was probably her fault for writing about the serial killer. She took a deep breath and hurried down the steps to the dog. He jumped up excitedly, wet paws on her trousers. The snow thickened; it speckled her hair and gave Sausage dandruff on his head and back. His tail was too waggy for snowflakes to settle on it. Kerri looped his lead around her wrist and ran on uneasy legs back to the house. She shot past Mark who was making Mrs Williams comfortable even though she had passed away, and pelted up the stairs and into the flat. No need to find her keys, the door was wide open.

She turned on the lights and let Sausage off the lead. If someone was hiding in here Sausage would find them. The dog trotted in and out of rooms, sniffing around furniture, tail wagging. No concern. Kerri took her phone off the charger which was plugged into the wall near the front door. She dialled 999 and explained to the operator what had happened. Once the call had ended, she relaxed a little. Maybe it was an accident. She frowned, trying to remember how she came to be downstairs. It was possible Mrs Williams had called for her and she'd gone down and then had a seizure. Sometimes there were blanks in her memory after a seizure.

The dog had disappeared. Even though Kerri felt safer, she didn't want to be too far away from Mark.

'Sausage, here boy!'

Kerri patted her thigh. The dog didn't come. She went to her room, flicked on the light switch, and glanced around. No dog, but the teddies that lived on the top of her drawers were scattered all over the room. Feelings of unease started to crawl back over her skin. She turned off the light and made her way to Mike's room.

'Sausage!'

Kerri poked her head around the bedroom door and turned on the light. The dog barked and leapt off the bed. Kerri's heart nearly exploded in her chest. 'You little shit!'

Sausage rushed past her and out the bedroom door. Kerri reached up to turn off the light, then caught a glimpse of her face in the oval mirror on top of Mike's chest of drawers. She walked towards the mirror. Staring back at her was a heavily made-up face, black smudges under her eyes, tear lines drawn through round blush on her cheeks. She looked like a drag queen. Her gaze flicked to the corkboard, a photograph of Mike and his drag friends was pinned at the top. A corner of the photo had been ripped away; one of the queens was missing her head.

Stress pains stabbed Kerri in the chest; she held her hand to it. The material felt strange. She opened her coat wider and found she was wearing a leopard-print top and jeggings. She didn't own either item of clothing. Were they Bea's? Had she borrowed them? This was getting weird. She couldn't remember anything. She held out her arms. This wasn't her coat! She thrust her hands into her pockets and her fingers found something folded up in the right one. She took it out. Fingers trembling, she unfolded a paper doll.

'Oh my God.'

Kerri's stomach turned and her tears splattered onto the doll's patchwork dress. She was shaking with fear, but relieved to see the headshot stuck on the top of the doll wasn't either hers or Mrs Williams. It was that of a drag queen. She held the doll up to the ripped photograph on Mike's corkboard. The feathers around the drag queen's neck matched the boa trailing down her body. More tears fell thick and fast. Kerri sniffed. 'What the fuck is going on?'

Sirens sounded outside. Kerri pocketed the paper doll and ran to the window. She moved the curtain to one side and pressed her face to the cold glass. Blue flashing lights lit up the snowy street. An unmistakable green and yellow ambulance was parked up under a streetlamp, with a police car behind it, snow on the roof.

'Kerri!' Mark's voice travelled up to her. 'Kerri! Come down here.'

Kerri hurried across the living room, her boots thumping against the carpet. At least the knee-highs were hers. She dashed out the door and slammed into the banister. Her heart sank at the sight of the scene below. Mrs Williams was still lifeless on the floor, and from where she was standing up on the landing, Kerri could see the spilt blood flowered around her landlady's lank body. Mark was on his knees, patting for Sausage to come to him. Sausage was under the Christmas tree with a blonde wig in his jaws. The dog wasn't coming out so Mark could take his best find of the day away from him. Kerri held her hands either side of her head, fearful her brain might blow a fuse. *This can't be happening.* Paramedics rushed through the door and Mark began explaining that they'd found Mrs Williams like this.

Kerri's mind raced. The killer had not only been in her home but had tried to frame her. Swapped clothes and left Kerri to face the music. There was no other explanation. Why kill Mrs Williams though? The head on the paper doll was a drag queen's not her neighbour's. Police officers piled in. They beckoned Mark out of the way and huddled in the doorway that led to Mrs William's flat. Kerri slowly made her way downstairs. She glanced back at the small Christmas tree on the landing. It was splattered with what looked suspiciously like vomit. Below her boots there was a trail of red like someone had dragged a paintbrush up the carpet.

Mark met her at the bottom step and she fell onto him. It was all too much. She gazed up into his worried eyes. He wiped a tear from her cheek. 'What's all this make-up?' She shook her head. She had no idea.

A voice from the front door caught their attention. 'Is there a Mike here?'

Another set of paramedics stepped into the entrance hall, which was becoming crowded.

Mark glanced at Kerri, she shook her head a second time, unable to push words past her lips. He waved his hand to the paramedics. 'He's not home.'

'He called an ambulance. Are you sure he's not here?'

Kerri found her voice. 'There's no one else here.' She tugged at Mark's shirt sleeve and whispered. 'Mike did this. He's the killer.'

Chapter Twenty-Four

Bea Conscious

Bea could hear someone crying, but she couldn't see anything. She was cold. Shivering. Yet she could not feel her body. The sensation was strange. Bumped along. Was she awake or dreaming? Voices. They sounded far away. Underwater. She was moving. Was she blindfolded? She couldn't move her arms or legs. She couldn't speak. Her ears were all she had. What were they saying? Who's talking? The voices faded. There was nothing.

Killer

The interview room is small and uninviting. Magnolia walls, beech desk, hard plastic chairs. Two uniformed officers stand behind you, ready to restrain you if you decide to attack. Across the table two senior officers in meticulously ironed navy suits, lanyards around their necks, are growing increasing weary. They sent you one of their representatives and you refused to speak until she was asked to leave. You don't need a lawyer. What the fuck can she do? Not guilty is never going to fly. You did it. You're guilty. Everyone knows it. End of.

A woman in a pencil skirt is lurking in the corner. Legs crossed, arms crossed and still as a lion watching its prey. You've been in the room for hours now. You're tired. You thought admitting to all the murders would be a cut and dried thing. She did it. Lock her up. They know more than you expected. They know about everything and everyone.

'Why did you kill Mrs Williams?' The detective chief inspector on the right, dark hair tied back in a bun, oozes with confidence and projects a 'don't fuck with me' vibe. The young sergeant on her left is faking confidence; he's obviously in training and she chose to introduce him as sergeant rather than trainee detective or whatever his title is. He looks more like a fresh-faced footballer about to play his first professional match than a member of the police force. He's shitting himself.

You drum your fingers on the table. 'We've been over this. I do it because I enjoy it. It's my superpower. I control whether they live or die. If karma existed, I wouldn't have to take matters into my own hands.'

'Mrs Williams deserved to die? That was you dishing out karma?' The inspector's suit is less formal than her partner's. She no longer needs to dress to impress but has to look smart. In her late thirties, mixed race, and judging by the frown dent between her eyebrows it had been more than a struggle to climb the ranks.

You slump down on the table and throw your arms over your head. This is exhausting, it's late, you just want to sleep. 'Can I change my clothes? Have a shower or something? I stink.'

'Answer the question.'

You sigh. 'No, it wasn't karma. I was trying to leave and she got in my way. Look, we've been in this room for hours, I've told you everything, just sling me in a cell and throw away the key. I'm done.'

Chief Inspector Clark crosses her arms. 'We need to talk to the others first.'

You tug at a strand of hair, twist it around your fingers, you feel naked without the wig. 'You know what, I should be treated better than this. Made a Dame or some shit. Actually, make me a Sir. Dames always makes me think of panto. I want to be knighted.'

The young guy pipes up. 'For murdering people?' He shouldn't have spoken. She's told him not to, her glare gives it away. His function is to observe and take notes. They're recording so he can look back at the footage, but the senior inspector has obviously instructed him to jot things down like a school kid. That was the way she learned.

You lock the young sergeant with an unflinching stare. 'For ridding the country of child molesters!' His gaze drops down to the notepad in front of him. He scribbles with a black ballpoint. You climb onto your imaginary soap box. 'You make me out to be some psychopath. Kids have been, no, *are* being, and will continue to be, abused while you lot allow scumbags to live. These men, and sometimes women, know there are no real consequences for their actions. They're not scared of you. That's why they keep doing it! Cut off a few dicks and some might be deterred…' You make a gesture like you're holding a needle. '…Those not deterred need a sharp scratch from a poisoned batch.' You pretend to stab the imaginary needle into your arm.

The young sleuth makes a face like he's peed his big boy pants. It was the idea of dicks being severed rather than your demonstration of a lethal injection. He's sitting opposite a serial killer who dismembers and disembowels men. Well, three men and two women. Perhaps he's attracted to you. Likes dangerous women. It would be fun to play cat and mouse with this little rodent.

He plucks up the courage to speak. 'Then you admit you're a paedophile hunter?' The inspector side-eyes the boy. He spoke again when he wasn't meant to, but this time she looks pleased with his question.

'You say that like it's a bad thing.' You swivel on your seat and throw your legs up on the table, cross them, knee-high boots resting on the edge. They don't ask you to move. They don't lecture you about feet on the table. You cross your arms. 'What's worse? Letting a child suffer or killing a paedo? Why does society continue to treat these monsters with more respect than their victims? Is a man's penis more important than a child's life?'

The senior detective chimes in. 'Princess, I think…'

You cut her off. 'No, you don't, none of you do. Do you know how many victims have committed suicide? They're constantly reliving it, in perpetual torture, remembering how it felt when the monster grabbed at their bodies…' You grab your breasts – the young sergeant's eyes widen with shock – you claw at your top. '…Pawing at them, forcing fingers, cocks, dildos, poles, bottles, anything and everything into their mouths, snatches, and into their arses! Little boys and girls are being raped, ripped, tortured and tormented. Do you know what that does to a person?'

Senior detective Clark clears her throat. 'I don't but…'

'But nothing!' You lower your legs and slam your fist down on the table. The young pig flinches and the older one blinks several times. 'You don't get to talk morals with me. You're not on the right side of them. You give rights to the monsters and leave the kids out in the cold. I protect children.'

Chief Inspector Clark tilts her head. 'What about the innocent man you almost killed and Mrs Williams?'

You stare at her smug face. Dumb bitch! She thinks she's so smart. You relax back in your seat.

'Friendly fire. A few innocent lives for many. Isn't that what society teaches with its wars? You think it's okay to send thousands of innocent men and women to their death for oil, but sacrificing a handful to save the children, that's not on?'

The stern woman sat in the corner speaks for the first time. 'Princess, can I speak to Mike?'

You scowl at her. 'I dunno. Can you?'

The woman has an Oprah Winfrey confidence about her. She puts you on edge.

'Ask Mike to come forward.'

You don't want to talk to this woman. She's going to try and get inside your head. Unlock your secrets. You do as she bids, close your eyes and whisper: 'Mike.'

Mike

'**M**ike?' Mike glanced around the room, twitchy, scared. He stared at the two strangers in front of him. The woman spoke softly. 'I'm Detective Chief Inspector Clark and this is Sergeant Woods.'

'What am I doing here?' Mike shrank back in the chair. He had no idea where he was or how he'd got there.

Inspector Clark leaned forward. 'Please could you confirm your full name.'

Mike rubbed his arm nervously and glanced over his shoulder at the uniformed officers standing behind him. 'Have I done something wrong?'

'We just need to ask you a few questions, okay? Full name and date of birth, please.'

'Michael Gloss.' Mike's stomach growled. It felt hollow, like he hadn't eaten for a week. He rattled off his date of birth, then turned to the sergeant. 'Has my stomach been pumped? I have a drinking problem, I admit it. I'll go to AA meetings. I'll go right now.'

Mike rose out of the chair. Behind him an officer in uniform placed his hand on Mike's shoulder. 'Sit down, Mike.'

Mike lowered himself back down. 'Yes, officer.'

Detective Chief Inspector Clark watched Mike with woeful eyes. 'You really have no idea why you're here?'

Mike shook his head. 'Did the ambulance bring me here?' He wrung his hands and glanced down at his stained top. 'Is this blood?'

A woman in a pencil skirt sat down beside him. 'Mike, I need you to remain calm.'

Mike pulled at his top. 'Whose clothes are these?'

'Don't worry about that now. You're in a safe place. The officers just need to ask you a few questions, okay?'

Mike nodded. 'Can I have some water?'

The sergeant opposite Mike stood and swiftly walked over to the cooler. The water trickled out as he pressed down the tab. He hurried back and passed a full cup to Mike. Mike chugged the cool liquid back and then wiped his mouth with the back of his hand.

The attractive young sergeant began jotting down notes. The inspector, who had soft features apart from some frown lines, came across as rather butch, probably a lesbian. Mike internally scolded himself for making such an assumption. He hated being judged, but here he was making judgments about others. If he was honest with himself he did this a lot. He really wasn't that good a person. He dropped his gaze, hangdog.

'Mike...' He glanced up. The inspector linked her fingers on the table in front of her. 'There's no easy way to say this... Your landlady, Mrs Williams, has been killed.'

Mike's mouth dropped open. 'Oh my God! What happened?'

The officers exchanged dark glances. The sergeant stopped scribbling to answer, 'She was murdered. Stabbed to death.'

Mike frowned. 'Who would do that to an old lady? She used to give me grief for coming home drun... I mean, late, but... Wait, am I a suspect?'

The woman next to him used a soothing tone. 'Tell us about your childhood, Mike. Was it a happy one?'

Mike shrugged. 'I guess.'

'Tell me about your mother and father. Were they good parents?'

'I-I don't know. I lived in a children's home for a while. Why are you asking me this?'

'Do you speak to your family much these days?'

'We're estranged. I wouldn't even recognise them if I passed them on the street. They shut me out, didn't want a gay son, I guess.'

'Where were you yesterday between 4pm and 10pm?'

Mike's palms felt sweaty. He was a suspect. They think he killed Mrs Williams.

'Um … I came home from the club early.' He held his hand to his throbbing forehead. 'I'm sorry, I'm hungover, I don't remember. I didn't do anything to Mrs Williams, I've never even been in a fistfight, let alone stabbed someone.' Mike took a deep breath; he didn't want to land an innocent person in trouble, but he had to say something, just in case she had done it. He wasn't going to be charged for a crime he hadn't committed. 'It's my flatmate, Kerri. She has dresses hidden behind a panel in her wardrobe. She's Princess. It's her.'

Mike sobbed into his hands. He couldn't believe Mrs Williams was dead and that he was a suspect. He'd thought his luck had changed and now this craziness was happening.

'It's okay, Mike.' The sergeant handed him a tissue. Mike dabbed away his tears and blew his nose. 'We'll get you cleaned up. You're not in any trouble. You're safe now.'

Mike nodded. 'Okay.'

Kerri

Kerri woke in a box room. It was cold and dull, but clean, at least. Her back ached like she'd slept on a bed of scattered Lego and her joints were stiff. Yesterday, Mark had brought her a change of clothes and told her to cooperate with the police and answer all their questions as accurately as possible. She hoped he would collect her today.

For breakfast she was given toast and a cup of tea. She was then taken to the same interview room she'd been in last night. She knew it looked bad, but she was sure the police officers had believed her when she said she was framed. Even so, she had spent the night incarcerated, and this meant she probably still needed to prove her innocence. Two officers escorted her to the room; she was glad they had not felt the need to handcuff her. Although she had red marks around her wrists so they must have cuffed her at some point. She couldn't remember.

The inspector took a seat opposite Kerri. 'How are you feeling this morning, Kerri?'

Kerri picked at her nails, which were chipped and chewed. 'I'm a little tired. The bed wasn't that comfortable. I've told you all I know. What happens now?'

The sergeant sat down beside the inspector. 'We need to speak to Beatrice and then we can decide what to do from there.'

Kerri held her forehead. A wave of dizziness blurred the room. 'Is Bea here? My head is a mess. I feel like I'm losing my mind.'

The inspector passed her a beaker of water. 'Try to stay calm. This won't take much longer.'

Kerri took a sip. 'You know I didn't kill Mrs Williams, right?'

'We know you didn't.'

Kerri sighed with relief. 'Do you know who did?'

Neither the inspector nor the sergeant answered her right away.

After a few long seconds, Detective Chief Inspector Clark replied, 'We're still piecing things together.'

The sergeant pushed a tablet towards Kerri. On the screen was a photo of a blonde woman dressed up in a sparkly gown.

'Do you know this woman?'

'No.' Kerri stared down at the image. She had no clue who that might be.

'Does she look familiar to you in any way?'

'No!' Kerri reached up and twiddled her hair anxiously. 'Please, I want to go home. I've told you someone tried to frame me for writing those articles. I thought Bea might have something to do with it when I found that bloody great knife in her room and she was writing about the murders … but the torn photograph was in Mike's room. Unless she went in there…'

The inspector tapped her finger against the tablet screen, her short nails making a clacking sound against it. 'Kerri, this is important. Try and stay focused. Her name is Princess. Do you know her?'

'Princess?' Kerri scratched the back of her head. 'I know that Mike was obsessed with a girl going by the name of Princess. Mike and I have never really clicked. Probably because I don't agree with his lifestyle.'

The sergeant cleared his throat. 'His lifestyle? The cross-dressing?'

Kerri scowled at him. 'His drinking. People don't use the term cross-dressing any more. It's kinda insulting.'

The sergeant's cheeks bloomed red.

The inspector moved the tablet back towards the sergeant. 'Kerri, why do you think Bea had something to do with the murders? Apart from the knife in her room.'

'I read her manuscript. It was intense. The only other time I've read writing as intense and as detailed as that was in a non-fiction book.' Kerri took another sip of water. The toast she'd had for breakfast only had butter on it, but it was causing havoc in her tender stomach. 'Of course, that's not true of all non-fiction. Some is embellished bullshit … the celebrity books, so over-exaggerated…' She paused and locked eyes with Detective Chief Inspector Clark. 'But when people have been though something horrific and they open up about it, it pops off the page like nothing else. That's how I felt when I read Bea's work. It popped right off the page and shot me in the soul.'

The sergeant flipped the protective cover over the tablet. 'Maybe she's just a good writer?'

'Have you read any of her previous work?' Kerri smirked. 'If you had, you would understand why this is different.'

'Thank you, Kerri.' Chief Inspector Clark stood up. 'We're going to leave you in Doctor Lamb's safe hands.' She pointed to the woman in the corner. It was the same one who had been there last night, observing silently. 'You've had a traumatic experience and she'd like to have a chat with you, alright?'

Kerri nodded and followed the tall woman out of the room. A wave crashed inside her head and rushed over her brain. Her eyes rolled back. *Oh no, not another seizure.*

Bea

Bea's eyes were glued together with sleep. She lifted her hand. It stopped way before she could reach her face. Her arm was stuck. She tried the other hand. That arm was stuck too. Panic pulsed through her veins. She kicked her legs and writhed, untucking the bed sheets.

'Kerri! Mike! Help! I can't move!'

'It's okay, Beatrice.' A firm woman's voice.

'Who said that?'

'I'll undo the straps. Don't panic.'

'Why am I tied down!'

'Try to remain calm…' the woman cooed. Bea squinted, vision blurred, the fuzzy figure stood up. 'I can't release your hands unless you agree to stay calm.'

Bea remained still, she blinked several times and the room came into sharp focus. She glanced around like a terrified rabbit who had woken up in a fox's den. There were empty hospital beds opposite her. This wasn't her local rundown hospital. It was modern and quiet. It had a floral scent rather than cheap disinfectant.

Two uniformed officers stood in front of the doors like statues, arms behind their backs. Sitting at her bedside was a young man in a navy suit, bored expression on his thin face, as if he'd been dragged to a lame gathering at the local community centre. An older woman in a navy suit, brightened by a pale blue silk scarf tied at her neck, was standing over Bea. She unfastened the bindings at her wrist. Then she strolled around to the other side of the bed, her heels softly clipping the floor. As soon as her other hand was free, Bea pushed herself up to a sitting position.

'I didn't mean to frighten you, Beatrice. The restraints are for safety.' The woman in the suit and silk scarf smiled as she made her way back to her seat.

'What am I doing here?' Bea's voice was suddenly croaky, her mouth dry, like someone had been pouring sand into it all night. She glanced beside her and reached for the jug of water and beaker on a small table next to the bed, poured herself a glass, and chugged. The water was warm but fresh.

The woman placed her hand on the front of her suit jacket. 'I'm Detective Chief Inspector Clark.' She pointed to the young lad next to her. 'And this is…'

'Sergeant Woods?' Bea guessed.

The inspector raised her eyebrows. 'How did you know that?'

Bea shook her head. 'I don't know. I feel like I've met you both before. It's like déjà vu. Please tell me what's going on. Why am I in a hospital? Why are you here?'

'You suffered a nasty bump on the head and you're not very well…' Chief Inspector Clark rested her hands in her lap. She gave Bea a strange feeling, as if they were playing poker and she knew Bea's hand before it had been dealt. '…But you're in the right place now, and the doctors are going to do all they can to help you.'

Bea reached for her head and felt around until her fingertips found a painful lump like a boiled egg under her hair. 'I don't remember bumping my head.'

'Beatrice, before we hand you over to the medical team, we've got some bad news…' Chief Inspector Clark paused and gave the sergeant a sorrowful glance. 'Mrs Williams has passed away.'

'*What?*' The corners of Bea's lips turned down. Tears fell before she could feel them well up. 'How?'

'She was stabbed.'

'*No!*' Bea shook her head and wailed. 'No, please! She's all I have.'

Inspector Clark gently placed her hand on Bea's arm. 'I'm sorry for your loss.'

'She was like a mother to me.' Bea sobbed into her hands.

One of the uniformed officers handed Bea a box of tissues.

'Thank you.' Bea pulled three tissues out of the box in quick succession, like a magician pulling scarves from inside a sleeve. She scrunched them up and blew her nose.

'Beatrice.' Inspector Clark stared at her strangely, the way someone does when they recognise your face but they can't remember your name or where they know you from. 'There's something else we need to talk about.'

Bea sniffed. The room shrank to the back of her mind as Mrs William's smiling face was all she could think about. 'I know what you're going to say.'

'You do?' The young man spoke for the first time.

'Mike never liked her. She used to yell at him for coming home drunk late at night and waking her up. He's involved, isn't he? I found a stack of vintage paper doll books in his room. One was missing several dolls with dresses that matched the ones in Kerri's article.'

Inspector Clark nodded. 'I see. How often did you and Mike spend time together?'

'Never, not in person. We lead different lives, but we message each other quite a lot.'

'How about Kerri?'

Bea wiped her eyes on a clean tissue. 'We're good friends.'

'When you message Kerri, does she reply right away?'

Bea's eyes moved skyward. 'No. We never have a back-and-forth messaging session, if that's what you mean. She always takes hours or days to reply.'

Inspector Clark glanced at a slender woman sitting cross-legged on a chair tucked in the corner near the uniformed officers. Bea hadn't previously noticed she was there. She stood up and picked up her chair. Her high-heels clacked against the floor as she approached. She set down the chair beside Bea's hospital bed.

'Hello, Bea.' She extended her hand. Bea shook it. 'I'm Doctor Lamb. I want to have a quick chat if that's okay?'

Bea nodded. As the doctor sat down, her pencil skirt tightened across her toned legs and she shifted in her seat in a bid to cross them. Doctor Lamb's dark-brown, almond-shaped eyes brimmed over with kindness, but her frown gave away the truth of there being something wrong.

'We think you might have a psychological disorder.'

Bea rubbed her throbbing temples. She could feel a tension headache coming on.

'Great. Another mental illness to add to the list.'

'We know you suffer with anxiety and depression, but there might be more to it than that. Do you ever feel like there are voices in your head?'

Bea threw the scrunched-up tissues on the small table. She'd balled them up so tight they looked like a pile of mini-snowballs. 'I'm a writer; there are nothing but voices in my head.'

'Of course.' The doctor linked her fingers over her knee. 'Aside from the writing, do you find your memory is patchy? Have you ever forgotten what day it is, or woken up in strange places?'

Bea twisted a tissue in her hands. 'Like now, you mean?'

The doctor adjusted her glasses on her wide nose. 'Like now, yes, but has it happened before?'

Bea nodded. 'Many times.'

The officers remained silent while the doctor quizzed her.

'Have you heard of Dissociative Identity Disorder?'

Bea shook her head. 'Can't say that I have.'

'It used to be called Multiple Personality Disorder.'

Bea tightened her grip, twisted again and the tissue in her hand ripped in half. 'Excuse me?'

Wasn't that some sort of schizophrenia? Is that why they tied her down? In case she flipped out? She might be depressed and anxious, but she wasn't a nutball!

The doctor nodded to the suited officers. They got to their feet. The sergeant left the ward. The inspector walked around the bed and stopped beside the doctor. She spoke softly to Bea. 'We'll come back and see you again, when you're feeling stronger. I think it's best the doctor explains what's going on.'

The uniformed officers by the door whispered with the inspector before she disappeared from the room.

The doctor gave Bea a reassuring pat on the hand. 'I know it's not the best time with losing a loved one, but if we don't make sure we have the right diagnosis you'll be facing a prison sentence.'

'For what? You think… *I* didn't murder Mrs Williams. I loved her like a mother!'

'I'll explain the best I can. I need you to answer a few more questions, okay?'

'Okay.' Bea couldn't believe what she was hearing. How could they think she might have killed her landlady? The first she'd heard of her death was when they'd told her just now!

'Beatrice Summers is your real name, correct?'

'Yes.' Bea nodded.

'Where there any traumatic experiences in your childhood? Any abuse?'

'No.' Bea shook her head.

'Do you remember much from your childhood?'

'Not really, but no one can, right? Because it was so long ago.'

'Sometimes. Okay, this might be to be difficult to digest, but from the information my colleagues and I have gathered, we think you have a personality disorder caused by childhood trauma. You were sexually abused by a family member over a number of years, weren't you, Bea?'

Bea shook her head vigorously. 'No, I wasn't.'

'Okay. That's what I needed to confirm. You don't have any memories of it because your brain developed a coping mechanism. The consciousness disassociates from the memories, feelings, thoughts and sense of identity to protect the person from the abuse. This is how the other personalities are created. You're the main personality and there are three other primary alters that we know of.'

'Alters? I don't understand.' Bea's heart pounded in her chest. Nothing was making sense. Was the woman saying her mind had been altered and that's why her memory was bad?

'Alters is short for altered states of consciousness. Kerri is one of them. Mike another.'

Bea frowned. What was she talking about? 'Kerri and Mike are my flatmates.'

'This is going to be a lot to take in. Tell me if you need me to stop at any moment and we'll have a break.' Bea nodded. 'People with D.I.D. normally have at least ten alters. We have only seen three of yours. Alters usually know about each other, but in this case it seems Princess was the only one who knew about you all.'

'Princess?' An image of herself wearing a princess dress flashed inside Bea's head. Pain throbbed over her skull. She held her forehead. Then came a flashback of Mrs Williams, lying on the floor bleeding.

'Beatrice? Listen carefully. Princess said she never blocked you out, not like she did the others. She said you were co-conscious. That she is your protector. She took control when bad things happened. We need to make sure of your innocence, prove that this disorder is what you have, otherwise the courts will try you for murder.'

Flashbacks flooded Bea's mind like a roller-coaster ride of nightmares. Knife plunged into an eye socket. Spencer's innards spilling over her hand. Strangling Bat with his tie. Fucking Kerri's boyfriend. Coffee with Donna. Sausage the dog. Mrs Williams hitting her over the head with a vacuum cleaner pipe like she had done to her uncle when she was twelve.

'*No!*'

Beatrice leapt from the bed and ran towards the door in her hospital gown. The burly officers blocked her way. Bea held her forehead. Blinding white-hot pain was striking through every neurological pathway.

The doctor was on her feet. 'Beatrice, I need you to come and sit down.'

Bea retreated to a corner behind an empty bed and cowered like a threatened animal. 'I'm not a killer!'

The room blurred like smeared paint. Bea stumbled sideways and vomited over the floor.

Killer

Sitting at the small desk in your room, you hum a nursery rhyme and colour a bow with the pink crayon. No books: you make your own dolls out of paper. Safety scissors. No sharp blades. This is because they've concluded you're a psychopath and that you manifested because of your uncle's abuse. You did your job as protector, but then took it too far. You wanted to protect all children from the monsters. Never again would a child be abused like Beatrice was.

You were the superhero and took the brunt of the abuse, so the others didn't have to feel it, so they could forget, but you never forgot and instead of being the punch bag, you became the puncher. It's unprecedented. It's never happened before. Sure, moviemakers have portrayed people with D.I.D. as having a dark side but it's bullshit. You're not Bea's dark side; your actions were driven by light. They say you lost your way, that Bea started writing to forget you. She hid inside her imaginary worlds, but her new book changed things. If she hadn't been asked to write crime would you have kept going? Kept giving her more to write about?

Beatrice is the main personality and can't be held responsible for your crimes. Bea is insane but you're evil. Whatever. *Tickle, tickle little fish, blame the killer and not Bea's wish.* She wished. You granted. You wouldn't be here if it wasn't for them and they wouldn't be here if it wasn't for you. You'd all be dead. Suicide or drug overdose or suicide through drug overdose the most likely outcome.

Still, everything turned out for the best. They all got what they wanted in the end. Beatrice's book is a global success and her new novel, *The Killer Within*, has just topped the charts. Kerri was upset; she denied the other alters existed for a while. She's coping better now, but she obviously can't be with Mark because we're locked up in this institution. You did the crime, all four do the time. They have to live in this place with you. It's not a bad place, and the four of you have a bigger room than anyone else. Kerri has made her peace with the situation and found success as a blogger. Her blog, 'Life on the Inside', is read all over the world.

Mike has found fame online. His channel has millions of followers. As for you, you're no longer needed. You spend your days colouring and designing clothes for your dolls, decorating your side of the room with them. Mike used you in his show. He filmed an episode about your paper dolls. No more photos of ugly paedos stuck over the top of the pretty drawn faces, though. No more death by your hands.

The therapists tried to make you fade into the background, merge with one of the other lesser alters who none of us know very well, or make you into a fragment. You stayed quiet for a while, to protect yourself from the therapists, but also because Bea doesn't need you to protect her any more. From time to time you feel guilt over Mrs Williams: she didn't deserve what she got. You hadn't intended to kill her; it wasn't planned. The girls will never forgive you. Mike is the only one who communicates with you, but sometimes, when there's a troll on Kerri's blog or Bea gets threatening letters, they let you come forward or 'front' as some doctors call it. What no one expected was people wanting to write to you. You're not allowed the privileges the others have, but Mike tells you what people say online. Many think you're a hero for killing those bastards. Copy cats have emerged. They're not killing, just catching, but they're doing it in your name. They are your princesses. This fills you with warmth like drinking hot chocolate on a cold day.

'Doll Hunters' is what they call themselves. Yesterday, an officer came to speak to Bea. Said there had been a death linked to these hunters. An accident, it would seem. You know it's not. Bea knows it's not. The police know it's not. That's why they came.

Someone has picked up the torch. Someone is carrying on your good work, and one day 'death for dolls' will be written into law. Children should get to kill their abusers. Laws need to change, and they will if enough people agree. Revolution is near … and you started it.

THE END

Acknowledgments

As with every novel, I have an army of people to thank. Thank you to my husband Chris for being my first reader and harshest critic. Big hugs to my family and friends who are always super supportive. Thank you to the team at Bloodhound Books for their hard work and dedication. Big thanks to the cover designer. I love the cover so much! Thank you to Chris Smith for his insights into the crazy world of journalism. Thank you to all those who didn't mind me pinching their first names for this story. Thank you to my editor and the amazing team of beta readers some of whom have been with me for years. This round of awesome readers included Leah Porter, Heather Alexander, Sandra Davis, Bea Coombes and Jo Raggett. Thank you to the super talented Lucy Hay for always having my back.

Lastly, thank you to my loyal readership and welcome to my new readers. You are why I do this. Thank you for buying my books and sharing your love of reading.

Author's Note

Do not read this page before you have finished the book. It will spoil the ending.

Usually people with the disorders talked about in this book are not dangerous. I urge people to remember that this novel is a work of fiction. I did some research, and what I found fascinated me. Those with Dissociative Identity Disorder seem like the loveliest people. I studied abnormal psychology in my twenties, and back then there wasn't much information about the disorder. There is dispute among some professionals as to whether or not it's a real disorder. Personally, I believe it is.

I write dark stories and so this one couldn't be anything other than a murderous tale, but I hope that readers will take an interest in D.I.D and the incredible people who live with the disorder.

If you have been affected by any of the disorders or mental illnesses described in this novel, please speak up and get help. If you're in need of assistance asap, I recommend The Samaritans. www.samaritans.org. The person on the other end of the phone helped me at a time of desperation. I'd never called a charity helpline before because I didn't want to waste anyone's time, and I felt there were others who needed the service more than I did. Don't be like me. Call them straight away. When you're feeling well, you can do what I did and say thank you by donating at a later date.

I hope you enjoyed this twisted tale. If you did, please check out my other titles. Happy reading!

9 781912 986217